THIS
CLOSE
TO
OKAY

THIS
CLOSE
TO
OKAY

A NOVEL

LEESA
CROSS-SMITH

GRAND CENTRAL
PUBLISHING

NEW YORK   BOSTON

Copyright © 2021 by Leesa Cross-Smith

Cover design and illustrations by Laywan Kwan. Cover copyright © 2021 by Hachette Book Group, Inc.

Grand Central Publishing
Hachette Book Group
1290 Avenue of the Americas, New York, NY 10104
grandcentralpublishing.com
twitter.com/grandcentralpub

First Edition: February 2021

Grand Central Publishing is a division of Hachette Book Group, Inc. The Grand Central Publishing name and logo is a trademark of Hachette Book Group, Inc.

The publisher is not responsible for websites (or their content) that are not owned by the publisher.

The Hachette Speakers Bureau provides a wide range of authors for speaking events. To find out more, go to www.hachettespeakersbureau.com or call (866) 376-6591.

Print book interior design by Tom Louie.

Library of Congress Control Number: 2020946458

ISBNs: 978-1-5387-1537-6 (Hardcover); 978-1-5387-1535-2 (ebook)

Printed in the United States of America

LSC-C

Printing 1, 2020

*For Loran and our babies, for little twinkling lights
in the dark*

PART ONE

THURSDAY

TALLIE

Tallie saw him drop his backpack and climb over the metal railing, the bridge. The gray Ohio River below them, a swift-rippling ribbon. She was driving slowly because of the rain, the crepuscular light. She didn't give herself time to think. Pulled over, lowered the passenger-side window, and said hey.

Hey!

Hey!

The *heys* increased in frequency, volume. To her left, the blur of traffic. She punched her hazards, climbed over the armrest and out of her car, leaving the passenger door peeled open.

"Hey! I see you! You don't know me, but I care about you! Don't jump!" she said, loud enough for him to hear, but she didn't want to startle him, either. The cars and trucks were loud, the rain was loud, the sky was loud, the bridge was loud—all those sounds echoing off it, rattling down and back up. The world was so loud.

He turned slightly, his face wet with rain.

"Hi. I'm Tallie," she said. "I don't want you to do this. Is there somewhere I can take you instead? And I could take your backpack. What's your name?" She was reluctant to touch the backpack. It was dark green and dirty. She reached for it.

"Don't touch it," he said softly. Far too softly for someone who was about to jump to his death. Why bother speaking softly when death is slipping its hand in your pocket?

Tallie put her hands out in front of her, surrendering. She wouldn't touch the backpack. Fine. A blessing.

"I'm sorry. Is there somewhere I could take you and maybe we could talk? Or I could call someone for you? Come with me. We can figure it out," she said, her voice climbing a rickety set of stairs.

She'd almost forgotten she was a licensed therapist until she said those words. *We can figure it out.* And how often did licensed therapists get to do surprise on-the-street sessions? A lot, actually. But this one was *on-the-bridge.* She'd never lost a client to suicide, and she wasn't going to start now. He wasn't her client, but he could've been. She began speaking to him as if it were true.

Instead of being out in the cold rain, she imagined they were in her cozy office with the calming lapis walls, the white-noise machine, her chair—a basil green. The shiny, honey-smooth hardwood floors; the soothing, soft almond suede couch. She had a scented-oil diffuser on a table by the window—lavender and a hint of lemon; she'd mixed it herself. There were potted spider and dracaena plants, bamboo palms, a *Monstera*, succulents in the sunlight—natural air purifiers. The bookshelves were packed neat and tight, with an amber salt lamp atop the one closest to the door. She pictured her office perfectly, transported herself there in her mind, willed that calm into her voice. Her receptionist's fingers gently clicked the computer keyboard, the rocky fountain bubbled in the waiting room.

Her older brother, Lionel, was a big-shot finance bro and had given her the money to design everything so beautifully from scratch; it made her feel guilty, like she could never do anything so important and pretty for him. She didn't want the man on the bridge to know she was a therapist with a rich big-shot brother and a calming office just yet, because that would separate them. She wanted him to think and know she was like him; they were the same. She had her share of want-to-jump days like everyone else, just had never made it over the railing before.

"No, thanks. Leave me alone," he said politely. Too politely for death. He hadn't completely made his mind up yet.

"I've had some shitty days, too. Some *really* shitty days. I just went through a divorce, and before the ink was dry, I found out my ex-husband got his mistress pregnant. I can't have babies, so it was literally the *worst* thing that could've happened to me. He's with her now, and they have a little girl. They moved to Montana to be closer to her family. Who lives in Montana? I can't even remember where it is half the time," she said, hating that she'd used the word *mistress*. She usually tried to avoid it, knowing how it cast a spell she didn't intend. *Mistress*—with its snaky curves and Marilyn Monroe breathiness—implied so much drama and romance that it seemed desirable.

"I'm sorry that happened to you," he said and paused, "but lots of people live in Montana. It's a regular state. I have friends who live there." His voice snapped. Politeness averted.

He was looking down at the river. It was cold and getting colder. Late October, the nights were getting longer. That alone made Tallie start to question whether life was worth living—God turning out the lights. Autumn was okay, but winter? Winter was too brutal to tackle alone, and this would be the second winter since her divorce. Joel would be spending winter in Montana with his new wife and baby.

"Right. I'm sure Montana is fine. Um, you said you had friends there. Why don't you come over to this side and tell me about your friends?" Tallie said, stepping closer to him.

He looked at her before giving his attention back to the river. It was the first time she'd seen his face full on. He had a smattering of light freckles, like someone had accidentally spilled cinnamon across his nose and cheeks, and he was wearing a jacket the same color as his backpack. Both his jeans and boots: syrupy brown. Shattered energy seemed to pulse from him like sonar. Tight blips of loneliness. Tallie translated the echolocation easily. She was lonesome and blipping, too.

"We should call them. I bet they'd love to hear from you," she said, moving closer and going into her pocket for her phone. "What are their names?"

"I don't want to talk to them right now."

"You won't tell me your name or how I can help you?"

"No, thank you."

"All right. Okay," she said, tapping around on her phone, wondering if there was something she could find that might help. She glanced at her car, the open door, the rain falling sideways against the seat. The dome light glowed a blurred white. She wiped her fingers dry, tapped around more.

"Have you heard this song? I love this song," she said, turning it up, stepping closer to him.

She was on the safe side of the railing; he was on the suicide side. She doubted he would be able to hear the music. It was a loud world. She was only a bit surprised no one else stopped, no one else pulled to the side and said hey. Everyone always thought everyone else would take care of things.

"A Nervous Tic Motion of the Head to the Left" by Andrew Bird played from her phone. She thought past the title having the word *nervous* in it, but early in the song he sang the word *died*, so she waited until that part had passed and only turned it up once Andrew Bird began to whistle. It was a quirky song with lots of whistling. She'd been flicking through the musical artists in alphabetical order and skipped ABBA, although "I Have a Dream," with its hopeful lyrics about believing in angels, wouldn't have been the worst choice. One scroll past ABBA was Andrew. She stretched her arm out so the phone would be closer to his ear.

"This guy. His name is Andrew Bird, and he's whistling like a bird in this song. It's a pretty song, but I don't know what it means," she said. The rain was wetting her hoodie, her cold hand, the phone. This man must've been freezing if he'd been on the bridge for even a short amount of time. She asked how long he'd been standing there.

"I don't know," he said, still looking down.

She let the song play, stopping it before Andrew Bird said the word *died* again. She put the phone into her pocket.

"I'm sure you're very cold. There's a coffee shop up the road. We could go get a coffee. I'd love to buy you a coffee. Would you let me buy you a coffee?" she asked.

He could be a murderer. He could be a rapist. He could be a pedophile on the run.

"You don't want to tell me your name? I told you mine. I'm Tallie. Tallie Clark."

"No," he said. Soft. The world was loud and hard, but he was soft.

"Would you like something warm? To hold or drink? I can't leave you here. I won't do that," Tallie said. She could reach out and touch him but was afraid. He could jump. He could fall. He could grab her and not let go, take her with him. She didn't want to go.

"Play another song, please," he said.

Tallie searched for "Jesus, Etc." by Wilco—a song she'd always found comforting—and held her phone out for the man to take. They stood there listening to Jeff Tweedy's flannel, languid voice together. She hugged herself for a moment, an attempt at warmth, before tucking her hands into the kangaroo pocket of her hoodie.

"Thank you," he said, handing her the phone back once the song was over.

She looked at the highway—the flashing gloss of minivans, SUVs, pickup trucks, four-doors—no police cars, no fire trucks, no ambulances. She didn't know what to do and told him that. Maybe it would make him feel better, knowing no one had all the answers. And if he was going to jump, he surely would've jumped already. Right? Right.

"You don't have to do anything. It's done," he said.

"What's done? What's going on?"

"I don't know," he said.

It made her want to laugh, the humanity and honesty of him saying *I don't know.* Tallie prayed to herself: *Jesus, You see us. You know us. Let this man know. Let him find a reason to stay. Surround both of us. Let me be able to do this. Abide with us.*

She held her hand out for him. Shaking, wet, cold. He looked at her, the river. The river, her. The backpack was at her feet. He was looking at the river, and he was looking at the river. He was looking at the river when he took her hand.

He smelled like the rain. There was a hood on his jacket that he never pulled up. Pointless if he was planning on dying soon. What's a wet head to a dead person? He picked up his backpack and followed her to the car. Sat and closed the passenger door.

"The seat is wet. Sorry," Tallie said, forgetting he was already wet. So was she. She closed her door, reached into the backseat. Grabbed the small towel in her gym bag and patted her face. She tried to hand it to him, but he refused. "So if you were looking for a sign not to take your life, the sign is me. Stopping. Taking you for a coffee instead."

"I wasn't looking for a sign."

"Why not?"

Tallie turned off her hazard lights and waited until it was clear. Pulled into traffic. This was potentially a terrible idea, but it was happening. It was scary and thrilling, and her heart zapped like her body couldn't tell the difference between panic and excitement.

"I didn't want a sign," he said.

"But you got one," she said, smiling over at him. Maybe her first *true* smile of the day. She was busy with appointments in the morning, smiled perfunctorily, ate a salad and a can of tuna in her office alone. She'd had appointments all afternoon, too, and before leaving work had logged in to Joel's social media account because Joel had never changed the password, and she clicked around on his new wife's profile like she always did. Looked at old photos of her pregnant belly and photos from the baby shower she hadn't seen before. She could make out Joel in the background of one of them, grilling. There was still a brand-new gas grill on Tallie's deck that Joel had bought and never used.

Joel's baby was almost two months old now, and in one of the new pictures with her, he had his hair pulled into a ponytail. A fucking *ponytail*. Tallie had closed her laptop and cried into her hands before leaving for the day. She'd run four miles at the gym across the river, disappointed in herself for not pushing for her usual six. And on her way home she saw Bridge—what she'd begun calling him in her mind since Bridge Guy wouldn't tell her his name.

He shrugged; apparently he didn't believe in signs, although clearly she had just saved his life. She'd never *literally* saved a life before; she felt warm all over thinking about it. She looked at him, considered his profile. He was probably handsome and could've been anywhere between twenty-five and thirty-five.

"Do you like coffee?" she asked.

She used a lot of different techniques in her therapy sessions—holistic, behavior modification, Gestalt, cognitive—but also believed in the power of simplicity: listening, a warm drink. Her clients opened up more when they were holding a steamy mug. She sometimes felt guilty billing them when all she'd done was boil water. The coffee shop she was taking him to was her favorite, a stop she made almost every day. A safe place. He couldn't murder her there; she knew the baristas.

"It doesn't matter," he said with enough breathtaking sadness to stop clocks.

"It matters. *You* matter. Your life matters. It does," she said and waited for a response. When she didn't get one, she continued, "Um...we're almost there. The coffee shop is just up the road. You may know that. Are you from around here? I'm kind of winging this, but I'm trusting God right now."

"What if there's no God?" he asked, looking out his window, the raindrops slicking down in a beaded curtain.

Then I don't know. That's why I have to believe there is, she thought.

"Your name is Tallie?" he asked after several moments of silence.

"Tallie. Tallie Clark. Short for Tallulah. It means running water...jumping water. But everyone calls me Tallie except my brother and his family. They call me Lulah." She could see the coffee shop ahead on the corner, the viridescent sign wrapped in neon, lit up and waiting for them.

"Huh," he said, turning to her. Transfiguration—a suicide smile. Kind of creepy. Kind of nice. Ted Bundy had a creepy, nice smile, too. So did the Zodiac Killer, probably, and most of the murderers who ended up on *Dateline*. "It's pretty. But my name *isn't* Tallulah," he said. The smile was gone.

She pulled into the coffee shop parking lot, thankful to be in a public place. She'd get him something warm, and she hoped to learn more about him in the process, figure out what kind of help he needed. Soon she'd be home in her pajamas with her cats, watching some trashy thing on TV, a soothing avocado sheet mask on her face, wine in her glass, feeling good about saving a life.

They parked and walked into the coffee shop together. He cowboy-walked slowly, and she matched his strides. When he held the door for her, she got a clear look at his face. Yep. He was Probably Handsome. Bridge was also probably five feet eleven, nearly the same size as Joel. Or maybe she was imagining it. Was she obsessed, making *every* man into Joel now? Bridge had shaggy hair, and she pictured Joel's new ridiculous little ponytail swatting her in the face.

Tallie could see Bridge was wearing a white undershirt beneath his flannel, the gold chain of a necklace peeking out. She would ask him his name again later, but perhaps if she talked to him more, he'd offer it up on his own. She used the same technique with her clients, the ones who arrived an hour early but then clammed up when they came into her office. The ones who would talk about their mothers but not their fathers. The ones who would talk about everyone else but not themselves. She sometimes turned down the lights or played soft classical music if the clients preferred. Bach's cello suites were disarming. Chopin, Mozart, Liszt, Haydn.

She had dark chocolate with almonds and hard candy in a sheesham wood bowl handcrafted by Indian women. She'd bought several for the office, and the money went to ending sex trafficking. She made a mental note to donate to the cause again as soon as she was in front of her computer. Those poor girls. Maybe Bridge was one of those disgusting creeps who bought little girls. Those guys could be anywhere. It sickened her, thinking about it.

She considered herself a decent judge of character when she trusted her instincts. She gave him a hard look to gauge his energy, tried to decide if he really had the face of a man who wanted to die. He had kind, redwood-brown eyes. Redwood called up cedar, her favorite smell. She'd bought Joel an expensive cedar-based cologne for their last anniversary. He wore it once and told her he didn't think he could wear it anymore because it got all over him. "It was everywhere," he'd said, and she'd thought, *That's the point.* She'd loved the day he smelled like it, when it was everywhere. She still had the bottle at home: a glass rectangle the color of sunlit bourbon. She wished she could give it to Bridge, tell him the cedar scent matched his eyes. Maybe he'd understand what that meant. Maybe his senses infused one another, too, leaked out, left stains. Like how the rain could make her go gray-blue and how the gray-blue left her with the cloying taste of blueberries in her mouth.

The coffee shop was warm and crowded, everyone busy on their phones or laptops or with their books or children or boyfriends or girlfriends or friends or cakes or cappuccinos. She'd gladly pay for his coffee and a snack if he was hungry. Did Bridge have money? A phone?

"So you'll drink a coffee if I buy you one? Or would you like a pop or a milk?" Tallie asked him as they walked to the counter together. His boots squeaked, the cuffs of his jacket dripped.

"I'll drink a coffee," he said, nodding.

"Black?"

He nodded again. She convinced herself she'd imagined his creepy smile. He didn't seem creepy in that coffee shop. His eyes were delicate, crinkled in the corners. He couldn't have been in his twenties. Definitely thirties. He seemed like a smoker, although he didn't smell like it. *Smoker's energy*, she knew it well. Her mom had it bad.

She couldn't text her best girlfriend, Aisha, because she was out of town on an unplugged Thursday-to-Sunday hippie yoga retreat. Tallie considered texting her brother, Lionel, to say hi and casually let someone know where she was, just in case. But she couldn't tell him about Bridge. He'd get really angry. He'd said something to her about being careless in the past week because she'd gone to visit him, parked in his steep driveway, forgot to pull the emergency brake. When she came out, she saw that her car had rolled down the driveway and into the grass, narrowly avoiding the front line of trees edging his property. "Sometimes you're so careless," her big brother had said. But Tallie wasn't careless. Lionel was obsessed with perfection, leaving no room for honest mistakes. Her mother and brother often insisted on saying what didn't need to be said. Hurtful things. It was one of the reasons Tallie had become a therapist—to help people be kinder to themselves and others. To make the world a safer, sweeter place.

Once when Tallie was ten and playing in her room by herself, content and humming, her mother had told her she was a lonely little girl. She'd never forgotten it. What an awful thing to say. Maybe someone had told Bridge he was a lonely little boy once.

"Did you want something to eat? Would probably be a good idea," she said. She stood at the counter and ordered two coffees from the barista after exchanging hellos. Bridge looked down at the glass pastry case. Without waiting for an answer, she ordered the last two old-fashioned pumpkin doughnuts they had left. She paid and went to the condiment station to pour soy milk in her cup, a small shake of raw sugar. Bridge followed her, and they found a table together. They sat in the corner next to a pole with white twinkle lights wrapped around it, their atomic halos softening everything in their glow. He peeled off his jacket. Thanked her for the coffee, the doughnut.

His shirt seemed dry. He had nice hands, coffin-square shoulders. A light brown-reddish beard that matched his freckles. He slicked his damp hair back, rolled up the cuffs of his sleeves. She waited for him to take a drink of his coffee. When he took a drink of his coffee, they could begin. This was a therapy session whether he knew it or not. He *had* to expect her to ask a lot of questions. They'd met under extraordinary circumstances; they were in this together. He sipped his coffee, broke off a piece of doughnut and ate it. He was very neat, careful to keep the crumbs on the plate.

"How are you feeling?" she asked.

"I need to take my medicine," he said after he'd chewed, swallowed.

Antidepressants? That's all this was. The chemicals in his brain were off-kilter, and his medicine would fix it. She'd had clients who went off their meds, and it wasn't until they had an extreme wake-up call that they realized how much they needed their prescriptions. Had the bridge woken Bridge up? She could take him to get his meds, pay for them.

"Where is your medicine?"

"My backpack," he said, tilting his head toward his feet, where it was. He kept eating. She mirrored him, dug into her doughnut, a treat she allowed herself only every now and then, but tonight was obviously different. The crumbs were sticking to her fingers, and she wiggled them to shake them off.

"We could get a bottled water. And um, is there someone you can stay with? Do you think you need to go to a hospital? I could take you there," she said. There were people she could call. She had connections. Doctors, a fireman who used to be a neighbor. She could piece a rescue together. Didn't he need to be rescued?

"Antihistamines. It's my allergy medicine," he said after he drank more of his coffee. Like, *Look, lady, why would I go to a hospital for allergy medicine? You are being crazy. I am fine. Please stop being crazy and let me drink my dark blend in peace.*

"Well, I mean because of the bridge." *Hospital because you were going to jump to your death. That's why hospital.*

"That was then. This is a new moment."

"Still important to discuss, though, don't you think?"

"I'm not from here. My family's from Clementine," he said. Tallie had heard of it, knew Clementine was a small city in southeastern Kentucky, about three hours away.

"You're half black? I don't imagine there are a lot of *us* in Clementine," Tallie said, leaning forward. She'd never seen a face like Bridge's before. Mixed with a million things—his thick, Kennedy-like dark blond hair blushed with red.

"My grandmother was black. And no, you're right. Not a lot of us, no," he said.

She liked that he told her something about his family and how he blew across the top of his coffee, the ripples it made. She liked watching him finish his doughnut. Her brain fizzed. This man wanted to die less than an hour ago, but now he was sitting across from her, careful not to burn his mouth. He seemed to purposely flood himself with more gentleness as he thanked her again. His necklace had slipped to the front of his undershirt—a small gold cross winking light.

"Should we call your family?" she asked, pulling her phone out of her pocket and setting it on the table in between them, though she couldn't say she expected him to agree. In order to keep him talking, she would have to tell him about herself. "My family is from here and Tennessee. Some are from Alabama. Do you get along with your family?"

"I don't care about things like that," he said.

"What *do* you care about?"

"I don't care about small talk."

"Neither do I. That's why I'm asking you about *big* things. So we don't waste our time together," she said.

The corner of his mouth rose and twitched. "I like this song," he said. The coffee shop speakers were playing Radiohead down low. "Knives Out."

"I do, too. It's so moody and strange," she said. *Commiseration. Empathy.* It usually worked, got people to bloom like flowers. "Was this your . . . um, first suicide attempt?"

"I don't know what it was. But I guess I feel better now. It's hard to say."

He felt better? This quick? She didn't believe him.

"I'm going to the bathroom." He stood, taking his backpack with him.

"Okay," she said, nodding.

When he was behind the bathroom door, she immediately moved to his chair and rummaged through his pockets. A receipt for his jacket. He'd bought it that morning. What kind of person goes out in the morning and buys the jacket he wants to die in? Tallie glanced up to make sure he wasn't opening the bathroom door. All clear. She was nervous and excited, the adrenaline rabbit-beating her heart, her hands shaking. In an inside pocket she found folded paper—a note? She didn't have time to check. She pulled it out and put it in her pocket, glanced at the bathroom door again, and put her hand back in his jacket. Another piece of paper. Another note? She took it. No way would he not notice both of them missing, but she'd figure that out later when she could get alone and read them. They were probably nothing. She sat in her seat, drank more of her coffee. Two minutes, and he returned with his backpack, sat across from her.

"Yeah, I'm definitely feeling better now," he said. "I splashed cold water on my face."

"Technically, you already had cold water on your face from the cold rain."

"I guess you're right."

Bridge was gaslighting her in a yellow-orange whoosh. Almost choosing suicide and now acting like it was no big deal? She was frustrated with him, felt connected to him. The idea embarrassed her. She had a habit of forming quick, intense connections to people she barely knew. Before GPS, worrying over whether someone she'd given directions to made it to their destination, or when she was in a bigger city on public transportation, not being able to stop herself from asking a crying person if they were okay, even when everyone else was determined not to speak or make eye contact with them. Occasionally, clients got intensely attached to her, emailing and calling at all hours of the night, wanting her to meet their families. She reminded them that clear boundaries were important for everyone to have, although she didn't tell them how hard it was for her to listen to her own advice.

Right after the divorce, Tallie had gotten mildly obsessed with Joel's new wife, going so far as to compulsively worry about her when she saw on social media that she'd been in a minor car wreck. Tallie kept checking in, making sure she was okay, reading and rereading her page, although she never posted about anything too intensely heavy or personal. Tallie learned generic things about her life by snooping around. And obsessing over those things was something that made her feel crazy. Crazier. When it got going, it was a loop she kept looping, a hoop she kept swirling around and around, never stopping.

"I like your jacket. It looks brand-new," Tallie said, brushing her hair from her face. She was sure she looked a hot mess and couldn't quite decide if she cared or not. A part of her wanted to go to the bathroom, fluff her hair, reapply her peachy-pink lip gloss, pinch her cheeks, but she didn't have the time for vanity right now, not when she was trying to get to the bottom of this. To figure out and help and love her neighbor as herself.

"I bought it this morning," he said. The receipt was from the giant camping store, Brantley's. It was eighty dollars even, an avocado-green rain jacket. He'd paid cash for it at 9:37 a.m.

"You bought a brand-new jacket when you knew you wanted to jump from a bridge?" she asked, surprising herself. She could've, and maybe should've, asked the question differently, or even let it go completely. She didn't want to upset him, but he didn't seem easily upset. If she'd stumbled upon him any other way, she would've remarked on his chill factor, how he seemed like he never stressed about anything. He was simply sitting in a coffee shop having a cup. He was simply in a red-and-black buffalo-plaid flannel worthy of apple picking, new jacket hung over the back of his chair, boots wet, but they'd dry. Everything dried eventually. Everything was fine. Relax. Shrug.

"I bought the jacket this morning. The bridge was the bridge. This is now," he said, as if there could be no other answer. His pacific presence soothed her, and she wanted to keep that feeling, trap it under a cup.

"So your family is from Clementine but you're not?"

"I was born there."

"Are you completely detached from your family? You don't feel like you can talk to them?"

"I don't want to talk to them right now."

"Okay. Mind me asking how old you are?"

"Mind me asking how old *you* are?" he asked. Raised his eyebrow.

"Okay. You don't want to tell me. So tell me this: Do you want more coffee? I can get you a refill. I'll get one, too," she said, taking his still-half-full cup.

"Sure. Thanks."

At the counter, when she was turned away from him, she touched her pocket, checking to make sure the papers she pulled from his jacket were safe. She got their refills, performed her whole coffee ritual at the condiment counter, gave him his cup. Black. Her initial nervousness had sailed away, and she wanted to cup her hands and say *Come back* to that little nervous ship, because that's what made sense. She *should've* been nervous. Was she *this* lonely? She had a respectable career, a nice house, her cats, her parents and brother and sister-in-law and a host of relatives and friends in her contact list. She had Aisha and a stocked pantry—which made her feel safer and better about the world. Losing her nervousness made her feel reckless, and feeling reckless fed her recklessness, leading her to feel the scariest, most thrilling thing of all: free.

"I'm forty," she said after she'd sat across from him again.

"I'm thirty-one," he said. Another layer peeled away.

Tallie fingered the folded papers in her pocket underneath the table, felt guilty for swiping them. She should put them back; they weren't her business.

"Wow, you're young!" she said. Jovial. Maybe it would rub off on him. She bubbled with desire to get to know him better, to unravel whatever it was he had tightly wound around his heart. She cared for Bridge. No matter what, he had something to live for. Estranged or not, he had a family in Clementine. He seemed interesting and intelligent. She tried her best to give everyone the benefit of the doubt.

"I *feel* old," he said.

"I feel old sometimes, too."

"Why did you stop me?" he asked. His eyes, hauntingly sad. It was almost as if a shadow fell across them. Supplicating. Like an oil painting of Christ wearing His crown of thorns.

"I care about you. I don't want you to die. I'm...so glad you didn't jump."

He took the lid off his coffee cup, blew across it. Drank and put it down before looking at her.

"Well, you were making so much *fucking* noise I couldn't hear myself think," he said.

He'd caught Tallie so off guard she was blushing as she laughed, covering her face. Voilà! She knew making suicide harder for people who were considering it was sometimes the difference between life and death. She'd read about the suicide rate plummeting in Great Britain after something as simple as swapping the coal gas stoves for natural gas, because too often, suicide came down to a matter of convenience. She was pleased that making so much *fucking* noise had made a difference. She thought back to her well-intentioned but slapdash therapy session and sloppy rescue techniques, almost choking on her coffee.

"Careful. You're going to spill everything," he said. She felt the table steadied and peeked out from between her fingers at him, drinking his coffee again like he hadn't said a word.

"I'm not apologizing for stopping you," Tallie said, once she finished laughing.

"I'm not asking you to."

"Good."

"What are you going to do now?" he asked after a moment. He leaned over like a sigh, let his weight press against the wall beside them. *Suicide casual.* He was a stranger, a strange man. Everything about him was oddly both new and familiar when held up to the other men in her life. Bridge had small ears like her dad and her college beau, Nico. Bridge, Nico, and Joel all had nice hands. Bridge looked the most like a storybook lumberjack from a deep forest who'd taken a wrong turn, ended up in the big city. And the rich, golden timbre of his voice reminded her of her brother's.

"What are *we* going to do?" she asked. The little boat of nervousness was gone, gone, gone. Bon voyage. She couldn't see it if she squinted.

They were en route to her place. He'd been quiet so far in the car, only replying to the questions she asked.

19

"So you have a house or an apartment?"

"I used to. Not anymore, really," he said.

"You don't have anywhere to stay?"

"I didn't say that. I just don't have a house or an apartment."

"You have a car?"

"I don't have a car here. Not in town," he said.

"How do you get around?"

"I get around all right," he said. He looked over at her with the backpack in his lap. He kept his hand on top of it. Tallie's fear scuttled back when she glanced at that backpack. That's where his torture devices could be—the ropes, the gun, the knives. *"Knives Out."* Creepy song to be floating across the coffee shop. Tallie kept hearing the chorus in her head.

It was full dark and still raining, although not as much as before. Halloween was on Saturday. What was she doing? Locked in her car, this stranger in her passenger seat, driving him to her house? This was a perfect horror film she had created, and when they got to her place he'd take whatever it was out of that backpack, murder her, and put her somewhere no one would ever find her. Her parents and brother would be on TV begging for her return. Years from now her brother would write a book about it. It'd be a best seller, get optioned for a movie. One of those kids from one of those teen vampire shows would play Bridge. He'd win an Oscar. Her brother would become a highly sought-after screenwriter and leave his family, start dating one of the young girls from the same teen vampire show.

And all that should've kept her from taking Bridge to her house, but none of it did. She never did things like this, and she was leaning into that chaotic energy, eager to see what was waiting for her on the other side. The wide mouth of the world was opening up! Something was happening, something beyond her control. She'd been given the keys to the lion's cage, and she was inside, petting it. Staring into its pale amber eyes.

BRIDGE

(Driving through the rain. Her car is clean, the radio off. There is light traffic, and Tallie looks both ways even when she has the green light.)

"Let's see...do you have any hobbies?" she asked him.

"This feels like small talk."

"You're right. Okay, big talk...after my divorce, I was so sad I didn't know what to do. My world was smashed, and it felt like I was blurred out, too. Couldn't see straight."

"And now you feel better?"

"Most of the time, yes."

(A fire engine's siren screeches the quiet red. Tallie pulls over to let it pass. Her hand is flat on the stick shift. She double-checks the rearview mirror, leaning closer to the churning hurricane in her passenger seat.)

TALLIE

When Tallie's house was built, the Fox Commons neighborhood was brand-new. A mixed-use community unlike anything else in Louisville. Most residents swapped their expensive cars for golf carts when they got home from work and used them to motor their children to the school playground or the walking trails at sunset, the fountain in the square, the amphitheater overlooking the fishing lake. There was a public pool, several tennis courts, two salons, and a building solely devoted to doctors' offices—dermatologists, neurologists, allergists, pediatricians, internal medicine, plastic surgery. Residents had their choice of fine dining with plenty of outside seating, including Tallie's favorite trattoria, Thai noodles, sushi, pizza, and an American bistro with the best burgers in town. There was also a pastel sweet shop where the gelato was made with local milk and an Irish pub lit up with enough lime-green bulbs to turn everyone into Elphaba from *Wicked* upon entering. Plans for two hotels—one leviathan, one boutique—had been drawn up. The grand-opening ribbon for six neat beige rows of condominiums had recently been cut with a pair of comically large scissors. Lionel was an investor, and he and his wife, Zora, had attended the ceremony, then stopped by Tallie's for small-batch bourbon and homemade Kentucky jam cake afterward.

~

The steps leading to Tallie's white-brick front porch were fringed with pumpkins—some orange, a few blued like skim milk. A fluffy wreath of orange-red-yellow-brown leaves hung on the wide yellow front door. On one wicker porch chair, there was a polka-dotted canvas pillow with the word HOCUS printed on it. On the other, POCUS. The welcome mat read HELLO in loopy black cursive on the stiff hay-colored brush.

"Um, I could make dinner. Are you hungry?" she asked him after they'd gotten inside.

Her house was immaculate because the night before, she'd dusted, swept the floors, beat the rugs outside. Was it her hormones? Perimenopause? She felt like nesting and had decided to bring Bridge home like he was one of her rescue cats.

Usually her two cats were skittish around new people, but they were curious about Bridge and sauntered around the living room with their tails up and hooked.

"The marmalade one is Jim, and the black one is Pam," she said.

"Like from *The Office*."

"Exactly."

In their short amount of time together they'd already gotten in the habit of ping-ponging their questions and answers. She'd ask him a question, and he'd ignore it completely, only to answer three questions later, both of them remembering where they left off. He was easy to like. He'd put his backpack at his feet and taken his jacket off. Tallie took it from him, hung it on the hook in the laundry room so it could drip.

"I could help cook. I'll eat," he said, sitting on the couch.

"Great! Okay. That's what we'll do." She went to her bedroom and returned with some dry clothes. "You can put these on," she said, handing them to him. "And I'll go to the bedroom and change, too. Then we'll make dinner."

~

Tallie closed and locked her bedroom door and put her ear against it, listening for him. Listening for what? Anything. She slid onto the floor and got the papers from her pockets. Opened the first one. He had standard man's handwriting—small printing, almost cursive. She looked at the bottom to see if it was signed. No. But at the top, a name.

Christine.

My dear bright Christine, my love and life. My world went dark when you left. You are my whole heart. I am broken and empty without you. What else is left for me to do? I miss you. I miss you. I miss you. I miss you. I'm so sorry for everything. Please don't be mad at me. I love you.
I love you
so
much
God.
Dammit.
Christine.

Tallie put her ear to the door to listen again. Nothing. She refolded the first letter, opened the other piece of paper. No name at the bottom. But at the top.

Brenna, my sunshine. It's dark now.
Please don't be mad at me.
I love you
so
much
I

The letter was unfinished. She pulled out her phone and googled *Christine* and *Clementine, Kentucky*, knowing it'd be impossible to find anything useful without any other information. She entered *Brenna* and *Clementine, Kentucky*, and nothing still. She tried both names together. A fruitless search. She took a peek at the *Clementine Most Wanted* list to scan for anyone resembling him. Nope. She widened her search to *Louisville's Most Wanted*, *Kentucky's Most Wanted*, *America's Most Wanted*. Flicked through, squinting to recognize someone. Thankfully, she didn't.

Tallie didn't have a strong internet presence, just a rarely updated, mostly private Facebook page and nothing online linking her to her therapy practice. On the practice website, she was listed as *Ms. T. L. Clark*, as it always had been, before and after her divorce. She hadn't taken Joel's last name, content with her own. If Bridge tried to look her up, he wouldn't find anything.

If he were her actual client, she would've been required to report his suicide attempt to someone else. If he were her actual client, she would be taking therapy notes. If their time together so far had been a scheduled appointment:

Client Name: No Last Name, "Bridge"
    Age: 31
    Bridge makes eye contact easily. Naturally quiet? He smiled once, maybe twice. Anxiety? Suicidal ideation. Depressive. The suicide attempt may have been his first, may have been impulsive. Bridge is funny and charming. He appears to be healthy, level-headed (despite the attempt), and thoughtful. His body language is relaxed, appetite normal.
    Medication: antihistamines.
    Bonus: the cats like him.
    Barriers to Treatment: won't give his name. Doesn't seem to think his suicide attempt was a big deal. Also…hasn't consented to treatment.

Family/Friends (?): Christine and/or Brenna?
Client's Goals: ??

Tallie put both letters in her top drawer, underneath the black lace she hadn't thought about wearing since Joel left. She took off her old clothes, put on new ones—a long-sleeved shirt with her alma mater's growling mascot on the front, a pair of black leggings. She went to her bathroom, peed, smoothed her hair down, slipped clear lip gloss across her mouth, and checked the mirror. When she walked into the living room, Bridge was sitting in the same spot in the dry change of clothes she'd given him, like they'd magically appeared on his body. The cats purred in his lap.

"You're up for cooking? Anything you don't like to eat?" she asked. She was hungry; he was hungry, too. They were just two people who needed to eat. Everyone needed to eat. It was okay for them to eat together. Joel never really cooked and could be a picky eater, depending on his mood. She thought of the picture of him she saw on social media, the one of him grilling like a jackass.

"I like to cook, and I'm not picky," Bridge said, tenderly lifting each cat and placing it on the couch next to him. Tallie bent to pick up the damp clothes folded neatly at his feet. "You don't have to—"

"Not a word. I'm washing these for you," she said, taking them. She went to her laundry room and started a load. "And even though we're to break bread together soon, you still won't tell me your name?" she asked when she was in front of him again. He was committed to the mystique. She was curious to see how long it would last.

"It's Emmett," he said. So easily, as if all she needed to do was ask kindly, one more time.

Client Name: No Last Name, Emmett.

"Okay, Emmett. Let's go to the kitchen."

EMMETT

Emmett could go to the bridge after dinner. He'd once wondered if the aching would ever stop and it hadn't, so wasn't the bridge his last hope? His *only* hope? Death and hope wrestled, tangled tight. Was there anything left but the bridge?

He'd peeked out when he was in the coffee-shop bathroom and seen Tallie going through his jacket, taking his letters. She was playing investigator and probably marathoned *Law & Order: SVU* with her cats in her lap. Probably worshipped Olivia Benson.

Tallie had given him a white T-shirt and gray sweatpants, a sweater. Leftovers from her ex-husband. He went into his backpack, got out his medicine, and took it by filling his hand up with what water it could hold and throwing his head back. Pointless to take his medicine, but so what? Tallie had reminded him of it, and she was being so nice.

Before climbing over the railing, he'd counted the vehicles as he stood on the bridge.

(Seven vans. Five pickup trucks. Four delivery trucks. Fifteen cars. One motorcycle, one bike. One hooded person in the distance, walking away. The bridge lights are on, but one is flickering. One of the cars honks. Someone has graffitied a neon-yellow dick on the steel next to an ABORTION STOPS A BEATING HEART bumper sticker.)

And now it was time to make dinner. Dinner with Tallie. Tallulah Clark. A stranger. He'd never met anyone named Tallulah before and predicted she'd act differently from the other people he knew, which was true. She asked a lot of questions and smiled at him like he hadn't just been standing on a bridge wanting to jump, wanting to quiet the noise, wanting it all to *end* somehow.

But the bridge would be there waiting for him, its arms outstretched. He didn't need to make an appointment. He'd chosen today for a specific reason, but later would work, too, or tomorrow. It didn't matter. Nothing mattered. He wanted it to. He wanted *everything* to matter, but nothing did. Grief had swung open a door in his heart he hadn't known was there, and it'd slammed closed behind him. He'd been on the other side for three years. Too long. Locked away, unable to escape, tackled and held down by the darkness that wouldn't let him go. Jumping from the bridge meant a chance to soar before the free fall. As he climbed over the railing, he'd been cold, wet, and alone; Tallie had shown up warm. And it was Tallie who got an eggplant from the fridge and pulled a handful of campari tomatoes from a box on the counter.

(A green cruet of olive oil, a tall brown, pepper grinder, a white ceramic saltcellar labeled SEL in raised capital letters. Dark and light wooden spoons in a fat mason jar. A viney plant hanging from a hook in the ceiling. There is a small dent in the floor, front of the sink—a tiny divot a hallux can dip into.)

"Everyone likes pasta, right? It's comforting," she said.

"I do like pasta."

"So you want to chop?"

"I'm a strange man in your kitchen, and you want me to take the knife?" he asked. He couldn't not ask. What was happening?

"I've been reading your vibes ever since I stopped my car, and I can't convince myself completely that you have violent energy. I've been trying to feel it, but I can't. I tried to *force* myself to feel it, but I can't. You seem like a kitten to me, honestly," she said.

28

Christine had told him that before. Not the kitten part—he wasn't sure how he felt about that—but she'd said he was a gentle spirit. And he'd assumed she was disappointed in him because of it. A dark macho signal he wasn't giving off but should've. Like he was some sort of phenomenon the weather radar couldn't pick up, leaving her flummoxed. Remarks like that felt like criticisms coming from women, but Tallie's hippie comment about *vibes* intrigued him.

"Reading my *vibes*?" he asked.

She pointed to the knife, and he picked it up, began slicing the onion as she filled a big pot with water and salted it before going into the cabinet for a box of rigatoni.

"It's a gift I have. People with violent energy give off this kind of dark green smoke. It *tastes* bitter. I can tell. And your jacket, your backpack...they're dark green, but they don't match your energy. Your energy is like...a lilac puff," she said, standing like a flamingo, leaning against the counter in her kitchen.

"And this energy radar's so strong...you feel comfortable giving a suicidal man a knife."

"Apparently so."

They were quiet, looking at each other. His eyes began burning from the onions. She got a tea light from the drawer, lit it for him, put it down.

(*A wide drawer full of tea lights and pens, pencils, a spool of gold thread with a needle poking from the top of it, a roll of masking tape, a tape measure, a deck of cards, a neat stack of bright Post-its. Her countertops: pale bamboo. In the corner, up against the fog-colored backsplash: a small crystal bowl of change and a pair of yellow earrings, two closed safety pins.*)

"It's unscented. It'll help your eyes. Technically, we were supposed to light it before you started chopping, but what the hell," she said and laughed.

"It definitely sets a mood," Emmett said. He glanced at the flame, kept chopping.

"I'll count it as a win!"

"So...a lilac puff," he said and nodded.

"No denying it," she said.

"What color is your ex-husband's energy?"

"Slut red."

"Slut red," he repeated.

He'd say he wanted to go for a walk after dinner to clear his head. He could go to the bridge, jump at night. Much less of a chance some person who could read energy colors would see him and try to stop him. His last meal: rigatoni alla Norma. He slid the onions to one side of the cutting board and rinsed the eggplant under the running sink water. Chopped.

"You're good with the knife," she said. "I've never chopped an onion that quickly and perfectly in my life."

"Do you mind if I have a glass of wine?" he asked.

"Well...you probably shouldn't, since you weren't feeling so well earlier."

"Thanks for the concern. I really do appreciate it. I think it'll help relax me, honestly."

"Have you ever had a problem with alcohol? I'm sorry, but I feel like I should ask."

"I understand. And no, I haven't. I promise."

"Maybe we could have just a little," she said, getting out a bottle of red.

"How long were you married?" he asked.

"Almost ten and a half years."

"How long have you been divorced?"

"Almost a year," she said.

Emmett thanked her as she poured two glasses and set his in front of him. She went over to the cabinet by the stove, pulled out a big pan, and turned the burner on next to the pasta water. He kept chopping as she added a glug of olive oil to the pan. He paused, drank some wine. He never drank wine anymore; it silked down his throat like a ribbon.

"Did you and your ex-husband live in this house together?" he asked.

"Yes. But it's mine. I lived here alone before. He moved in when we got married...and then he moved out."

"Simple enough," he said.

"I should probably salt the eggplant to make sure it's not bitter," she said.

"We don't need it. Rarely is an eggplant bitter enough to need salting."

"Settled. I'll take your word for it."

"Do you like living alone? You don't get scared?" he asked as he finished chopping.

(*A knife block by the stove. One wide white-curtained window in her kitchen, another on the door leading to the deck. The back light comes through. Large arch-top window in the living room, the streetlamp light comes through.*)

The olive oil pan was hot, waiting. He went to it, used the knife to slip the eggplant cubes and onions into it. They bubbled. Sizzled.

"Okay, now tomatoes," she said, holding out her hand for the knife. He turned the handle so it was facing her, handed it over slowly. "I have a gun. And a security system," she added.

"And these two ferocious attack cats," he said, looking down at them winding their way between his legs. He was careful not to move too much, didn't want to spook them. He leaned against the counter drinking his wine.

When his eyes met Tallie's, he was thinking he could still be dead by morning if he wanted. Could she tell?

It'd be easy.

One.

Two.

Three.

"Exactly," she said. She began chopping the tomatoes as he tended the stove. He turned up the burner on the water, added a lot more sea salt, covered it with the lid.

"It's good for a woman to have a gun," he said. "Now I have to ask. Do *you* have violent energy? Can you read your own? I don't know how it works."

"You'd have to check with my ex-husband about that one," she said.

"Ah."

"I'm afraid of *some* men, but I'm not afraid of you."

"Because I'm a lilac kitten puff," he said.

She pointed the knife at him.

"Emmett what. What's your last name?"

"It's just Emmett. Like Bono."

"Okay."

"You've been very kind to me. Not a lot of people would do what you're doing. I realize that," he said.

The vegetables hissed in the pan as the pasta water came to a rolling boil. He opened the box of rigatoni, rattled them in. Tallie finished chopping the tomatoes and stood there drinking her red wine, looking at him like she really *could* read his colors. His mind.

They ate their dinner with Parmesan and mozzarella cheese, drank their wine, and sat on the couch when they were finished. He sat on one side; she sat on the other. She tucked her feet underneath her and tuned the TV to the World Series. It was soothing how she never ran out of things to ask. Their talk didn't feel so small anymore.

What's your favorite movie? Where's your favorite place you've ever been? Do you have a favorite book? What other kinds of music do you like? If you won't tell me your last name, will you at least tell me your middle name?

Hers was Lee. Tallulah Lee Clark. TLC. He told her his middle name was Aaron and his favorite movies were *Back to the Future* and *Badlands*, but he didn't tell her how much Sissy Spacek reminded him of his mom. His favorite place besides Kentucky was Paris. He loved too many books to pick a favorite. He liked other kinds of music besides Radiohead. Frank Ocean, Sturgill Simpson, Solange, John Prine, OutKast, Alabama Shakes, A Tribe Called Quest, the Roots, Free.

Emmett rarely listened to music anymore. Hadn't read a book in a year. Couldn't remember the last time he watched a movie.

"Your turn," Emmett said. She'd lowered the volume on the TV, but he could still hear the murmurs. The wine in his bloodstream— an eraser that had lightened him, like he could balloon-float away. He could almost mistake it for happiness.

"I love a *lot* of movies and musicals. Every James Bond. *Singin' in the Rain* and *Funny Girl*…those classics…I've seen them all a million times. When I was growing up, my mom and I would watch them together. That's why California's one of my favorite places…because I love old Hollywood so much," she said. She kept talking, mentioning that she was an official member of the Jane Austen Society of North America and how Austen's books were her favorite. She talked about the *Outlander* series and how she listened to a lot of folksy, quiet music and oldies.

"Also Sade, Patty Griffin, Aretha Franklin, Ella Fitzgerald, Etta James, Ben Harper, Florence and the Machine, One Direction—"

"One Direction? The what…British boy band?"

"Yes, and don't try to tease me, because I have a Harry Styles mug I can legally use as a weapon. Absolutely One Direction, the British-Irish boy band that was," she said, rolling her eyes at him. "I make no apologies for loving sunny, happy music! The world is dark enough. But I can tell I probably shouldn't let on how much I love ABBA, though, at least not yet."

Emmett raised his hands in surrender and laughed. An accident. It was the wine. The fake happiness held him under his arms, lifted him up and up. He couldn't help but smile, betraying the darkness in his heart. He nodded, kept drinking. The goal was to get as drunk as possible without making himself sick or blacking out. Two more glasses should do it. The Yankees ace threw a wild pitch, allowing the Giants a run. Emmett went into the kitchen, ferried back the warm bottle of red to the living room after asking Tallie if it was okay. She'd hesitated before relenting.

They drank. It rained. They drank more. It rained harder.

"What color is *all* my energy now?" he asked. The *all* stumbled out because his blood was wine. The room was wine. He, Tallie, and the cats, along with the entire house, would dissolve into a puddle of wine, drip and slip off into the rainwater.

"Oh, it doesn't change. Well, not usually. You're still a lilac puff," she said. He poured more wine into her glass, his own.

"You'll tell me if it changes? Promise?" he asked.

He wasn't flirting. Not intentionally. He liked to imagine he'd transcended sexual desire, since this could be his last day. He liked the sound of the rain against her windows; maybe it would never stop raining. The water would rise and rise and rise and rise and lift them up, float them away. The whole earth would be covered in water and no one would complain. *This is our new normal*, the world leaders would say. Or maybe he'd drown, maybe they'd all drown. Then he wouldn't have to make the decision himself; the rain would do it for him.

"I promise," she said.

"But a self-destructive suicidal man such as myself"—he touched his chest—"my energy must be reading *somewhat* unpredictable and crooked. Isn't it like I'm a radio station that won't come in all the way? Shouldn't this be where you tell me what's wrong with me?"

The Giants scored another run. If the Giants came from behind to win the game, he would wait to return to the bridge. And if he waited...and the Giants won the World Series...what then? His impulses buzzed on and off like neon as he considered his past, his present, a future that didn't exist. All that could happen. How his world could change in an instant. He'd lived it and he was fucking tired. Didn't he have the right to be tired? After what he'd been through? Regardless, his alligator tomorrows waited with open mouths, toothy snaps. Nothing wrong with waiting a few days.

"You don't need me to tell you what's wrong with you. Do you want to tell *me* what's wrong with me?" she asked.

Her cat hopped in her lap, purring as Tallie smoothed the hair on its back.

"There's nothing wrong with you. Well, wait . . . you're too trusting," he said.

"Clearly," she said, opening her arms wide. "But I'm more distrustful of people in general than I might appear. When it comes to you, I'm just going with my instincts, which are much better now post-divorce. I trust those above all. And honestly? It's kind of one of my rules now . . . not to be afraid to live my life."

The Giants scored again, tied the game. Like the rain, maybe the inning would never end.

"Were you ever afraid of your ex-husband?"

"Ah, good ol' Joel," she said.

"Were you afraid of Joel?"

"Not really. He was never violent, but he had these heavy moods. Sometimes it still feels like a dream to talk about because it all happened so fast. I found out . . . he moved in with her . . . we got divorced. They got married and had a baby," she said, miming a head explosion. "We didn't really talk about it. There's so much left unsaid, and now it feels too late. What's the point? It's baffling how you can think you know someone and not know them at all. Maybe not even a little bit . . . but that's not what you asked. However, I do still stalk him on social media," she finished, her words clomping out with sticky boots. She was buzzed like him. They were two tiny bees touching antennae. Buzzing.

"I'm not on social media," he said.

"Smart move. I don't enjoy it, but I snoop around on there. Joel never changed his password, so sometimes I look at his account."

"What do you see?"

"Everything," she said.

"And how does it make you feel when you look at that stuff?"

"Sounds like something I would ask *you*."

"It makes me feel curious when you tell me you stalk your ex-husband on social media," he said, stroking his chin.

She smiled and told him she was trying to stop spying on Joel, but he'd changed so much in such a short amount of time that she could hardly believe they were ever together. *Montana Joel*, she called him, saying it as if he were a new species of Joel that needed to be taxonomized, tagged, tracked.

"How can he be a *completely* different person now? He grew his hair out, and now he has this stupid ponytail I hate so much. He's a father; they have a horse. He bitched about my two cats, and now he has a *horse*?" she said, raising her voice. Buzz.

"His loss," he said. There was a reason for cliché—sometimes there was nothing else to say.

Where had Tallie put his letters? He looked at his backpack on the floor by his feet, touched his toe to it. He was wearing the fresh dry pair of socks she'd given him—white with a skinny gold stripe across the toe. Pitching change. The ball game went to commercial.

"I'm not the only person this has happened to...things like this happen every day, I know. But I need to find a way to completely move on with my life, I guess. I'm almost there," Tallie said. She was staring off, like she was alone and daydreaming, not talking to him.

"What would help you move on completely?"

"A little more time," she said and paused before adding, "and it would be nice if Joel would admit none of this was my fault and I couldn't have done anything differently to stop it. I'd especially love to hear him say it wasn't the stress of in vitro fertilization that pushed him away," she said and stopped. Emmett didn't say anything, just listened as she continued. "I know it in my heart, and I know better than to think I can control what anyone else does, but it would feel good to hear him say it. However, I'm never going to tell him I want that, so—"

"Maybe you'll tell him eventually. Tomorrow can bring something new," Emmett said, posturing. Wishing he believed his own lies.

"For you, too," she said.

"I guess so."

"Are you feeling better?"

"I guess so," he said again. He poured the last of the *This is my blood* wine into his glass and looked at it in there for how long?

"Emmett, are you comfortable staying here tonight?" Tallie's voice said, fracturing the deep ecclesiastical spell he'd gone into.

"Only...if you're absolutely sure it's okay. I do like it here."

"Would you like to sleep on the couch or in the guest bedroom? Forgive me for not giving you a proper tour." She stood and pointed, ticking off the rooms for him. "Laundry room, my bedroom, guest bedroom, office. And the hallway bathroom is yours. I have my own in my bedroom."

"I'll take the couch. I appreciate it," he said.

Tallie disappeared down the hallway. Emmett heard a door click open, the slip of fabric across wood. She reappeared with three thick-knitted blankets: purple, brown, and gray. She put them on the couch and went into the closet again, returned carrying a pillow.

"I knit these," she said, touching the blankets. "Knitting calms me down. I always have a project." She reached into a basket by the couch, held up a thick ball of yarn attached to rows of neat knitting hanging from a circular needle. "I've started giving most of the blankets away to the homeless shelter. For Christmas and Valentine's Day, I knit tiny red hats for the hospital nursery."

"Oh, wow, so you're actually, like, a *good* person," he said. "You aren't worried I'll, at the very least, rob you blind while you're sleeping?"

"Not really. I'm kind of a hippie about that stuff. It's not like

I have a trove of jewels here. The most precious things to me are myself and these two, and we'll be locked behind the door," she said, nodding toward the cats.

(*A truck shifts and grumbles down the street. The ocean-deep bass of a slow-moving vehicle rattles through the rain, thumping Tallie's windows.*)

"I...um...I wrote my parents a suicide letter and mailed it to them. They'll get it tomorrow. Saturday at the latest," he confessed once it was quiet again.

"Oh, no."

"So yeah...that's awkward."

"How did it make you feel, writing the letter?" she asked. Her presence—a cool, minty balm working its way onto his skin, through his muscles.

"I hated it, but I didn't feel like I had a choice. If I didn't write it, that wouldn't be fair. If I *did*...if I had to write it, period, that would be awful, too. So I chose the *least* awful choice."

"How do you feel about it now? They'll get it and you're still here. I'm so glad you're still here," she said, tilting her head to the side.

"Shitty, I guess," he said.

"Well, don't you want to call them and explain? Try to intercept it somehow? We could do something," she said.

"I don't know yet." So much darkness, Tallie couldn't possibly understand, even if he laid it out for her. And he didn't. Wouldn't. "But yeah, I'll sleep on the couch. I appreciate this. I would never...look, I promise not to uh...kill myself in your living room," he said, noticing her pale pink toenails—Brenna's favorite color. His eyes burned and welled; he put his head in his hands. He couldn't believe the thing that broke him open, what finally made him cry, was the color of Tallie's toenails. That whisper of pink, those screaming memories. Emmett was embarrassed he'd told her too much by crying in front of her. The Giants scored, taking the lead in the bottom of the eighth.

"Listen to me. I hope you've heard it plenty of times before, but it's okay to *not* be okay. And it doesn't make me uncomfortable, you crying. So I don't want you to worry. I'm totally fine with emotionalism," Tallie said, her voice soft and sweet as that pink polish.

"Do you have to work tomorrow? I'm assuming you have a job," Emmett said. Sniffed.

"I do have a job. I have the day off tomorrow, though."

"What do you do?"

"What do *you* do?" she asked.

Emmett sniffed again. His throat was thick and wobbly. Hot. He wiped his nose.

"I've worked a lot of places," he said.

"But not anymore?"

"Not anymore."

"I teach high school. English. I scheduled tomorrow off so I could have a break from teenagers," she said. She drank some wine, put the glass down. Picked it up again and finished it, wiping her bottom lip with her thumb.

"Easy, tiger," he said.

"Ha! Why do men think women can't hold their alcohol? It's like you guys depend on us being weak and vulnerable even when we're not. *You're* drinking tonight, but I can't?"

"I'm sorry. I was only kidding. Really. I didn't mean it like that. You don't seem vulnerable. Maybe you should behave more like it, but you don't," he said.

"Wait...I *should*?"

"Hell, yeah. You invite a stranger...a man to your house? A *suicidal* stranger. I know you can't stop thinking about that part. Look at me. I'm not all there up here, apparently," he said, pointing to his head. "I could be anyone."

"And so could I."

"Yeah, but it's different and you know it."

"Okay, so...want to arm-wrestle?" she asked, squinting.

(The blue mood of the room flashes and catches the light. Prism-quick.)

They got on the floor, cross-legged, with the coffee table between them. She put her elbow on the wood.

"Drunk arm wrestling," he said.

"You expected something else entirely when you woke up this morning."

His eyes still burned from crying, his temples throbbed.

"I did," he said. "And I'm left-handed, so you have the advantage here."

"Yes, a southpaw. I noticed," she said, grabbing his hand. "I should warn you that I can handle myself."

"I don't doubt it."

He wrapped his hand around hers, the pales of their wrists kissed. Tallie counted to three. He put up a decent fight before letting her win, and she knew it. She didn't say it, but he knew she knew. She stayed there on the floor and so did he. Quietly, they watched the Giants pitcher retire another batter and another before winning the game.

So it was official.

He'd wait.

When Tallie said she was getting sleepy, she showed him how to unlock the front door if he needed to get out for fresh air. Told him he was welcome to anything in the kitchen.

"I have lots of snacks," she said, pointing to the pantry. "And I'll toss your clothes in the dryer."

"Thank you. And is it okay if I use your computer if I promise not to nose around?" he asked. Her slim laptop sat on the coffee table— a glowing silver island on that cherrywood ocean.

"Of course. Feel free," she said. "Good night, Emmett."

"Good night, Tallie."

Emmett watched her walk down the hallway, go into the laundry room, then her bedroom, and close the door. He listened for the click of the lock. When he heard it, he opened her computer and broke his promise.

Tallie was logged in to her ex-husband's Facebook account for stalking purposes, like she'd said. Joel had to know Tallie stayed logged in, snooped around. Probably wanted her to. Emmett clicked through Joel's messages first. Found some from Tallie. Her profile pic was of her with Jim the cat held next to her face. She had her hair pulled on top of her head; her lips were a cranberry red. She looked pretty. Her full smile wasn't a total surprise like some other people's. It was natural, as if her face preferred it to frowning. He liked that she wasn't one of those people whose profile pics didn't look like them, the people who used all sorts of filters and camera-angle tricks to lie to the world. Tallie looked like Tallie.

Emmett had finished his glass of wine and was drunk enough to stop drinking. He was now in a happily tipsy state he would live in, if possible. He made himself more comfortable on the couch. Tallie had also given him a new pack of boxer shorts and a cozy, thick navy-blue cardigan sweater that Joel had never worn. Still had the tags on it. She'd taken a small pair of gold stork scissors from the kitchen drawer and cut them off. He loved it on his arms, so heavy and warm. He snuggled into it more, put his feet up on the coffee table, the laptop screen robot-glowing his face as he read Joel's messages. The most recent one from Tallie was written over the summer.

last call. if there's anything else still in the house you need, just let me know. there's a box of books and some of your old albums. i'm donating this stuff to goodwill if i don't hear from you. there's nothing left to say i guess.

Joel had responded:

You can give it to Goodwill. I have everything I need. And I know this is weird, awful, etc. I've told you it was never my intent to hurt you and trust me, I know it sounds like a load of real bullshit. I've asked you to forgive me, knowing how huge, undeserved and probably impossible it is. You can message me anytime you want. Odette doesn't mind and even if she did, I wouldn't. I don't mean that in a nasty way. She's fine. We're fine. I still care about you. It doesn't matter if I'm in Montana or that we're not married anymore.

He clicked back to Joel's profile, enlarged his photo. It was of him, a woman tagged as Odette, and their new baby girl. Odette had her head on his shoulder. The baby was sleeping. Joel was looking straight into the camera, and Emmett had no opinion of his face. Joel could be anyone. He scrolled through Odette's profile, finding photos of her pert face alone, with friends, with Joel. Photos of her pregnant and smiling, photos of her holding the baby. Odette seemed so different from Tallie. He imagined Joel would've had to split himself in two to ever love them both.

Emmett decided against googling *Tallulah Clark* to let the mystery of her play out by itself. Maybe he'd google her on his way to the bridge, find out he'd spent the night with a wacko who pretended to be normal but regularly posted to dark conspiracy theory message boards using her real name. And she wouldn't find *him* online. Since he wasn't on social media, there was nothing for her to discover if she attempted to look him up, which he was sure she'd done already. Would've been the smart, reasonable thing for a woman to do.

Emmett opened an incognito browser tab, created an entirely new email account. He tried to think of something Tallie would choose. Looked around the living room, minimized the browser, and checked out her desktop photo. It was of Jim and Pam sleeping on the couch he was sitting on. He maximized the browser window, chose the new email name.

Talliecat. He heard it chime in his head like the chorus of the Grateful Dead's "China Cat Sunflower." He'd need to add some numbers, too, just in case it was already taken. He glanced at the DVDs on the shelf beside him: all the James Bond movies in a neat row, in order. *Talliecat007*. Password: *Thur$dayOctober2nine*.

He went to Facebook again, found Tallie's profile photo, and saved it to the desktop. Uploaded it so it would show up as her photo with her new email address. He got Joel's email address from his profile, copied and pasted it into the recipient box.

From: talliecat007@gmail.com
To: joelfoster1979@gmail.com
Subject: i still care about you too

hey joel, this is my new personal email address. starting fresh. i've been thinking about your last message and obviously i still care about you too. and thanks for letting me know it's okay to write...when or if i need to. it's weird not being married to you anymore. you're montana joel. a father. you have a baby and a ponytail!

Emmett laughed at this part. He couldn't help it. He put his finger to his lips and shushed his drunken self, which made him laugh harder. He turned to look at Tallie's locked bedroom door, wondered if she was asleep. He walked down the hallway quietly and listened. Heard nothing but his clothes in the dryer, tumbling hot. Getting back to the email, he wrote: *so i'm open to talking.*

but it would be nice if you'd admit none of this was my fault and i couldn't have done anything differently to stop it. i know better than to think i can control what anyone else does...but it would feel good to hear you say it. the way you went out and got another woman pregnant because you think i'm broken? crushing. i'm still working on my heart about it. it's baffling how you can think you know someone...and not know them at all. maybe not even a little bit.

are you coming back to town anytime soon?

do you miss me sometimes?

He didn't sign her name. The *do you miss me sometimes?* hovered there at the end, unpinned. Sent.

Tallie and Joel weren't Facebook friends, and there wasn't much on her page, but under "work and education" it read *TLC*, which Emmett thought was pretty cute. Under "family and relationships" her brother was listed: *Lionel Clark*. Emmett clicked on his profile, read Lionel's announcement for a big party he was having on Saturday.

It's time for the Annual Clark Halloween Party again! Best costume wins $2500 with another $2500 donated to the charity of the winner's choice!

Emmett scrolled through Lionel's page until he found photos of Tallie. A guy tagged *Nico Tate* had his arm around her in one, and she was smiling a different smile. Blissful. Emmett felt a twitch of jealousy. He clicked on Nico's profile. Half of his page was in Dutch, some French, a bit of English. Flipped through photos of him kayaking and rock climbing. He was a tennis coach, and there were links to his website. Photos of him on the court with his students, at fund-raising events with Roger Federer and Serena Williams. There were also more pictures of Tallie: Nico and Tallie on a tennis court, Nico and Tallie at a wedding. A younger Tallie, scarfed in an orchard with her head thrown back laughing, a bright blurred apple in her hand. The picture could've been a movie poster—an autumn romance with a happy ending. Emmett leaned closer to the screen.

He was careful to sign out of the new fake email account, deleted the photo of Tallie he'd saved to the desktop. He deleted everything in the browser history that revealed his snooping, clicked through sports news, looked at the box score for the baseball game he and Tallie had watched together. Closed the laptop, set it on the coffee table.

Emmett got his phone from his backpack and entered the new email information so he'd know when Joel had responded. And if he didn't, who cared? Nothing mattered. He stepped to the window, wishing the moon was out. Would he ever see it again? The forecast called for rain off and on all weekend. If this was really it for him, no more moonlight. Felt like years since the last time he'd drowned himself in it. Day or night, he loved looking up at the sky, being out underneath it. He'd taken so much for granted.

He lay on her couch, covered himself with the blankets she'd brought out for him, felt himself sinking. He still had the nightmares from time to time—his own metallic voice screaming, detached. Demonic. Every dark, demented horror of all he'd seen and been forced to do. The violence and loneliness stabbed at him, left invisible gashes for the soul leak.

But thinking about the future was a comfort to him as he drifted off, everything ending soon. Sleep being so much like death. No nightmares that night. He slept in the cardigan with the weight of Tallie's hand-knitted blankets on him in what felt like smooth, zipped-up, dreamless darkness, like he'd never been awake.

PART TWO

FRIDAY

TALLIE

In the morning, Tallie saw a text from Lionel—a reply to a question she had forgotten she'd asked before the haze of Emmett excitement. The thought of *I let a strange, unstable man spend the night* had tapped her on the shoulder and woken her up long before her alarm had a chance to.

Same thing every year, so quit playing. I'm not telling you my costume. It's a secret, her brother had written before dawn, the forever early riser he was.

i know you never tell, but i like asking...to annoy you! Tallie texted him back.

Annoyed. You got your wish.

aaand you love me.

That, I do.

Her cats purred down by her feet like two fuzzy engines. Tallie held her breath, attempting to listen for Emmett moving around out there on the couch. Had he bolted in the night? She tiptoed to her bedroom door, unlocked and opened it slowly. From there, she could see Emmett's hair, set like a red-gold paintbrush against her pillow and the lavender fabric of her couch. She closed and locked the door, went into her bathroom. As a way to self-soothe, Tallie took baths as hot as she could stand every night when she got home from work. Usually, she steeped herself like tea until she was blushed and loose, limbs limp from the heat, eyelids heavy. Since she'd skipped her ritual the night before, it was time for a shower. She undressed and stepped into the white-tiled coolness.

~

Afterward, she took her time brushing her teeth and washing her face. She used her apple toner, her hyaluronic acid, her caffeine under-eye treatment, and moisturizer with sunscreen. Squeezed the skinny tube of coconut lip gloss onto her finger and swiped it across her lips. She liked coconuts in the morning and mint at night. She didn't change or shorten one thing about her morning skin-care routine. The glass serum bottles and smells soothed her. Joel used to ask, *But what's it do?* as he inspected the teeny print on the labels. He liked to claim skin care was a scam, but he didn't understand that she used it to organize her mornings and evenings. It wouldn't even matter if her routine *did* anything or not. But it did! Her skin had been clear, soft, and smooth for almost the entirety of the two years since she'd started paying more attention to it and taking time for herself. The fertility drugs she'd been prescribed had reconfigured the precious science of her body and, in turn, wrecked her skin. She needed the exfoliators, boosters, ampoules, acids, and essences. Eye creams, sunscreens, and night creams. Retinol and sheet masks. Morning and night, the ritualistic three or five or ten steps she could control when she couldn't control anything else.

~

Careful not to make any extra noise, Tallie walked past Emmett camped on the couch with his backpack underneath his knees. She stood in her kitchen, replied to texts from a couple of her girlfriends. Texted, i love you, miss you, to Aisha, knowing she wouldn't see it until Sunday. Tallie took her laptop to the kitchen table and checked the browser history—sports websites and articles. Emmett certainly hadn't googled *how to murder the woman who bought you coffee last night*.

She walked into the living room, got on the floor across from him. She was eager for him to wake up so she could gauge his mood, to see if he was feeling better. His head was turned toward her, and she resisted the urge to get closer. To lean in and inspect him more, to see how he smelled as he slept. To whisper *Who are you?* into his ear so he'd dreamily open his mouth and scatter his secrets across the morning light.

EMMETT

He woke up to Tallie trying to be quiet in the kitchen and the smell of coffee, bacon, eggs. He had a full-blown, throbbing red-wine headache. He took himself and his backpack to the bathroom first thing.

"Hi, Emmett, good morning. I hope you're feeling well. I put a new toothbrush on the counter for you. You probably see it," she said from the other side of the door after tapping on it.

Peeing, he spotted the red toothbrush still in the package on the counter.

"Good morning. Yes, I feel okay. Thank you. I see the toothbrush."

"And I have coffee and breakfast when you get out."

"Thank you," he said again.

Emmett brushed his teeth using her cinnamon toothpaste, his reflection blinking back at him. He hadn't intended on being alive to see himself in a morning mirror. He pictured the bridge in cloudy daylight, the cars whizzing by. Was there a chance he'd be conscious after hitting the river? He'd read about the rare survivor stories, but he'd also read that the impact from jumping off a bridge was the equivalent of getting hit by a car, that his body could be falling at the rate of seventy-five miles an hour. He would accelerate as he fell, then his bones would break, his organs would tear apart. Simple physics. And by chance, if those things didn't kill him instantly, his last breath would be water.

He wasn't scared.

Emmett splashed his face, wiped it dry on her hanging towel. Looked around at the little glass bottles and plastic tubes she had in there. Everything smelled like flowers, a girl garden.

(The hallway bathroom. Two candles: one half full of wax, one with a wick that hasn't been lit. A photo of her and another woman hangs in a white frame next to the light switch. A hook next to the frame, holding two wooden necklaces, one beaded one. Pearly white liquid soap in the dispenser. Pale blue bath mat. Four fat bulbs of white light above her mirror. A postcard of Michelangelo's David *tacked next to it. The bathroom door handles are curved silver with curlicues on the ends. Swan's neck faucet, silver. White floor vent, white tile. A full-length mirror on the back of the door. A wall outlet with two plugs, one holding an auto night-light. A small garbage can in the corner next to the toilet. A shower curtain matching the bath mat. A round frosted window fit for a ship.)*

He was greeted by the cats sitting side by side in the hallway, watching the door. He petted them on their heads, rubbed behind their ears. When he walked into the kitchen, Tallie handed him a Harry Styles mug of coffee. Emmett pointed to Harry's face and thanked her one more time, took a sip as she sat at the kitchen table.

(A plate of bacon, eggs, and toast. On the middle of the table—butter and local organic blackberry jam, almond butter. A carafe of water, two glasses, and a bottle of ibuprofen.)

"Red wine gives everyone a headache," she said, touching the plastic top of the medicine. She motioned for him to have a seat. "Do you like breakfast?"

"Only a psychopath wouldn't like breakfast," he said. He took two ibuprofen. Last night he'd wondered if dinner would be his last meal, and now? He was ravenous for breakfast.

Emmett and Tallie ate and discussed the rain, the weekend forecast. She asked him again how he was feeling.

"Better...I feel better," he said.

"Glad to hear it."

He remembered the phony email to Joel and felt like garbage for it, wondering if he could make it all go away. His feelings shuffled like a deck of cards—diamonds of embarrassment, overreacting clubs, stubbornness in spades, the ace of guilt. And his heart, their hearts, still beating. Somehow. But hope. Hope was the real joker. Had he confused exhaustion for hopelessness? Maybe they felt exactly the same in the cold rain, darkness creeping.

"Just wondering...do you ever talk to Joel anymore?" he asked after a moment, attempting to make the question as casual as possible—a continuation of their conversation from the night before. If she talked to Joel via some other form of communication, she'd figure out what he'd done real easy.

"Oh...no. I actually blocked his number in my phone out of pettiness. Maybe the occasional message online, but not really. Last time he wrote me, I didn't feel the need to respond. Nothing more to say," she said. "On a nicer note, did you sleep well?"

The sweetness in her voice inspired a violent tenderness inside him.

"I did. Did you?" he asked.

"Yes."

"Well, you did beat me at arm wrestling...so maybe tonight *I* should be behind the locked door," he said.

"Oh," she said. Her face went plain.

"Not that I'm trying to stay here tonight. I was kidding. I'll be on my way soon, no worries," he said, not fully able to decode how he wanted her to respond. Ask him to stay? Ask him to go? Leave it up to him? He ate, drank his coffee.

"No, that's not what I meant. You're more than welcome to stay. I'm worried about you. Maybe you need a couple days to feel back to your old self?"

Emmett swallowed and took his time. "I don't ever want to feel back to my old self."

"Of course not. Right," she said, nodding. "Well, okay...so my brother, Lionel, has this huge Halloween party every year. It's on Saturday. Tomorrow," she said, as if he were an alien and didn't know how the days of the week worked. "It's a lot of fun, tons of people in wild costumes..." She stopped talking and put her elbow on the table, her chin in her hand, before sitting back in her chair and beginning again. "A proposal: How about you stay here at least until then and go to the party with me? That would be fun and something to do. It's always good to have something to do...to look forward to. It keeps our brains happy."

They smiled across the table at each other like old friends.

"What'd you dress up as last year?" he asked.

"Dorothy from *Wizard of Oz*, and my best friend, Aisha, was Dorothy, too," she said. "My brother always goes *way* overboard since it's his favorite holiday. Last year he was Houdini and rented a water tank. And! He has this friend who grows his beard out specifically to dress up like Gandalf every year, then he shaves it the day after. He even comes with his own little hobbits. The whole thing is beyond."

"Okay, wow. Big leagues. So what's your costume?"

"Absolutely no clue. I usually know, like, *months* in advance, but this year I'm so slow...with work and...everything else on my mind, I haven't figured it out yet. And time's a-tickin'. But it'll all work out, because now you and I can look for costumes together."

"I'll do it," he said. What did it feel like to have a happy brain? He couldn't fully remember, although there was a flick of it somewhere inside him. But it was too small, too far away.

"Good. That's what we'll do today."

~

(An outlet mall costume shop, but this one isn't as sad as it could be. The costume shop is sandwiched between a shoe store and a candy store. There is a sporting goods store across from it, a kitchenware store next to that. It is a wet morning, and the world seems to have not woken up yet. The college kid working the register has his feet up on the counter. He is wearing glasses, reading a Superman comic book.)

They wandered up and down the aisles, Tallie stopping every now and then to inspect costumes a little more closely.

"See anything that looks good?" Tallie asked him from the end of a row of gorilla costumes.

"Not really," he said, putting his hands in his pockets.

"Last time you dressed up for Halloween...what were you?"

"Few years back, I was Beetlejuice."

"I *love* Beetlejuice. That's so good. Okay, what about *Star Wars*? All boys love *Star Wars*. You love *Star Wars*, right?"

"I do," Emmett said.

"We're just riffling through the leftovers at this point. I waited too late," Tallie said, walking away from him and down the other aisle. He could see the top of her head bobbing. And when she got next to him, she popped up over a rack of spooky signs. "There's nothing good over here. Okay...I *know*, I know...but what if we do a couples costume? Not a *couples* couples costume, but you know what I mean...related costumes for two people going to a Halloween party together. Is that weird? Would you maybe do that?" she asked.

"I'd do that."

"Really?"

And when he nodded she said, "All right. Come on this side with me," and waved him over.

"What about Clark Kent and Lois Lane? Those are easy and don't require too much," Tallie said after they'd circled the store once with their new goal in mind. "It's either that or Sandy and Danny from *Grease*. I can't actually win the costume contest since it's my brother's party and it wouldn't be fair…so be warned, we don't have to have the *best* costumes, but let's make a valiant effort we can both be proud of."

"Right on," he said. She had a pair of black plastic-framed glasses in her hand, shiny black leggings thrown over her arm, purse hanging off her shoulder. "I'll wear the glasses."

"Try them."

Emmett took the glasses and put them on. He would've done anything she asked in that moment. He looked at her, his new surprise friend Tallie.

"Perfect. Okay, we need suspenders. Or maybe we don't need the suspenders, but we *do* need a Superman shirt to put underneath a white dress shirt, and you can throw your tie over your shoulder. Windswept. Like Clark Kent transitioning into Superman." He realized how seriously she was taking this. She'd walked into the store like it was casual, but now she was down to business. "I have a pencil skirt and the rest of it, but I need, like, a newspaper badge or something. Let me go ask this kid if they have those," she said, taking the glasses off Emmett and putting the shiny leggings back where she found them. She walked to the front of the store. Emmett let *pencil skirt* hang out to dry in his brain momentarily, having absolutely no clue what those words meant put together like that. He was baffled and impressed by all the secret things women knew about the world.

The cashier guy followed her and pointed. "We have these badges. FBI *X-Files* badges."

"Oh! Let's be Mulder and Scully instead!" she said, grabbing two FBI badges from the rack next to them. The cashier guy straightened a shelf of ridiculous jester and skull hats on his way to the front of the store.

"We can basically wear the same things, but not the glasses or Superman shirt. Mulder wears a lot of black or gray suits, but I do have a navy suit at home that'll fit you."

"Joel's?"

"He never wore it."

"Why do you still have so many clothes he never wore?"

"Because I haven't gotten rid of them yet and I wanted him to be something he wasn't, and he only wears black or gray suits," she said sharply—a needle through paper.

"I like Mulder. I'll be Mulder."

"You'll be a *perfect* Mulder," she said with steely confidence.

Emmett followed her to the counter.

"I have plenty of money. At your place. In my backpack. You don't have to pay for my stuff all the time," he said. He pictured his backpack at Tallie's, safely snug in between her couch and the end table where he'd left it. It didn't make him nervous leaving it at her place. She lived alone; there was no one there but the cats to nose through it.

"Nonsense. I'm making you go to a Halloween party. It's my job to buy this."

"You're not *making* me go. I want to go," he said, surprising himself by meaning it. He couldn't remember the last time he wanted to do anything like go to a party.

She touched the top of his hand and took the badges to the cash register; he insisted on carrying the slick orange bag out of the store.

~

"Y'know, you can be honest with me. About anything," Tallie said.

They'd stopped at Poodle Skirt, a '50s-themed hamburger joint at the end of the outlet mall. It was all lit up, an oasis for the shoppers who could make it that far without killing themselves. Bravo.

"Weird. I was going to say the same thing to you," he said, smirking.

"I'm serious, okay?" she said in a kind of whine he found endearing. She gooped her french fry with ketchup before eating it.

"I'm serious, too. You tell me something honest, and I'll do the same. Right now," he lied.

"You want to go first?"

"Absolutely. I'll go first. We could've passed each other on the street or at the grocery store or whatever so many times...and *now*...here we are," Emmett said. He looked around, noticed the family in the booth diagonally across from them.

(An older couple with their adult son, his small children. They have their food already. The older woman orders a milkshake from the waiter. Chocolate. The children drink from plastic cartoon cups with bright red lids. An Elvis clock swings its glittery hips on the wall. Tick, tock. Tick, tock. Tick, tock.)

"You come to Louisville a lot?" Tallie asked.

"Enough."

"Well, I would've remembered you."

"Remembered what?"

"Your face and hair and eyes. Your whole thing," she said in between bites of food. She pointed a limp fry at him. "You're *striking.*"

He loved looking at her but refrained from saying it for fear of making her uncomfortable. Her listening face was pretty and consistently reassuring, like a familiar character from a pleasant, uneventful dream.

The waiter stopped by their table, refilled their drinks.

(The waiter's name is Greg. Greg has short brown hair. Greg is wearing blue-and-yellow running shoes, jeans, a white T-shirt, a red half apron with buttons on it. One of the buttons reads ROCK AROUND THE CLOCK TONIGHT. Another button is a fluffy pink poodle drinking a milkshake against a black-and-white checkered background. Another: ASK ME ABOUT POODLE SKIRT REWARDS POINTS.)

"Can we get two beers and two shots of bourbon?" Emmett asked the waiter before promising Tallie he'd give her money as soon as they got back to her place.

"Uh...um. Okay, look. Swear you're not an alcoholic?" she asked after the waiter was gone.

"I'm not an alcoholic, Tallie. Are *you* an alcoholic?"

"No. I'm not. But day drinking is rarely a *super*good idea."

"I'm breaking all the rules," he said.

"Mmm-hmm...and you had the nerve to 'Easy, tiger' me last night. Oh, wait! You've never been here before, right?" Tallie asked.

Emmett told her no, he hadn't.

"Then you have to try their dipping sauce. Sometimes you have to ask for it...I'll get it for us. It's so good. I almost forgot! You *have* to try it," she said, politely waving the waiter back over.

Tallie doing something small like that made him feel loved. The costumes, the food—someone else was taking control, even about tiny decisions. For so long with Christine he had to make *every* decision, check every lock, pay every bill, make every breakfast, every lunch and dinner. All of it had wrung him out, but he didn't have to worry about that anymore.

Christine: a bucket filled to the top that he'd been asked to carry through a war zone, over fiery coals, in a hot air balloon, on a shaky roller coaster. Their relationship, doomed from the start. She spilled out and over, and there was nothing he could do about it. The inevitability of it had borne down and crushed him. But now, Christine was gone, and none of that mattered. He missed her. And the mere pinch of any kind of forgiveness or mercy flooded his heart with watery light.

TALLIE

Emmett began to cry and used the paper napkin to wipe his nose. He pressed the heels of his hands to his eyes and left them there.

"Did I say something that upset you?" she asked as his chin shook.

Client cries easily, is tenderhearted. Demeanor quicksilvers.

Too many questions? Or was he thinking of the letters, those women? Or his parents, the letter he'd written them? Guilt? Remorse? It could've been anything. On the drive to the outlet mall, she'd asked him again if he wanted to try to intercept the letter and he'd shrugged, said he didn't think so. She couldn't persuade him otherwise. His poor parents. Once they got that letter, they would think there was nothing they could do. She hated imagining the depthless doom of it. But there he was in front of her, perfectly alive and safe.

Tallie was an empath. She closed her eyes, put her hands out, read the braille of her clients' hearts. It was a gift she had; she'd made an entire career out of it! She was soul-connected to Emmett already, instantly. He'd cried easily but was surprisingly *not* needy, not in the way so many of her clients were. Not like the ones who craved constant reassurance and coddling. A part of Emmett seemed *confidently* depressed, resigned to it, but he also had clear instances of buoyancy and boyishness that led her to believe there was still a lot to work with.

The waiter brought their drinks and the sauce for Emmett. He downed his shot immediately, chased it with two big draining gulps of his blond beer. And although she wasn't sure exactly why, Tallie did the same thing to keep up with him. The waiter had only just made it to the next table when Emmett motioned for two more shots of bourbon.

"It wasn't anything you said. I'm all right," Emmett said. He dipped a bit of his burger into the special sauce and ate it. Told Tallie how delicious it was before turning his attention back to his beer.

"Um. You...*we* shouldn't drink too much. It's bad news," Tallie warned. She'd never go to lunch with a client or let a client spend the night at her house. And of course she would never drink with a client. Even the thought was absurd. It would've been unprofessional, borderline unethical! She always held herself to such strict boundaries of living, but really...what had it gotten her in her relationships? Hadn't it left her feeling alone? No one else seemed to follow the rules, so why should she? What was the harm in a teeny-tiny act of rebellion? What right did she have to tell a grown man what to do? "I mean...no more after this. That's enough, don't you think?" she tacked on the end.

"Sure. I gotcha. I'm going to step outside and smoke. I think that would make me feel better," he said, like he was asking for her permission. And something about him doing that made him seem so small in the moment, even though he wasn't.

Coping mechanism: aha! Cigarettes, as suspected.

He stood and touched his pocket, went in and found the treasure of an almost-empty soft pack.

"Okay. Whatever you need. I didn't know you smoked. I thought, maybe, but you didn't smell like it, and you haven't smoked since we met. Have you? Maybe you smoked while I was sleeping?" she asked. She looked up at him, awash with the absurdity of having her feelings hurt because she didn't know this *one* specific thing about him. She knew absolutely nothing about him outside of the little he'd told her. And those could've been lies. But the purloined letters—which he hadn't noticed were missing yet, or at least hadn't mentioned—those weren't lies.

Before she fell asleep the night before, she'd tried Google again. Searched for his name alongside *Clementine, Kentucky*, but found nothing about him. She'd tried *Emmett* and *Christine* and *Brenna*. Tried them all together, paired up—it didn't matter. With no last names to search for, there were no hits, no news, no websites, no social media.

Emmett shook a cigarette out of the pack. "No. I didn't smoke while you were sleeping," he said, teary and sniffing, the cigarette bobbing in his mouth.

"Do you mind if I smoke with you?"

"Do you smoke?"

She shook her head; she hadn't had a cigarette since college.

He motioned for her to follow him, and the waiter returned with their shots. Emmett stepped to the table again, slipped the cigarette behind his ear, and downed the gold as if it were water. Tallie downed hers, too, feeling enormously guilty and irresponsible but also loving the burn.

～

Outside, Emmett lit the cigarette and took a drag before he held it out for her. He French-inhaled as he leaned against the restaurant brick. The French inhale was a luxury, although nothing about the afternoon was fancy.

The sky: hoary and mizzling.

The air: apple, tinged with grilled beef and onions.

The cider aroma was from the coffee shop next to the restaurant and smelled like that from the middle of September until the day after Thanksgiving, when it was swapped for pepperminty Christmas coffee.

Tallie could've told Emmett she was a licensed therapist, that TLC Counseling Services had been her forever dream, how proud she was of it, how it would soon grow to house two more therapists. But knowing that would change how he interacted with her. She made a living keeping other people's secrets, and it was exhausting. Isolating. She had secrets like everyone else, and Joel had kept his. Emmett was keeping his, too, so why shouldn't she? It was finally her turn.

The danger: a frothing aphrodisiac.

A secret shock of lust ran through her. Inside the restaurant, Emmett had shaken the cigarette out of the pack and put it between his lips with this kind of handsome, loose motion that reminded her of Steve McQueen, and she loved Steve McQueen, found him irresistible. Those hypermasculine old-Hollywood types smoked constantly in the classic movies she loved so much—huffed and puffed like dragons. She wished she could see Emmett shake his cigarette out again. Or that she'd recorded a short video on her phone so she could watch it on a loop before she went to sleep.

She took an extra breath and let herself imagine being in bed with him. A tonic of flickers, this fantasy. What did he smell like underneath his flannel forest of clothes? Like the flooding autumn river filled with leaves, cut with camphor? White soap, sweat, and one drop of gasoline? Cigarettes braided with wood smoke? She imagined his hot, rhythmic weight on top of her. His face between her legs, hers between his. Him behind her, hairy and grunting as he came and pulsed. The two of them, feverish. Wilding.

~

It'd been over a year since the last time she and Joel had been together, and a month since she'd been with anyone—she'd had *I'm recently divorced and have no clue what I want right now* sex with

Nicodemus Tate. *Nico.* They'd dated off and on in college for years. Back then, they'd floated away from each other instead of snapping apart, and in the past, she'd always had excellent, efficient sex with Nico. As excellent and efficient as a Target run—everything she needed in the right place, and occasionally there was an extra treat on clearance, making the whole trip more than worth it. But the post-divorce sex with Nico? Absolute rockets. The kind of orgasms that made her go deaf and dizzy for two full minutes afterward.

Nico and Tallie were in love in the '90s. Dave Matthews Band concerts, Lilith Fair, mixtapes. They threw a Y2K party together. Nico had played tennis in college, finishing seventh in collegiate rankings and reaching fortieth in the Association of Tennis Professionals rankings at one point. Tallie and Aisha went to his matches even long after college, when he wasn't her boyfriend anymore, to drink icy gin and tonics while they—*quiet, please*—watched Nico sweat and grunt on the green clay. One night after one of those winning matches, they went out for more celebratory drinks, and Tallie had ended up in his bed again, although they didn't have a name for what they were.

Three months later, Nico called to let her know—surprise!—he was engaged to his childhood sweetheart, Saskia. Saskia, the attorney. Saskia, her name like scissors slicing wrapping paper; Saskia, the sound one makes after chugging extra-bubbly pop. To her surprise, Tallie drank only a thimbleful of jealousy but had expected to feel more of it. Her strongest feeling was genuine happiness for him, and when he and Saskia got divorced, Tallie and Nico reconnected. But then there was Joel. When Tallie and Joel got serious, she began to feel for him the jealousy and territoriality she hadn't felt for Nico. Joel inspired urgency. She got drunk quick on the liquor of those new-to-her emotions.

Over the past summer, she'd bumped into a bearded and single Nico at the gym she'd recently joined, and he asked if she was still married after glancing at her ringless left finger. He showed sweetness and sadness over her divorce. Made her laugh by reminding her that she said she'd never take his name and change hers to Tallie Tate if she married him because it sounded like a bratty children's book character. She let Nico know everything about Joel's affair because she couldn't keep it in. In turn, he told her about Saskia having an early miscarriage and the guilt he felt at being relieved. Angry, Tallie spilled out her struggles with infertility to him for the first time. He apologized profusely, and she found it hard to stay mad at him. Nico was so familiar and safe, a true friend, a sort of accidental constant in her life somehow, even when they didn't keep in touch. She didn't know how it worked, but she knew it was a bit of magic. And she could trust Nico, the cool drink of water to put out her fires.

There were nights when she was feeling low and Nico could detect it in the atmosphere. Knew to bring her flowers or chocolate and wine. Food. He'd stop by her favorite noodle shop without asking, order the spicy pad kee mao with tofu and basil fried rice with shrimp. Calamari and dumplings. He was a proper, much-needed companion in those dizzying mushroom-cloud months after her divorce. She'd lost Joel—her *husband*, her lover, her partner, her friend, her company—the person she'd shared her entire life with. The person she'd slept next to and gone to the movies with. The person she'd told everything, the person who'd become a part of her family. The person she'd eaten dinner with every night and who went with her to the grocery store on Saturday afternoons. All the big and little things. The stupid, annoying things. The important things. Now she had to do them all alone.

But Nico had been there when she needed him, like a stashed first-aid kit.

Nico knew Tallie wasn't ready for a real relationship or anything close to one. She was up front with him from the beginning, letting him know she hadn't been with any man besides Joel in the past thirteen years. She told Nico that he was the last man she'd been with before Joel. She told Nico she was afraid she couldn't even remember what it was like to be with any man besides Joel. Nico had said he'd help her remember. He'd said "good thing I'm not Joel" before kissing her mouth like he'd done when they were undergrads with spicy ramen breath and stinging eyes from staying up too late studying for finals. It was like a well-written short story: Nico had been an assistant to Tallie's French professor, and Nico had also become her French tutor with benefits. *Oui*, they were adults now, with adult lives and the freedom and problems that came with, but. Part of him would always be College Nico.

College Nico in the emerald library light with his *belle bouche* and slow, stomach-swooping kisses. College Nico's wide eyes when Tallie learned to translate and repeat his dirty talk. *J'ai envie de te baiser.* College Nico in a berry raglan sweatshirt, a pencil behind his ear; College Tallie turning into a soft candle watching him slip it there. College Nico in that fisherman's cable-knit sweater heathered like static—the one she'd wanted to roll around like a dog on, cover herself with his scent. Espresso, peppermint, paper. *Nico, je suis à toi.*

Nico had been married for only two years when he and Saskia got divorced, and although their divorce wasn't as gasp-scandalous and drama-filled as Tallie and Joel's, Tallie and Nico found the same comfort in their similar broken *afters*. He called and texted Tallie often, checking in on her, and it was supportive and encouraging, not smothering. They'd slept together three times since her divorce, all three times at his spacious, glassy loft downtown. Him, breathless and naked on his back, reminding her before she left the second time that he was down for hooking up whenever she needed to remember that Joel didn't have the only cock in the world.

It'd been a month since she'd seen him. He'd texted a few days before, telling her he might swing by Lionel's costume party. Before meeting Emmett, she would've almost certainly gone home with Nico afterward, but Emmett was her "date" to the party now. Nico wasn't nosy and wouldn't ask too many questions. Their relationship had always been casually intense. Intensely casual. And if Nico wanted, Tallie was sure he could easily find a fun woman dressed like a taco or a clever woman wearing a white slip with the word *Freudian* written on it and disappear with her down Lionel's long driveway at the end of the night. Thinking of Nico leaving the costume party with someone who wasn't her didn't exactly flick Tallie's jealousy switch, but somewhere inside—somewhere she couldn't specifically give voice to—she prickled.

Nico could be exceedingly stubborn and obsessive, fixating on an argument until he felt his point had been made one hundred times, but he was also self-aware and quick to apologize. He was handsome and desirable, like the men from her beloved Jane Austens. She imagined Miss Austen anachronistically describing him as tall, with cowlike Sinatra-blue eyes and long lashes—and an amiable countenance to match them. Nico's energy was as blue as his eyes. Tallie sometimes found herself wondering why she didn't go ahead and marry Nico when he asked, but they were in college. Couldn't get the timing right. And now, any sort of serious relationship with anyone, even Nico, would be too soon after Joel.

She hadn't acted out after her divorce besides unabashedly leaning into her natural tendency for woolgathering, crying while eating too much ice cream, indulging in a glass or two of wine in the middle of her off days, and spending too much money on yarn, pajamas, and French and Korean skin care. She was secretly jealous of her divorced girlfriends who'd gotten plastic surgery, splurged on tropical vacations and luxury cars, had mindless sex with men they'd met on hookup apps. One girlfriend of hers disappeared to Paris with a dashing Frenchman for more than a month. Aisha cut her hair after her breakups and repainted the walls of her bedroom, burned sage and smoked away even the faintest memories of her lovers. Tallie hadn't gotten a prescription for sleeping pills when she'd been struggling; she hadn't even gotten a post-divorce haircut. She hadn't gone wild yet, but she'd been feeling the pinball lever of it pulled out tight, ready for release after years of ignoring her own feelings and listening to everyone else's instead. She could be wild! She could do something! Anything could happen!

~

Emmett French-inhaled again, and it was sexy. Why was he doing that? *So* sexy. Oh, the rebellious paradox of her not wanting him to harm himself but also loving to watch him smoke. Tallie turned away with blushes. Was he doing this on purpose? Was he seriously this sexy and didn't know it? Knew but didn't care? He had plenty on his mind. He could lean there, smoke sexily, and it wouldn't matter to anyone in the world. He was depressed, and depression wasn't sexy. She saw so much of it every day that she didn't have a romanticized idea of it. People died, people were miserable, people gave up. Forgot how important and loved they were. Depression was a vacuum that sucked out everything—leaving nothing behind except the burdening weight of nothingness.

They'd been quiet, smoking by the window of the restaurant. She was afraid Emmett would be able to read her mind because of the look on her face, so she relaxed it. A technique she used often with her clients: projecting placidity. And when he smiled at her it wasn't the creepy one. It was toothsome and tricky. Like he was saying, *I told you so.* Tallie smiled in accord. *Absolutely. You told me so.*

~

"Thanks again for this. The food and spirits, figuring out the costumes," he said as they wandered around the outlet mall after lunch, the air like cool water.

"Don't mention it," she said, pausing only for a moment before blurting out, "Yesterday I told you I feel better, but sometimes I still have a hard time with my divorce."

"Honestly? He sounds like a dumbass. You're too good for him," Emmett said, as if he'd been waiting for permission to say it.

"You sure about that?" Tallie asked, snickering.

They stopped in front of a candle store. Tallie felt like she wasn't a proper steward of her money when she went in there and inevitably paid fifty dollars for candles that made her house smell like campfires, pumpkins, apple trees. She looked at the window display and saw a limited-edition fall candle they were sold out of last time. She pushed her nose to the glass.

"Hell, yeah. I would've given anything for a wife like you. That's me being honest," he said, looking at the same candle with matched intensity.

"Oh, please, you must be drunk," she said, giggling. "Let's go get this candle. This store is so overpriced. Let's go inside." She took his hand and he let her.

~

She'd worn comforting clothes to the outlet mall that made her feel pretty, like a forty-year-old Hermione Granger on a day trip to Hogsmeade for butterbeer. A toasty, oversize cardigan she'd finished knitting during the heat of summer. The color a deep goldenrod. She wore it over a long-sleeved gray bodysuit, dark skinny jeans. She'd chosen her trusty brown waterproof boots over the toffee-colored oxfords she'd wanted to wear, proud of how she'd gone with the more reasonable, practical choice for once in the past twenty-four hours. She didn't want to make it look like she was trying too, too hard, but it *was* a special occasion— Emmett was alive! And so was she! She'd put on hoop earrings, concealer and powder, eyeliner and blush. And lipstick, always lipstick. She never left the house without at least some nude color and gloss.

After Tallie got the candles, they wandered in and out of the other stores, only touching things, mocking, occasionally agreeing when anything cool and interesting was discovered.

"So you've been married?" she asked him as they made their way through the rest of the mall and to the parking lot, returning to her car. She'd bought him a fuzzy blue snow hat with ear flaps, pulled it on top of his head, and he still had it on, looking like he had owned it his whole life. She'd gotten herself a red one to match.

"I've been married," he said.

Christine? Brenna? Both?

"What happened?" she asked.

"What happened is . . . I'm not married anymore."

She smiled at him, playfully swatted at his elbow.

"That's all you're giving me?" she asked.

"Your turn to tell me something honest."

"I'm thinking of adopting a baby," she said. She'd told only one other soul: Aisha.

"Whoa. Big talk. *Huge* talk."

"Yep. I go to the same websites every couple days and think *What if?*"

She liked to click around reading about the pregnant women, some of them not due for months and months from now. How if they made a good match, that baby could be hers anywhere from twenty-four hours to three days after it was born. She loved thinking about converting her spare bedroom into a nursery and knitting tiny socks and hats with bamboo yarn. It didn't terrify her, as it had in the not-so-distant past, thinking of how much her life would change, thinking of doing it as a single woman. The trauma of Joel's betrayal and their divorce had made her feel as if she were starting her entire life over. She'd tried to fight it off, but now? Now she was finally ready to do just that.

∾

Emmett was driving her car. Tallie was too buzzed, and despite her recent behavior, she really wasn't a natural risk taker. She'd been on safety patrol in elementary school, forced her family to practice fire drills in every house they'd lived in growing up. She'd convinced Joel they needed to start traveling with a portable carbon monoxide detector when they stayed in hotels after hearing about couples who had been killed by the murderous gas on vacation. Tallie, comfortable in her own passenger seat, clicked on the radio and searched for a song she thought Emmett might like.

"Tell me when to stop," she said. She flicked through the stations one by one, and he didn't make a peep until she landed on Sam Cooke singing "Bring It On Home to Me."

"This one. I like this one," he said.

"I like this one, too."

"Why did you say you would've given anything for a wife like me?" she asked before she could talk herself out of it. They were at a stop sign. The wipers, a sleepy heartbeat. In the side mirror, red and blue lights spun through the rain. The siren chirped.

"It's okay. It's all right," Emmett said calmly, both hands on the wheel.

"Shit, are you drunk? Look at me." He obeyed. His eyes weren't bloodshot or glassy.

"I'm fine."

Tallie turned around to see the officer approaching the car. She knew he'd ask for license and registration and proof of insurance next. That's what happened, that's what always happened. Emmett had taken his new fuzzy snow hat off, quieted Sam Cooke, killed the engine, rolled the window down. When had he done those things? There were gaps in her memory. She should start doing more crossword puzzles or download one of those apps on her phone to help— some kind of brain booster. Maybe vitamins? She needed to re-up her vitamin stash. Organic, food-based. She'd place an order later. She'd donate money to protect young girls from the sex slave trade *and* put in a vitamin order. She'd do it as soon as she got home and have everything delivered and taken care of by Sunday evening in order to start off the new week right.

"I've pulled you over because you failed to come to a complete stop at the sign back there. License and registration and proof of insurance," the officer said once he was at the driver's-side window.

"Sorry, Officer. Here's the registration and proof of insurance," Emmett said after reaching into the glove compartment and getting the paperwork. Tallie hadn't told him where it was; he'd opened the glove compartment and found it himself.

Tallie sat with her hands quiet in her lap, looking at them like they didn't belong to her. Like she'd gotten new hands zipped onto her wrists and it was her job to inspect them, to make sure they were the hands she wanted. She looked at her bare left ring finger, her short nails she'd recently painted burnt orange.

"Your license?" the officer said.

"I don't have it on me. All apologies."

"Is there a reason you don't have your license on you?"

"No, Officer. I just forgot it."

"You should always have it on you when you're operating a motor vehicle," the officer said to Emmett in a voice Tallie was sure should be used only for disobedient children.

"Right. Yes, sir."

"What's your name?" the officer asked after sighing and pulling out a small pad of paper.

"Okay...can I talk to you for a second, please?" Emmett asked. "I can step out?"

"Absolutely. Why don't you do that, huh? Go on and step out for me," the officer said, opening the door from the outside.

The officer was clearly in an awful mood, and Emmett was going to get handcuffed and arrested because she'd gotten buzzed at lunch and let him drive. It was her fault. Shame on her for letting Emmett drink alcohol in her presence after last night. Maybe he *was* an alcoholic. Maybe he had a drug problem. She shouldn't have been drinking with him, period. But! Emmett *wasn't* one of her clients, and she deserved a break, too! Truly. Or she could end up on the bridge like him. Still—guilt, shame, foolishness—the intensity of her emotions warmed her face.

She could bail him out if he didn't have any outstanding warrants. But...maybe he'd committed heinous crimes with a woman who looked a lot like her? The officer would handcuff her and take her in, too. The residents of Fox Commons would have an emergency meeting and tell the media they'd always suspected her. *She wore so much yellow, and she recently went through a divorce. Pity. She clearly snapped.* She'd have to shut TLC Counseling Services down. She'd get lectured by her brother about how careless she was, again. She didn't bother wiping the tears away. She was crying about Lionel never mincing words, about Joel's new baby girl, about Emmett feeling hopeless and lonely enough to stand on that bridge yesterday.

"It's okay, Tallie. It's all good," Emmett said quietly when he saw she was crying. She nodded at him, and he got out of the car, was polite to the officer. Tallie turned away from them and watched the rain slide down the passenger window. She glanced in the mirror and saw Emmett with his hands on his head as the officer patted him down.

"Do you have any weapons on you? Anything that's going to poke me?" she heard the officer ask Emmett.

"There's a knife clipped to my pocket," Emmett said.

He had a knife and Tallie hadn't seen it—but of course he did. Pretty much every man she'd ever known had carried a knife with him, as if they all got assigned one at birth.

"Is that all you have?" the officer asked.

"Yes, sir."

"No guns, drugs?"

"No, sir."

After Tallie turned to see the police officer slip the knife from

Emmett's pocket and heard it thunk on the top of her car, she was careful to remain perfectly still. Emmett and the officer walked toward the patrol car. On Emmett's face: serenity. Tallie saw it before he got in. She kept crying and watching the rain, which was letting up. What else was there to do? The red and blue lights were still spinning. On the sidewalk across from them, there was an old man in a raincoat walking a dog wearing a matching raincoat—the kind of thing that would usually make Tallie squeal with joy and snap a pic to send to Aisha or Zora. But no, Tallie was still, still, still as a statue.

Would the officer come to the car and give her instructions? Check to see if she was drunk? If she could drive properly? Tow her car if she didn't pass? She hadn't had a speeding ticket in fifteen years. She had no clue how any of this worked.

After what felt like forever, Tallie looked in the mirror and saw the officer and Emmett shake hands before he got out of the patrol car. The officer turned off his lights and drove away, waving at them; he smiled at her as he passed. She heard Emmett get his knife from the top of the car, and he sat behind her steering wheel, stretched back so he could reclip the knife in his pocket. She was still crying.

"Hey. It's all right. I told you it was all right," he said, putting his hand on her arm. It began raining harder. So hard it seemed as if the rain were coming up from the ground to meet the water from the sky somewhere in the middle.

"What did you say to him? What happened? He was being such a dick, then he waves at us?"

"I told him the truth. It's fine. Hey. It's all right," he said again.

Tallie directed Emmett to her place. He turned the radio back on—Motown, Four Tops—as if they didn't have a million things to discuss. He was frustratingly calm, as if nothing out of the ordinary had happened. Tallie wiped her eyes, tapped the radio off.

"Emmett, what the hell happened? Tell me! I was sitting here freaking out, afraid to move!" she said, raising her voice.

He put his hand on her leg and continued driving carefully. She couldn't imagine how anxious she would've been if she didn't have leftover bourbon sluicing through her bloodstream like medicine.

"I'm sorry you got so upset," he said. Before returning his hand to the wheel, he squeezed her thigh so tenderly she wondered if she'd imagined it.

"Turn left," she directed him. "And turn right up there."

"I didn't want you to get upset. The officer was nice. He asked if I'd been drinking…if *we'd* been drinking. I didn't tell him the truth about that because it would've gotten me into trouble. I lied to him about it, but that was all. I'm not buzzed anymore. Sometimes alcohol blows straight through my system. I'm a quarter Scottish." Emmett shrugged. "He asked me how I knew you. I told him you were a friend. He'd heard about your brother's Halloween party, by the way."

Tallie pointed, and Emmett pulled into her driveway, turned the engine off.

"And he let you go with what, a warning?" she asked, sniffing.

"Yes, he did. Bring it on home to me, Tallulah," he said, wrapping his arms around her and pulling her close. He was so warm, so comforting, doing the perfect thing at the perfect time. They'd touched but not hugged. And she'd been correct when she imagined his smell: the forest, the river. This forever rain with a hint of coolness, an antiseptic flashing pale blue and starry white as she closed her eyes tight.

Client seems patient and relaxed, even in stressful situations. Not easily rattled or overstimulated. Comforts others.

"But I should be the one comforting you," she mumbled into his sleeve.

"Because of yesterday?"

"We don't have to talk about it right now," she said.

"I would've given anything for a wife like you because of your openness…your sweet heart," he said with his voice melting against her ear.

EMMETT

From: JoelFoster1979@gmail.com
To: Talliecat007@gmail.com
Subject: Re: i still care about you too

Tallie, I'm glad you wrote me. You know how I feel about hoping we can still somehow be friends although like I've said before . . . I realize that's a lot to ask. I promise not to talk too much about the baby because I know it hurts you. I am so sorry.

Of course none of this is your fault. You absolutely couldn't have done anything differently to stop it. Do you hear me when I say this? Do you really hear me? I made these choices and they were completely separate from you. And that was my biggest problem . . . not considering you the way I should've. It was cruel. I don't think you're broken. I didn't get Odette pregnant on purpose. It was an accident.

You do know me. You may feel like there are parts of me you don't know, yes, but you do know the heart of me. I separated myself . . . in order to deceive you. I even thought about those damn horcruxes in Harry Potter. It was like that. I split myself. I should've said no to Odette from jump. But I didn't. I couldn't believe how hard it was to say no. I'm weak. But you do know me, Tallie. You do. Think about all we've been through together. It doesn't just go away. And even if it did, where would it go? One of us would still keep it.

I think you are an amazing woman who deserves far better than me, but I must admit there was an incredibly selfish part of me always hoping I could somehow remain in your life. And your email really lit up that part of my heart. So thank you. I am trying to fix my mistakes . . . the mistakes I've made in this Universe . . . I'd like to correct them by doing (at least some things) right.

Talk soon,
Joel

PS: I'm coming back to town for Christmas and of course I fucking miss you, Tallie. Of course I do. You were my wife for a long time. I'll love you forever.

PPS: I hope you have a good time at Li's party tomorrow.

~

Emmett drank a glass of water in front of Tallie's kitchen sink after she disappeared into her bedroom.

(The police officer had celery-brown eyes. A high and tight haircut, clean-shaven. Gun on his right hip. Last name stitched into his uniform in white: Bowman. His front tooth, slightly crooked. The tip of Tallie's nose gets hot pink when she cries. Her fingernails are short and painted deep orange. She wears earrings, but no rings. A light confetti of orange and black cat hair on her jeans, below her knees. And she sparks electric . . . like a woman.)

TALLIE

The orange streetlamp drenched Tallie's large living-room window with rainy, honeyed light. The gloaming spilled over her houseplants and bookshelves, poured across the floor. She loved that window, the holiness. She sat there in it, watching Emmett sleep. He breathed slow and deep with the ball of his foot pressing the armrest, as if he were kicking to a swim and would splosh the couch to water. She'd told him it was good for him to get extra rest. Tallie spoke with her clients often about their sleep schedules and how important they were to both their mental and physical health.

Like a fever dream, Emmett was on her couch with his backpack tucked next to him, and Joel was in Montana with his hair up in a ponytail, holding his new baby girl. She'd blocked Joel's number from her phone, but it lived on in her mind alongside the other number minutiae she had memorized. Joel wore a thirty-two thirty-two in pants but could wear a thirty-two thirty also, depending. Joel wore a ten and a half in shoes. Joel had thirty thousand seventeen dollars in his savings account when he and Tallie got married. Joel's parents' address was seven zero four. Joel's brother was two years older. Joel's birthday was nine nine. Tallie and Joel were married on six six. Tallie and Joel suffered through five failed IVF cycles—numberless injections and hours on the phone with the insurance company, innumerable days in bed, crying, wishing, praying—before they fully believed the *unexplained infertility* diagnosis. Tallie and Joel were married for ten years and five months. Joel had finally admitted to his affair on ten one, but only after Tallie told him she'd suspected it; she'd caught him texting Odette at two in the morning. Tallie and Joel were separated for the Kentucky-required sixty days, plus four more. They went through uncontested divorce proceedings on twelve four.

Tallie and Joel had gotten married in June in the wildflower gardens by the river, promising *I'll love you forever* in front of practically everyone they'd ever known. Joel and Odette had gotten married in December, mere weeks after the divorce. Joel had called Tallie, said they'd gone downtown to the courthouse, told her over the phone that Odette was pregnant.

"Tallie, it was an accident," he'd said, as if he'd done nothing more than knock a glass of red across a white tablecloth.

"The pregnancy or the marriage?"

Joel was quiet on the phone.

"Marriage doesn't mean anything to you, Joel."

What he'd done was catastrophic and brutal. Tallie ended the call before he could hear her cry.

She hadn't talked to Joel since their last Facebook communication over the summer. They weren't friends on there anymore. She couldn't imagine seeing Joel or Odette or their baby pop up on her timeline as she casually scrolled through the photos and anniversaries and recipes and political discussions. She had to be mentally prepared and ready for emotional battle when she looked through Joel's posts. She'd tried to frame it as a cleansing ritual she eventually wouldn't need anymore, but she needed it now.

She logged in to Joel's account on her phone. He'd updated the night before about seeing the latest superhero movie. She and Aisha had gone to see it, too, and Tallie had even gone back to see it again alone. It was perfect candy-coated escapism. But of course Joel picked it apart like he always picked everything apart, even using the word *doryphore*. No surprise, since Joel was the kind of person who thought the Grand Canyon was overrated. ("I just thought it would be bigger, that's all.") Tallie read the whole post, rolling her eyes, wondering if she could pass out from annoyance. She read it again before going to Odette's page.

Almost everything Tallie knew about Odette she learned from social media. She knew surprisingly little about the details of Joel's affair, feeling like it was better for her mental health to not have all the answers. Besides, she'd already been haunted by imagining them together—the gruff, chesty sound Joel made when he came, the seashell suck of his ear pressed against Odette's when he was on top of her. And she'd gotten all she could bear to know from Joel regarding when and where he and Odette had been together: never in their home, always at Odette's. One compact September-to-October month of clandestine sex, from how Joel told it.

Tallie had been frustrated with herself, half wishing she were the kind of person who wanted him and Odette to die and disappear forever. Or at least the kind of person who could hope for the possible future schadenfreude of Joel eventually cheating on Odette, or their marriage falling apart. But none of that would change what had happened, and she knew the toxicity levels of hating Odette would poison her and her only.

Odette had grown up summering in L'Isle-sur-la-Sorgue with her grandparents. Odette liked romantic comedies and cheesy Christmas movies. Horses and coffee. Skinny casserole recipes, makeup tutorials. She had favorite Pilates instructors and Zumba classes. Sometimes she posted things Tallie fervently believed in and agreed with, too, like climate-action petitions and Taylor Swift videos. It was a dizzying swirl of intense emotions, knowing she and Odette had *anything* in common besides Joel.

There were photos of him and their baby up and down Odette's page.

Tallie clicked the picture she looked at more often than the others: Odette in the hospital bed, holding their baby girl, Pearl. Pearl had her father's nose in miniature, his ebony curls. Joel, in a navy-blue V-neck sweater Tallie'd bought for him, had taken the picture, leaning over to make sure he made it all the way in. She'd loved that navy-blue V-neck sweater and nibbled Joel's arms when he wore it; she'd wanted to eat that sweater.

Back when she'd seen that they'd named their baby Pearl, Tallie couldn't get the word *pearl* out of her mind. It manifested itself and rolled around in her brain like a real solid pearl glinting catchlight. Tallie had imagined she and Joel would have a baby with those same curls—a baby whose tender head she could feel heavy in one hand. *Joel has a daughter forever*, Tallie had found herself thinking. Joel had done something hugely permanent with his life, changing everything. Sometimes it felt like the thought was too big for her head to hold, but she couldn't let it out until it gave her a headache. *Joel could have more children with Odette. Joel could have children with other women.* The thoughts would motor around and around in a circle until Tallie exhausted herself.

She was upset by the photo again. Restless and lonely. She logged in to her work email, although she'd promised herself she wouldn't, and she'd already let her clients know she would be unavailable until Monday. Bored, she wanted to make sure she wasn't missing anything important. She had several clients who leaned on her for extra assurance when making big decisions and others who would connect when they needed to be talked out of panic, or when a family member or friend or problem or fear they thought they'd previously conquered appeared again, haunting them like a ghost with a grudge. Occasionally a client would email, simply wanting encouragement or permission not to overanalyze things so much.

Being a therapist allowed Tallie to dig into the common sense so easily clouded by mental illness, depression, obsessiveness, anxiety. She encouraged clients struggling with obsessive-compulsive disorder to take time-stamped photos of their turned-off ovens and locked doors so they could revisit them during the day. She suggested to one OCD client who worried about leaving her coffeemaker on every morning to unplug the coffee machine or whatever small appliance worried her and take it with her to work. That way she knew for certain it wasn't left on at home, ripe for fire starting. So much of therapy was practicality and giving people a much-needed pass to relax when they needed to or be weird when they needed to. To free their minds from doing what they felt like they *should* be doing if it always went against what they *wanted* to do. To ask questions like *why* when the client had never considered it.

Tallie scanned her emails, relieved to find nothing urgent, and repromised herself she wouldn't peek again until Monday morning. She logged in to her personal email account and flicked through a few newsletters before pulling up old emails from Joel. As annoying as he could be on social media, he'd always been short in his emails, even the sweet ones. He wasn't much of a texter, either. And he was impossible on the phone. During their marriage, they'd always had their best and most important conversations over dinner or while cleaning up afterward. Or on walks, in the car, the bed. Over coffee.

She'd typed *Joel* into the search bar and clicked on a random message that popped up. It was from two years ago, when he'd gone to Chicago to visit his brother the same weekend Tallie and Aisha had gone on a girls' trip to Asheville.

To: TallulahLeeClark@gmail.com
From: JoelFoster1979@gmail.com
Subject: :(

Too late to call and my phone is out in the living room anyway, but I was thinking about you, your body, how good you smell. And I'm in this guest bedroom with this laptop all alone. :(Next time come up here with me.

Your poor, lonely husband,

J

And another from not long after that. He'd forwarded her an article on art deco architecture with pics of the American Radiator Building.

To: TallulahLeeClark@gmail.com
From: JoelFoster1979@gmail.com
Subject: Look

The building we saw from Bryant Park. Next time we go up there, we should do one of those art deco walking tours. Would be so easy to talk Lionel and Zora into going back up with us. Make a whole thing out of it? You're so fucking fun to travel with.

They'd never gone back up to New York together. Maybe Joel was planning to go on an art deco walking tour with Odette in the future. Maybe she was so fucking fun to travel with, too. He could walk next to her while she pushed Pearl in an expensive stroller. Maybe he'd strap Pearl to a baby carrier on his chest while he and Odette looked up and pointed at skyscrapers stabbing the blue.

It was imagining Joel with Pearl strapped to his chest that really did it.

Tallie hummed something quick and low to herself to stop her thoughts. Emmett rolled over, opened his eyes, and looked at her. Sat up, rubbed his face.

"I never take naps. Not really a nap person," he said, his deep voice still stretching and waking up.

"Today, you're a nap person," she said, thankful he'd distracted her. "Can I get you anything? Food? Water?"

Emmett smoothed his hair and looked around her living room before focusing on the doorway to the kitchen.

"Actually, I'd like to make you dinner. I'd like to go to the grocery store and come back here and cook for you."

"Oh, you don't have to do that. I have plenty of food. You don't have to go out in this mess," she said, motioning to the blurry, wet window. He leaned forward and opened his backpack, fiddled around in there, and held up money to show her. He handed her five twenties, explaining that it was for lunch and everything else earlier, putting the rest in his pocket.

"It's the least I can do. If you're okay with me borrowing your car? I'll leave—" he trailed off, rooting around again in his bag. He pulled out a small box and opened it. Inside was a ring with a diamond chunk the size of a pencil eraser. "I'll leave this ring here. So you know I'm not running off."

"You don't want me to come with you? I could drive if you insist on doing this," she said. He slid the ring box across the table so it was closer to her.

"I'll take care of it. Steak okay?" he asked, standing.

"Sure. Steak sounds great. Oh, and keys. My keys," she said, remembering her purse on the kitchen counter. She got it, unclipped them, and let her fingertips graze his palm as she handed them over. His grab quieted the jingle.

"Be back in half an hour. Promise."

"Do you want me to tell you where the grocery store is?"

"I'll find it."

He threw his backpack over his shoulder and headed toward the door.

There was no reason to believe him. The ring could be a fake; he could be going to the bridge to jump. He could run off with her car forever, and she'd have to explain to the police that she didn't know him or if Emmett was even his real first name.

She was trusting him, completely.

A crinkle flattened inside of her.

EMMETT

Fake, scritchy-looking black spiders had their legs wrapped around the lit-up letters of the sign spelling MARKET. From the outside, it looked like they sold only pumpkins and chrysanthemums. Emmett sat in Tallie's car in the parking lot, mindlessly scrolling through the news on his phone although he hated it. But if last night had happened how he wanted and they'd found him in the water, his face, his story would be splayed across the front pages. The news was so fucking depressing, and that was part of the reason he wanted to jump. How did anyone survive anything? Anxiety began itching at his neck, and his body ached with grief, a fact he'd gotten used to after years of living with it. "Grief hurts…physically," his dad had warned him.

Before his vision turned grotesque, he saw Christine and Brenna separately, then together, safe with their eyes closed, pale and sleeping. Reliving it was a cold shock of light before utter darkness, the cage door of his heart left swinging. Emmett put his forehead against Tallie's steering wheel, focused on deliberate, slow breaths in the engine-off coolness, looking up only when he heard a car pull next to him.

(A *white car. A redhead, a black-and-white polka-dotted raincoat. A car seat. The dome light ticks off. A blanket hangs over the car-seat handle, protecting the baby from the rain. The blanket is white with yellow ducks on it. The ducks are smiling.)*

~

Hitting the produce section first, Emmett picked up a small bag of red potatoes, put them in his basket. A woman stopped her cart beside him, swearing he looked familiar, that she'd seen him somewhere before. He kindly told her he was from out of town before turning away. Being out in the world heightened his desire for the comfort of Tallie's warm, clean, good-smelling house. He grabbed two steaks, Irish butter, a bottle of red. Stock and cognac for the sauce. He zipped through the wide, smooth seasonal aisle with its masks and motion-detector skeletons jiggling and rattling on both sides of him. Beeped himself through the self-checkout and left without speaking to another human.

~

At Tallie's, he promptly kicked her out of the kitchen.

"You're probably *always* taking care of other people. I say *probably* because I don't want to come off like a know-it-all, mansplaining your own life to you, but I know it's true. Look at what you did for me. You didn't have to do that. So let me do something for you," he said.

As soon as he'd returned to her place, she'd handed Christine's ring to him, and he'd put it into his backpack before bringing a big pot of water to a boil. Chopping the potatoes, dropping them in.

"It's hard to admit how much I love you making dinner so I don't have to think about it. I usually make little meals. Or just snack all day. Some days I get takeout. It's still kind of weird cooking for one. I'm not good at letting people take care of me," she said. She kept

88

her toes out of the kitchen, had them lined up perfectly where the tile turned to hardwood.

Emmett let the gentle faucet water run over the steaks and patted them dry with paper towels before rubbing them with olive oil. Tallie leaned and watched. A small yellow meow from one of her cats floated across the kitchen air. Emmett turned on the stove, dropped a pale cube of cold butter into the skillet, and poured himself a glass of water as the butter warmed and sizzled.

"Yesterday, the bridge, did that have something to do with your marriage?" Tallie asked as he put both steaks in the skillet. Bloody. Browning. Searing.

"In a way, it did. In a way, it didn't," he said.

"That clears it up."

He turned to her. Smiled. Tallie sat on the floor outside the kitchen and shook her head at him.

When it was time, he transferred the steaks to the oven, then he took the empty skillet off the stove and added glugs of stock and cognac. Used the wooden spoon to get the delicious crispy bits from the bottom before returning it to the burner and turning the heat up, bubbling it down. Tallie talked while Emmett cooked, and he pulled the steaks out of the oven when he knew the insides were still pink and cool.

"We'll let them rest," he said.

"How did you and your ex-wife meet?" Tallie asked.

"Are you going to tell me how you met Joel?"

"Do you *want* to know how I met Joel?"

Emmett nodded.

"Do you want me to go first?"

"Yes," he said.

When Tallie met Joel, he was a marketing manager at the health insurance company where Lionel was chief financial officer. They played on the company's intramural soccer team together. Tallie saw Joel at the soccer matches when she would go, thought he was cute.

"Joel had these black curls that bounced when he ran and an overly exuberant running gait, like a puppy. After I'd been to a couple of their matches, Joel asked Lionel if it'd be okay for him to ask me out. Lionel told me, 'He's a good dude. Kind of boring, but he's a kick-ass soccer player. He's smart, strong, wiry. He's pretty, too,'" Tallie said.

She had Lionel's comments memorized. Emmett watched her mouth move as she talked. She told him how picky Lionel had been about her boyfriends, taking forever to warm up to them, and she admitted to being pretty awful to some of his girlfriends as well. But she talked about how much she loved her sister-in-law, Zora. She told him Zora was more than a sister-in-law to her; she was a real friend. Tallie mentioned Zora coming over and staying with her one night after Joel had moved out. How Zora had cleaned Tallie's kitchen and made dinner for her, let Tallie cry in her lap while she petted her hair.

"How many dates until you knew Joel was the one?" Emmett asked after listening.

"I don't know...maybe two months' worth? I was seeing someone else off and on for a bit, but Joel was handsome, flirty, funny. Really sexy and aggressively confident, and he wore suits...a lot," Tallie said. "He's brainy and intrepid, too."

"Wow...intrepid," Emmett teased in a deeper voice.

"I *know*. But he is! Trust me, I'd never use that word to describe anyone else but Joel."

"Well, it's a great word."

"Agreed." Tallie paused. "And yeah, so...I'd had serious boyfriends, but being with Joel made me feel like I'd won something in a way I can't explain. Like in choosing between him and the other man I was seeing...Joel made me feel like it *had* to be him. How could it *not* be him? He was Joel! He'd somehow convinced me he was the only man in the world."

"And now?"

90

"Now I know better," she said. "Your turn."

"Well...our story is that I used to work with one of her best friends, who started dating my best friend...they're the ones who moved to Montana. I told you about them on the bridge. That's how Christine and I got to know each other," Emmett said, saying her name aloud for the first time to Tallie, filling in the relationship blank his letter had left open for her.

"*Christine*," Tallie repeated, like she enjoyed how it felt in her mouth. "And you haven't changed your mind about giving your best friend a call? What's his name?"

"His name is Hunter. And I love him, but I don't need to talk to him right now."

Hunter would want to beat his ass, dead or not, once he got wind of Emmett's letter to his parents. An irreverent laugh knocked at his stomach, and he put his hand there.

"How many dates until you knew Christine was the one?"

"One," he said.

"Really? Wow...the *dream*."

Emmett turned to the stove, watched the potatoes rolling in the water. When they were soft enough he used a masher to smash them, added more butter, sour cream, salt, and pepper. He put their steaks and potatoes on the plates he'd gotten from her cabinet, spooned the skillet cognac sauce over the meat.

～

"My wife, Christine...what happened is...unfortunately, she died," he said after sitting at the table and taking his first bite. Swallowing.

Talking about Christine's death was a surefire way to get him thinking about his own. Grief was so tedious, and his own death was the only escape from it. He told Tallie some truth and let it out— even if only a little—to avoid detonation. The only other option was to move forward with his original plan to make it all stop.

He watched the cloud swish over Tallie's face before she put her fork down. He'd suspected that Tallie would be a cloud-swish person, although some people gave a sad gasp. Others seemed to be attempting the quick math in their heads, turning away or lowering their eyes as they considered his age and how young Christine might've been. But Tallie didn't turn away. She looked right at him, and her eyes were so sweet. Her bright heart, tender and open, spread across her face. Emmett sat there, staring back, vibrating from the small comforts of normal domesticity. Unlocking in that safe space felt both as dangerous and as freeing as speedily descending a hill on a bicycle and letting go of the handlebars, holding his arms out straight.

TALLIE

"I'm so sorry. Completely. How heartbreaking," Tallie said, holding her hand to her chest. "The ring you left me earlier? That was hers?"

Emmett nodded and drank more water, took another bite of his steak.

"Bless your heart. Bless *her* heart. How long ago, if you don't mind me asking?"

"Three years."

"How long were you married?"

"Four and a half years."

"You...didn't have children together?"

He shook his head without looking at her.

"How old was Christine?"

"Twenty-six," he said, meeting her eyes again.

"Lord have mercy, that's too young. Do you...want to talk about how she died?"

"No."

"Okay. *If* you want to talk about it, I'll listen."

"Thank you."

"Grief is complicated...bizarre...it can make us do all sorts of things," she said.

Acute grief from the death of his young wife three years ago. An accident? Cancer? Can't ask who Brenna is, but dyyyyying to know.

He stared at his plate.

"This is unbelievably delicious, truly hand-to-God the best steak I've ever had, by the way," she said after waiting a respectful amount of time to mention it.

"Glad to hear it. It's my favorite thing to cook and eat. I haven't cooked like this for a long time, so this is nice."

"No, really, though. It's literally the best steak I've ever tasted. Like, wow."

"My pleasure," he said, modest as fresh-cut green grass. "I'll do the dishes, too."

"No. You absolutely don't have to do that. You're my guest."

"Guest," he repeated.

"Yes. Like the candle singing in *Beauty and the Beast*. You're my guest."

"Lumière?"

"Exactly," she said, laughing. "I should've known you were a Disney fan. I knew I liked you."

"Not to brag, but I'm a wealth of pointless knowledge."

"How are you feeling tonight? Compared to yesterday?" she asked before taking another bite of food.

"I don't have anything to say about it."

"Are you feeling anxious or worried? Unbalanced? Like you want to hurt yourself?" she asked, realizing she was sliding into tricky territory. These were the same questions she asked her clients, carefully, in her office. Emmett put his elbows on the table, laced his fingers together. Not his energy, but deep in his spirit, hidden away—it was Vantablack, and he was protecting it. Tallie couldn't get there on her own; he was going to have to take her hand.

"Do I seem unbalanced to you right now, Tallulah?" he asked after eating more of his steak and taking a drink of water. Each shiny gold syllable of *Tal-lu-lah* that escaped his mouth tingled her thighs, the top of her head.

"Not really. Does this happen to you often, these huge shifts in mood?" she asked, hoping she sounded more like a concerned friend than a mental health professional.

"Yesterday was a difficult day for me."

"You understand why I'm asking, though."

"Yes. You have every right to ask. I don't want to make you uncomfortable," he said.

"It's fine. We can stop talking about it."

Tallie was so looking forward to taking Emmett to the Halloween party. Imagined the two of them there together, away from the stress of the world, not worrying about anything. The party would be a great distraction, and she knew it. And she tried not to think past Saturday night, Sunday morning at the latest; the weekend could be a hermetically sealed capsule floating in space.

"What else would you ask Joel if he'd open up to you?" Emmett asked, that gravity returning her back to earth.

"Wow. Well...," she started. She wanted the spotlight to be on Emmett, his feelings, but she didn't mind having someone listen to her for once, either. *Pop!* A ticker-tape parade of expletives and frustration went off in her brain. She took a deep breath. "I'd like to know if the love he feels for her is different from the love he felt for me. If it's the same love, but it shifted from me to her. Also, I'd like to know how it feels for him to be a father. I know how much he wanted it. Now he has it. What happens when you get what you really want?"

"But you've gotten what you've really wanted before, right?"

"I have. But specifically this...having a baby. It was something we wanted so much...together. Now he has it *without* me. What's that like? Doesn't it feel kind of...I don't know...*wrong*?"

"Heavy."

"Too heavy." She let out a flat, nervous laugh.

"Let's lighten it up again. I really am going to do the dishes," he said, looking toward the sink.

"And I'll make us pumpkin spice tea. What else can I do?"

"You can keep me company. Keep talking to me. Do you feel like talking some more? We can take a break from the too-heavy stuff. I won't tell if you won't tell."

"I won't tell, I promise. Sure. I mean, I guess. Or ... I don't know. I could read. I could read to you. Too weird?"

"Nope. I dig it. And you'll have to try harder than that to weird me out," he said, standing.

"Okay, challenge! I'll be right back."

~

She reread at least one Harry Potter book every October because they were autumnal and she'd read them so many times that revisiting them was soothing—no surprises. She was halfway through the illustrated version of *Harry Potter and the Prisoner of Azkaban*, so she went and got it from her bedroom. After making the tea, she sat outside the kitchen with the mug next to her, the book in her lap.

"Talking Disney and now you're reading me Harry Potter. We're some grown-ass people tonight," Emmett said and laughed—one peppy *ha*—and turned to look over his shoulder at her. The water hushed hard into the sink as he rinsed the dishes. He'd taken his flannel off, stood in her kitchen in his own white T-shirt. Clean, fitting him perfectly, his shoulder blades angel-glowing, making two low, snowy peaks.

Tallie sat cross-legged on the floor, drinking her tea. Opened the book and began reading. She had to raise her voice so he could hear her over the rain, the faucet water, the sparkling, chippy clatter of dishes.

~

When he was finished loading the dishwasher and washing the skillet and pot by hand, he threw the dish towel over his shoulder.

"Well, I'm invested now," Emmett said, pointing at the hardback book in her lap.

"I'm way too old to be this in love with them, I guess? I don't have kids. There's really no excuse," she said, feeling her heart light dim. It was still a bit embarrassing, her body failing her in that way. And it'd taken her awhile to stop feeling guilty about it. She focused on the positive, the possibilities. She hadn't looked at the adoption websites since Wednesday; she'd return on Monday, click around and daydream.

"Well, I don't have kids, either, and I loved listening to you read it to me. So thank you," Emmett said gently.

Tallie flipped through the book for a moment before closing it and putting it down. "So did you tell your family you were leaving town?" she asked him.

"No. And if they got the letter today, they'll think I'm dead. If they didn't get it today, they won't be worried yet," he said. He wiped his dry hands, unnecessarily.

"They haven't tried to call or text you?"

"It's a new phone. I didn't want anyone to have the number. Clean break."

Tallie wanted to ask him about his childhood, more about his family. But when he was done answering questions, she couldn't get anything new out of him. She went to her bathroom, googled *Christine* and *Clementine* and *obituary* and got several hits for years going back, but none of them mentioned an Emmett, and the ages were off. Too old or too young to have been his wife. She searched for *Clementine* and *man* and *missing* and found old Golden Alerts. And she knew attempting to search for Hunter would be a waste of time. The internet wasn't helping. After she peed and washed her hands, she stood outside the kitchen.

"Emmett, if you gave me more information, I could reach out to your family. Maybe that would help? If you don't want to do it...I could do it for you," she said.

"I won't let you," he said with that shadow falling across his eyes. The rain was sideways now—striking the windows with horror-movie intensity.

EMMETT

A large section of Emmett's heart had been wrapped with concertina wire. Compartmentalization: it's how he got through his life *after*. Talking about *Beauty and the Beast*, listening to Tallie read from Harry Potter, those things smoothed inside him like a letter opener, peeled back, ripped him open. The tears that came in Tallie's presence were only a peek at the whole story—the teeniest tip of glowing ice blue poking out of the inky black.

He looked at Tallie and smiled slightly, left her there outside the kitchen watching the rain against the window and excused himself to the bathroom with his backpack and his phone. He hadn't responded to Joel's email when he was in the parking lot of the grocery store because he hadn't wanted to make Tallie seem desperate, waiting around for his reply. She was a busy woman.

He closed the bathroom door, stood against it.

From: talliecat007@gmail.com
To: joelfoster1979@gmail.com
Subject: Re: i still care about you too

hi joel. i'd like to start out by saying i agree! I AM AMAZING.

you obviously blew it. but yes, you already knew that.

i will never understand how you can say i know you, even though there is a HUGE part of you i obviously don't know. the part of you that decided to break our marriage vows. i didn't do that. i would've never done that to you. but like i said before, we've been over this.

i do have more questions for you since you're opening up. the love you feel for her...how is it different from the love you felt for me? is it different? it's the same love, but it shifted? also, how does it feel to be a father? i know how badly you wanted it. or how badly you thought you wanted it. well, now you have it! without me. doesn't it feel kind of...i don't know...wrong? what happens when you get what you really want? do tell.

i appreciate the sentiment of your email. you seem to finally be...trying. men need to get better at taking care of the women they claim to love so much.

tallie.

He was stung by those words, his own choices. Tallie had invaded his privacy, and now he'd properly invaded hers. Started it drunk, but still keeping it up sober. Maybe he could spin and sweeten what he'd done by forwarding the emails to her real email address as a gift when he left her. Spill the secrets of what Joel obviously hadn't been man enough to tell her before, help her heal.

Emmett used the bathroom and ran his hand through his hair— an oil slick. He poked his head out the bathroom door.

"Miss Tallie, it's okay if I take a shower? I haven't taken one since Wednesday. I plumb forgot to this morning, with everything going on," he said loud enough for her to hear him. The *Miss* had escaped accidentally, out of country-boy habit. The cats walked down the hallway to investigate what the fuss was about. He opened the door all the way and crouched to pet them as they purred and filled the hallway with their tiny-thunder meows.

"*Miss* Tallie? That makes me feel old," she said, now standing across from him.

"Forgive me. I promise I don't mean it that way. I'm from the country."

"Yes, you can take a shower," she said, stepping toward him so she could open the linen closet he was leaning against. In such close quarters, her arm slipped across the hem of his shirt; he felt the warmth.

"Sorry," he said, moving for her.

"You're fine," she said. She got out a folded fluffy towel and gave it to him. "Body wash, shampoo, conditioner, it's in there. All of it smells really lovely." She pointed toward the ruffly curtain behind him. He thanked her before closing the door and stepping into the entirely new and confusing planet that was someone else's shower. Took him a second, but he got the right pressure, the right temperature.

(*Five bottles of body wash: wild cherry, apricot, lavender, peppermint, Chanel. A thick cake of pressed-flower soap. A frilly pink pouf resembling an overripe peony. A translucent shower mat that looks like bubble wrap. Clean. Everything is very clean.*)

He imagined living there, making a life with Tallie. He imagined taking a photo of himself, soapy and dripping in Tallie's shower, sending it to Joel. Emmett smiled thinking about how much Tallie hated Joel's ponytail as he lathered up his hair with her shampoo. He held the bottle in his sudsy hands, mouthed the words as he read it: *orange blossom and neroli, a lemon tree by the ocean.* The water steamed up like a jungle, rained him clean.

∼

Once Emmett got out, he realized he hadn't asked Tallie for any clothes to put on. He could wear what he slept in last night, but those clothes were out there on the couch. He dried off completely, wrapped the towel around his waist. He'd dripped on his white shirt. He put it over his head and stepped out into the hallway. The TV was down low; British accents and a sharp laugh track. Tallie's argument of dark curls hung loose over the side of the couch.

"Could I put those same clothes back on? Is that okay?" he asked.

One of her cats stretched up on the arm of the couch, sniffed the air, the cloud of citrus following him. The rain had eased up, but the gutters were overflowing, rushing and dripping against her windows. He was sleepy and dizzy from the heat of the shower, from her cozy house, their dinner. From the emotions of yesterday and now tonight. He felt simultaneously light, like he could float away—and so heavy it was as if he were sinking into Tallie's blond hardwood floor, her plush rugs. For the past three years he'd been suffering from lingering headaches, black-hole moods. His body weight felt doubled and cursed by the burden of gravity. He swallowed the little fire in his throat, petted the cat's head with one hand, rubbed behind its ears. He kept his other hand wrapped around the towel knot at his waist.

(*The laugh track on the television show erupts. A character on the show is eating popcorn, listening to his office mates argue. Another character enters the office with a look of shock. The laugh track roars. Tallie giggles lightly, shakes her head.*)

"Everything was fine?" Tallie asked, putting down her refilled mug of tea and reaching for the clothes. When she saw he was wearing only a towel around his waist, she turned her head away and cleared her throat.

"Your bathroom is so nice. This whole house is super nice. I shouldn't have glossed over it yesterday."

"Thank you. And I promise it's okay. You've got plenty on your mind. My brother made a *lot* of money when he was younger.

Finance, stocks, investment stuff I don't fully understand. He's a math whiz. I couldn't have bought this house without his help. You'll get to meet him *and* the rest of my family tomorrow at the party."

Emmett got the charger from his backpack and plugged his phone in, leaving it on the living-room floor. He took the clothes from her and went to the bathroom to change. Did looking forward to something feel like this? Living had felt so much like dying that he could hardly remember. Did it feel like concertina wire unraveling? Like his heart was a cracked, tipped cup, running over?

TALLIE

Tallie told herself she wasn't going to watch Emmett walk down the hallway. He'd surprised her, being in a towel. Joel's favorite red towel; Joel, pre-ex, pre-baby, sans ponytail. Had she really given him that towel? Had it been an accident or on purpose? Sure, Emmett may have walked out dripping like a romance novel, but he had mental health issues he needed to deal with—so many scarlet warnings that he might as well have been a matador in a *traje de luces*. Still, her stomach dipped when she saw the towel and the way his water-dark hair curled behind his ear. Bridge, Mr. Probably Handsome, Mr. *Definitely* Handsome, Emmett No Last Name, steamy hot and blushing like a peach.

While he was in the bathroom changing, Tallie picked his phone up off the floor, clicked to see if it was locked. Yes. His background, a default photo of the earth. She turned to make sure the bathroom door stayed closed. She tried *1234* to unlock his screen. Nope. And no notifications. Nothing. She heard him move around in the bathroom, and she put his phone back. She went to her bedroom, got his letters from the top drawer of her dresser. His green rain jacket hung on the hook by the front door. She couldn't remember which letter went where, but she split them up, putting one in the inside pocket and one in the outside. She prayed Emmett wouldn't come out of the bathroom at that moment, and she huffed out a breath of release when, thankfully, he didn't. She returned to the couch.

~

"Can I ask you a question? About yesterday?" she asked him gently after he came out of the bathroom and sat next to her, but not *too* close.

"Sure."

"Do you feel like being on the bridge was a proportionate response to whatever it was that sent you there?" She knew her question probably sounded too much like a question a therapist would ask, so she turned the TV volume down and added, "There's no *right* answer, by the way. I'm just curious."

"I do," he said easily.

"How else do you deal with stress in your life? How did you handle your wife's death when it happened?"

"I haven't properly handled her death yet, really. I can't. I try, I guess...but none of it makes sense. She was there and now she's just gone? Everything gets too slippery. My brain can't...hold it. It feels both final and eternal at the same time. I can't process it so I just let it...sit there...dark."

"I understand," Tallie said and paused. "Emmett, do you feel compelled to go back to the bridge?"

"Right now? No."

"Do you have anyone you share your feelings with? Anyone you can trust?"

"I used to...Hunter...we lived together before I got married, but I don't talk to many people anymore," he said.

"Why not?"

"I don't have a short answer for that."

"But you have a long one?" she asked.

"Maybe."

"Okay. Do you *wish* you could talk to someone you could trust?"

"I'm naturally quiet," he said.

"Do you like being naturally quiet?" she asked, digging in like they were in her office and she was getting paid to learn every little thing about him.

"No one has ever asked me that before. I think so?"

"And I get it. I understand. You're clearly a self-soother, but everyone needs someone. We need each other. It's not good to feel abandoned or alone."

"I *don't* feel abandoned or alone right now. I really don't," he said.

"Have you ever considered therapy?"

"I've been to groups where people sit in a circle and talk about their feelings. I don't like them. Have you been?"

"I've been in therapy sessions before...in the past, yes," Tallie said, her blood tingling.

"Was it good for you?"

"Yes. Very much so. A game changer. But it was one-on-one therapy. Have you tried that? Do you think it could help?"

Emmett shrugged.

"Have you been single ever since you lost your wife?" she asked. She was so curious about Brenna, trying to find a way to get him to mention who she was.

Emmett held up his no-wedding-ring hand.

"I know you're not married, but not even a girlfriend?"

"Do I seem like the kind of guy who could be a decent boyfriend?"

"Well, you're an amazing cook, charmed yourself out of a traffic ticket, *and* you do dishes, so yeah, maybe," she said, thinking of him in that towel, how his hair was almost dry now. Thinking of his thighs beneath the soft gray fabric of those pants intended for Joel. Now Odette bought Joel's clothes, knew his sizes, knew not to buy him cologne because it *got everywhere.*

"But what if I'm only doing that stuff to impress you, Tallie?"

"You're not," she said, leaning into that dreamy fog of friendly flirtation.

"My mama raised me right."

"Clearly," she said. The fog cooled quick at the thought of his poor mother. "That's why I can't bear the idea of her getting a *suicide* letter from you in the mail when you're here, perfectly fine."

"Thanks, but it's not for you to worry about, so don't. Can we talk about something else? Please?"

"Yes," she said, turning the TV up for a moment before muting it. "Should I be scared of anything you have in your backpack?"

"Absolutely not," he said.

"But you won't tell me what's in there?"

"It's unremarkable, really. Nothing that would mean anything to anyone but me."

"Okay," she said, nodding and eyeing him a bit longer. He didn't seem uncomfortable with it, and she liked that; it made her feel safe.

"I like this. I've always liked this," Emmett said, allowing some quiet before the subject change. He was pointing to the framed postcard sitting under the creamy glow of the lamp next to them.

"Gustav Klimt."

"*The Kiss*," he said, looking away, refocusing on the TV.

"I love art history, even though I know that particular Klimt is everywhere. Loving that piece doesn't make me all that original. I also love *Danaë*," Tallie said, pointing to another shimmery Klimt she had framed on a shelf. "One of my favorite things to do is go to the art museum alone and share space with the work. In the quiet. Sometimes I cry there," she said. She knew talking about her own feelings helped others to be able to talk about theirs, and sharing her pure love for the art museum was an easy thing to gush about. "I don't know why I do it—I just get...*overwhelmed* by my own feelings and everyone else's and all the history of the world."

Years ago she'd made an important connection with one of Lionel's fancy friends who had helped Joel—unhappy with his marketing job—get the curator of contemporary art position at the museum. Joel and Odette had met working there, but that museum was *Tallie's*, not Joel's. It meant too much to her. It was the one she'd grown up going to, the one where she fell in love with sculptures and light installations and Dutch Golden Age paintings, especially the flowers. All of it! And now that Joel and Odette were gone, Tallie had reclaimed the space completely by re-upping her membership and going every Sunday after church.

"It's popular for a reason. It's beautiful. And you're plenty original, trust me," he said.

Her face warmed at the compliment. "You are, too."

"I like Frida, Basquiat, Andy Warhol, too," Emmett said, motioning to a stack of books by the table that included Frida's journals, a Basquiat hardback, a thick book of Warhol Polaroids, and a biography of Augusta Savage. "Awesome. Augusta Savage. I really love sculptures. It blows my mind how someone can take a block of marble and make it look soft or like someone standing in the wind. An *exact* replica of the human form," he said, lying back on her couch like he was her boyfriend.

"Right, like Michelangelo's *David* or *Winged Victory of Samothrace*. They're two of the most popular sculptures on earth, but it knocks me out if I imagine seeing them for the first time. I don't ever want to get over it! I never want to get tired or bored of beauty and goodness. That would worry me," she said. "I don't like to use the word *obsession* lightly because obsessiveness is a real problem for some people, but I'm so in love with *David*'s right hand, down on his thigh. I love looking at it! You're going to think I'm a weirdo, but I have an entire section of my secret art history Pinterest board dedicated just to close-ups of his oversized right hand."

Photos of *David*'s right hand soothed Tallie—the tip of his middle finger touching his thigh, the snaking veins—imagining how the cool marble would feel. She liked thinking about holding

David's hand. She also loved his nose, his entire face, those haunting eyes holding hearts. That taut torso, perfect ass, and glorious *contrapposto*. Some nights when she couldn't sleep, she listened to music and scrolled through her Pinterest. It was one way she took care of herself.

"We've already established you're the *best* possible kind of weirdo," Emmett said.

"Oh, have we, now?"

"Definitely," he said before continuing. "Yeah, I've been overseas once. Paris for a short time when I was in high school, so I got to go to the Louvre and see the *Nike*, the *Mona Lisa*, the *Venus de Milo*."

"That sounds lovely. I want to go to the Louvre someday and the Accademia Gallery in Florence to see *David*, although I'm afraid seeing it in real life would make me get Stendhal syndrome or...what's it called?...hyperkulturemia? Seeing something like that in person can cause some people to have an art panic attack. Art attacks...art palpitations. I'd be the one to faint. It's *seventeen* feet tall. Thinking about seeing it in real life wears me out." Tallie put the back of her hand to her forehead, mimed a fainting spell.

She let her hand slide to her heart, racing a little faster from the conversation, which often happened when she talked about art. Her face got hot, and she wanted to burst out of her skin. *Rubens syndrome.* She had erotic postcards tacked to the wall next to her bed; they'd been hanging there for years, held above the lamp with flat metal pushpins, the gloss glowing every time the wide triangle of light shone up and out. In the past, they'd reminded her not only of romance and dreams but also of fantasies of a steamy anniversary vacation with Joel. The two of them going overseas to spend mornings in bed and entire days visiting art museums, dining al fresco, completely immersed in another culture and language. Perhaps a second honeymoon. Tallie had accepted that fantasy as bust but had recently surprised herself by considering going alone.

"Whenever I'm in an art museum, I feel like that scene from

Ferris Bueller's Day Off, the one when Cameron is staring at Seurat's *A Sunday Afternoon on the Island of La Grande Jatte* and it keeps zooming in and in and all meaning disappears. I like how nothing else matters when you're looking at a painting...you can just forget the world completely," he said. He'd curled his hands into loose fists and held them up together to one eye, closed the other, and looked through to Tallie.

"Absolutely. I love that scene...let's watch it."

She pulled up the movie from her digital library, clicking to the art museum scene: the instrumental cover of the Smiths' "Please, Please, Please Let Me Get What I Want." Flashes of Hopper, Picasso. Cassatt. Gauguin. Pollock, Matisse. Cameron melting into the Seurat while Ferris and Sloane kiss in front of the night-blue stained glass of Marc Chagall's *America Windows*.

When it was over, Emmett had tears in his eyes. Tallie said oh, no and apologized for unintentionally upsetting him. She turned the TV off.

"No. Please don't. I wanted to see it. I'm okay. And maybe next time I'm in town we can go to your art museum together and try not to have art attacks," he said, sniffing. Blinking and blinking. He reassured her he was okay once more.

"If you're around Louisville on Sunday afternoon, I'll take you. Our own *A Sunday Afternoon in Louisville at the Speed Art Museum*," she said.

"We could roast a Sunday chicken and pretend like this is our real life?"

"Exactly. Then poof! Back to reality for me on Monday because I have to go to work."

"Back to school?"

Tallie knew he was picturing her as a teacher in a high school classroom full of rowdy, colorfully shirted kids—a sugary, bubbling gumball machine of hormones and long limbs, acne and braces. She thought instead of the morning therapy appointments she had scheduled for Monday. One of her favorite clients, whom she'd watched courageously tackle and conquer her agoraphobia over the past two years; another with self-diagnosed attention-seeking issues and selfitis—an addiction to taking and posting selfies on social media. Then there was one new potential client—a black woman struggling with the stress of living in America and the long-lasting damaging effects of racism—who was coming in for an initial consult to see if they clicked. Tallie was looking forward to it and already feeling like they were a perfect match if their emails were any indication. She had black clients who specifically sought out a black therapist, needing that understanding and connection. The beating heart of her therapy practice was helping people feel less alone.

On Monday, she and her receptionist would be in the office at eight, like usual. And soon after, Tallie would be taking her endless therapy notes and listening. Letting her clients tell her their secrets and asking them the questions that would lead them to more questions. More answers. And, she hoped, more healing.

Where would Emmett be on Monday?

"Yes. Exactly. Back to school," she said, then nodded, cleared her throat. "I've never been to Clementine. I've heard of it, though. How'd you end up in Louisville? I guess I could've asked this yesterday, but I was already overwhelming you so much."

"I like Louisville."

"When did you get here?"

"Wednesday night," he said.

"Where'd you stay?"

"Nowhere. I just walked around."

"In the rain?" she asked.

"Yeah."

"Is that what you wanted to do?"

"Pretty much," he said.

"You were happy doing that?"

"Are *you* happy at this moment?" he asked.

"Pretty much."

She smirked and turned the TV back on, flicked through the channels until she found the World Series. "Here we go. I hope the Giants win," she said as the rain snapped to a stop. Emmett looked like he was going to say something when it started up again, harder.

The electricity popped out with a swoosh.

EMMETT

His mom's maiden name was in slim blanched capital letters over the doorway of the restaurant. Previously owned by his great-grandparents, it'd been there since 1950 as part of the lake resort. A prime spot right on the water. Emmett had grown up happy inside those walls, learned to cook from his grandparents, his mom, and her brothers. High-end southern food, a hot tourist spot in the summers.

Christine's uncle had been mayor of that lake town for years and before him, her grandfather. Her great-grandfather before that. Her mom was a debutante; both of her older brothers were high school football stars. Christine—with her heart-shaped face, big brown eyes, and honey-brown hair—was the town princess. Her beauty: spectacularly normal, timeless. Practical and clean, like a girl on a bar of soap.

Emmett's mom, Lisa, and Christine's dad, Mike, had grown up near each other, and Lisa had never liked him or his crew. "A bunch of spoiled bullies," she'd say. Everyone knew Christine and her family, but she went to the private high school on the other side of town, and Emmett hadn't spent much time with her, although he'd grown up hearing stories about the brawls their dads had with each other when they were in high school together. The first time Emmett had ever heard the word *nemesis*, his dad, Robert, had said it about Mike. Emmett was raised with the details of how much his parents didn't like Christine's family, but neither of them had anything bad to say about Christine. Occasionally, Emmett saw her at a summer party or ran into her and her brothers at the ice cream shop, the movies, or football games.

~

Emmett's best friend, Hunter, worked at the restaurant alongside him. Emmett and Hunter lived together in a small apartment by the lake. Emmett was twenty-two, anchored by the restaurant; Christine was twenty-one and wandering. She would come to the restaurant to hang out with her friend Savannah, one of the waitresses, who was also friends with Emmett. Once Savannah began dating Hunter, they made a sunshine-on-the-lake-happy foursome.

There were long stretches of seemingly last-forever summer days when Christine and Savannah would show up smelling like coconuts and beer after hanging out on a pontoon all morning and afternoon. Bathing suits blooming wet patterns beneath their sundresses, plastic flip-flops slapping. The humid summer nights wrapped them up in the same strange magic: nightswimming in the navy coolness, smoking sticky bud, sharing cigarettes. The boys would reopen the restaurant in the wee small hours and cook for the girls, the four of them sharing salty fries and suds in a corner booth.

Some nights, Emmett, in his clogs and kitchen whites, knocked back a strong IPA underneath the lake lamplight, listening to Christine talk about her life. The dopey, rich ex-boyfriend she was glad to be rid of. Her ignorant, racist family. The ones who had never left that town, didn't want to leave that town, would never leave that town.

Christine flirted and complimented Emmett's food, asking for more. Emmett happily obliged. Wood-fired pizzas with basil and shrimp. Coconut fried chicken. Fish and chips. Pan-fried rainbow trout. Pasta bianco with extra pepper. Steak au poivre. Christine loved pepper on everything. Emmett couldn't see or think about pepper without conjuring Christine, the pepper pinprick beauty mark on her left eyelid, her scrunched nose when her food was *too* spicy. They'd fallen in love at the lake restaurant.

~

His mom reassured him that she had nothing against Christine and her brothers; their family wasn't their fault. And for as long as Emmett could remember, Robert had always told his son—as part of his routine Dad Speeches—that if you didn't want the bad shit in life to win every time, you had to keep your eye out for a bright thing. "Sounds like Christine is your bright thing," his dad had said to him after Emmett gushed about her. "You and your mom have always been my bright things," his dad frequently reminded him.

~

"How did you learn to cook like this?" Christine asked, laughing on their first date alone. Before summer blurred gold into autumn, Emmett had asked Christine if she wanted to do something, just the two of them. They'd smoked a bowl and, like always, ended up in the kitchen.

"What? Girl, you know this is my family's restaurant," he said. He'd made her a full plate of mac and white cheese with freshly ground pepper clicked over it. She sat there, lake-tan and pretty, her hair tied back with yellow velvet.

"Duh. I know. But how'd you learn to cook like *this*?" she said, taking a big drink of water, pointing her fork at him. The restaurant was empty, the lights low. It was nearly 1:00 a.m., and they had walk-and-talk plans to get coffee at the twenty-four-hour diner afterward.

"Because I like you. A lot. That's why it tastes so good," he said, in a purposely sexy, deep voice. And as soon as the words left his mouth, the power went out. Christine squealed and giggled wildly, her shiny sounds echoing off the hanging army of copper and stainless steel.

"It tastes even better with the lights out," she said. He heard her fork tip-tap the plate. His adrenaline flashed, being alone, together like that. Terrified of the strong feelings he had for her. She moved toward him through the black, kissed his mouth for the first time. He could hear the sirens of his heart on high alert, blinded by this bright thing, even in the dark.

∼

Tallie gasped.

"You're okay?" Emmett asked her, sitting up.

"Oh, yeah, I'm fine. It just scared me. Candles! I'll get my new candles," she said. Emmett saw the shadow of Tallie drift past him on the couch, into the kitchen.

He'd loved cooking in her kitchen. He'd missed being in a kitchen. He was thinking about being with Christine in the kitchen, being with Brenna in the kitchen. *Kitchen, kitchen, kitchen, kitchen.* An obsessive, dizzying carousel of memories. He needed fresh air. He got up and opened Tallie's front door, closed it behind him. Leaned over the side of the porch, and the rain wrapped around him, wetting him quickly. Had it really been raining for this many days? What day was it?

Paranoia. He knew what was happening, although there wasn't anything he could do to stop it. The intense awareness made it worse. Like always, he felt both numb and as if he had hypersensitive antennae out, touching everything. Every negative emotion powered up inside him until he was fully charged. Sadness and anger fighting for room and the persistence of Emily Dickinson's "I felt a Funeral, in my Brain" beating, beating inside of him. He was wet from rain? Sweat? Tears? His imagination? He got cold and hot at the same time, his body unable to properly regulate its temperature. It'd started after Christine and Brenna were gone. He'd read it was perfectly normal, but that didn't stop it from sending him into a panic when it happened. The suffocating feeling of doom, the vision of his body going from bloody and hot to stone, cold as tombs.

Emmett had left his backpack inside with Tallie, next to the couch, but he couldn't bring himself to go in there. He was paralyzed on that edge in the rain, like that edge was the bridge. He'd jump. It was time to jump. He'd fought and fought and fought to no avail. A couple of signs weren't enough to fix him. Maybe they were just coincidences anyway. *Remember, nothing matters. Fuck it—*

"Joel?"

Tallie called him by the wrong name. He couldn't move. He was only cold now. Shaking. It was brighter outside than he'd imagined it would be.

(The slurred orange light of the streetlamps still glowing, reflecting off the leaves stuck like stickers to the sidewalk, the street—the wet glass windows of the cars lining it. Four cars: two four-doors, two sports cars. A yellow fire hydrant with blue caps. Rainwater running over the gutters. Rainwater sweeping to the sewers. One sharp bark from a dog.)

"The streetlamps are on," he said to himself, wondering if he'd hallucinated the power going out. Had he heard the letters PTSD with a question mark on the end? Had he hallucinated that, too? Had any of it happened? Hadn't he faked taking his meds, stopped going to the support groups?

"Emmett?" Tallie said. He could hear her moving around in the house.

"The streetlamps are on," he said a little louder. He couldn't get warm.

Tallie snatched the door open, saying his name again.

"The streetlamps are on," he said to her, still leaning over the side of the porch. "And...and you called me Joel."

"I'm sorry. I meant Emmett. You're wet. Come out of the rain?"

TALLIE

"Have the streetlamps ever stayed on before when your lights have gone out?" he asked her, still leaning into the rain. "I needed some air."

Tallie had visions of him darting into traffic, harming himself, being gobbled up by the night. There'd be no way to find him, no way to tell anyone who he was. She'd blame herself forever for losing him.

Coping mechanisms: cigarettes, fresh air.

She often asked her clients how much fresh air they got, especially when they felt panicky or claustrophobic. Opening a window or stepping outside for a few minutes could change a client's mood, as well as her own, when exposed nerves scintillated.

She felt as if she'd escaped her own darkest period of divorce-depression, but there were cracks that let the shadows creep in. Like if she spent too long looking at photos of Joel's new life, new wife, new baby. Or if she heard a song that reminded her of Joel or one of their dates or their wedding or any of the weddings they went to together. Any Celine Dion. Any Luther Vandross. Any Faith Hill. Any drippy duets. They were together for practically *thirteen* years. *Thirteen* years of a life so easily triggered it might as well have been a loaded gun. She understood the anxiety of mental land mines, and that understanding helped her connect to her clients.

Tallie had trained herself to get out under the open sky as often as she could when she was feeling restless or downright miserable, and it always helped. She'd allowed herself a few weeks of skipping her normal runs after her divorce, but she found that the days she felt like staying in bed the most were also the days she benefited the most from getting out and moving her body for perspective. It wasn't a cure-all, because nothing was, but it helped. And she never brought up getting out for fresh air to her overwhelmed agoraphobic clients until they were ready. She was glad to see that Emmett took himself outside when he felt the walls closing in.

"I'll give you some space. But when you feel ready, come back inside." She left the door open a smidge for him. Her notifications lit up with flash flood warnings for the other side of town. She played solitaire on her phone in the dark until Emmett stepped inside after exactly eight minutes. Tallie had been eyeing the time. "I thought you'd left," she said, putting her phone down and standing. She was more upset than she expected. "And yes, sometimes. Sometimes the streetlamps stay on."

"I've thought about leaving. I really don't want to burden you. But I wouldn't go without saying goodbye," he said.

"You're not burdening me. I've asked you to stay. Do you promise you won't up and disappear?"

"Promise. I promise," he said into the candle-dark. She'd lit the ones they bought together at the outlet mall. One was pumpkin, the other, sugary cinnamon.

"I was scared," she admitted. Relieved. She'd enjoyed his company so much; she felt exposed by how hurt she'd be if he left without warning. Like her heart would turn to gray ash and blow away.

"I was, too, in my head. The fresh air helps. I'm going to step outside again and smoke." He moved through the darkness toward the wall plug, retrieved his phone. Went inside his backpack for his cigarettes.

"Smoke for fresh air?"

"Exactly," he said. "I'll be right back."

"Okay," she said, sitting on the couch, narrowly missing planting her butt on top of Jim. "You don't need the Wi-Fi password? For later? When power's restored? Are you calling someone?"

"No, but thanks. And I'm not calling anyone."

"I'm being nosy."

"It's your house. You have a right to ask," he said. "I was going to listen to the World Series outside. Join me. I may stand under the open sky."

He shrugged his jacket on, zipped it, put his hand in the outside pocket. Paper crush. One of the letters. He kept the look on his face plain, took his hand out. Tallie had a duckish-yellow rain slicker in the closet by the front door, a pair of tall black wellies. Once she put them on, she felt like Paddington Bear.

Before she could get out on the porch, Jim ran through the door crack in an orange blur, disappearing into the bushes.

"Shit. He used to do this all the time, but not anymore," she said.

"He ran to the neighbor's. Where's the flashlight? I'll go get him."

Tallie found the flashlight for him and handed it over.

"Jim would be a no-good, terrible outside cat. He's too lazy. I don't know why he does this," she said, squishing through her wet front yard. She made a clicking noise with her mouth. Puckered her lips and kissed the air, said the cat's name in a high, baby voice.

"I've disturbed their routine. Plus, this rain. And then the power goes out. It made us all a little crazy for a second," Emmett said.

They walked next door, saw an orange flick behind the burning bush in front of her neighbor's windows.

"There he is," Tallie said, pointing and bending over. Emmett stepped ahead of her and went to the other side of the bush, shining light into the darkness. "Come here, baby," she said to the cat she could now see was sitting behind the hedging, shaking rainwater off his head. Jim took a step back and licked his paws. "He's very stubborn." She reached for him.

Emmett handed her the flashlight and got on his hands and knees. With his longer arms, he stretched and gently took Jim by the scruff. Lifted him, cradled him. Tallie heard her neighbor's front door open.

"Tallie, is that you?" her neighbor asked from the porch.

"Yes. Sorry. Jim...my cat...he ran over here, but we have him now," Tallie said. She looked at her neighbor, touched the top of the cat's head. She glanced up at Emmett, wondering if he was feeling okay. Having something specific and distracting to focus on—like hunting a cat in the rain—could help put the brakes on anxiety attacks and anchor a person who was disconnecting. It was dark, but Tallie could still tell he'd lost the spaciness he'd held in his eyes when the power had gone out; now his eyes were warm with color. He stood there, petting the cat, whispering to it.

"Oh, you're fine," her neighbor said. She wasn't her nosiest neighbor, but Tallie knew she'd wonder who Emmett was since Tallie didn't have many new visitors. "Power's supposed to be restored soonish, but you know how they are. I just reported it."

"I'll report it, too," Tallie said.

"Hi there," her neighbor said to Emmett.

"Hi."

"This is my friend Emmett. And now we have the cat. Sorry for rummaging around in your bushes," Tallie said. She smiled and pushed the dripping branches back where they belonged.

With the streetlamps glowing, she could make out her neighbor staring at Emmett for a little too long before turning to Tallie smiling, waving. "Good for you, Tallie...on everything," she said.

~

Once they were on her porch, Emmett gave the soppy cat to her. She cradled Jim's head and fussed at him before taking him in the house. The cat sauntered into the kitchen and stopped to clean himself some more. Pam was unbothered, still sleeping on the couch next to Tallie's phone. She grabbed it, opened the electricity company app, found her neighborhood and house on the little cartoon map, reported her power outage.

She and Emmett went outside and sat on the steps. He lit a cigarette. After loading the live radio feed of the game on his phone, he told her the Giants were winning, three to nothing. He said it like the score was good luck. She checked the electricity app again and told him the power should be back in an hour or so, but he didn't seem concerned about her lights being out anymore. People with anxiety and mood disorders, people who were struggling, fighting hard against suicidal ideation and depression, often had wide mood swings. She had loads of experience with clients who went from fine to unwell in a matter of seconds.

Coping mechanisms: cigarettes, fresh air, finding cats in the rain, listening to the baseball game.

The baseball commentary made her feel better about the world, too, all those numbers and the neat way they rattled them off at the end of the games, shrinking the big business of the innings into small, organized boxes. He adjusted the volume of the play-by-play as he stepped down, leaned against her house, looking up.

"If you have a ladder, I'll clean your gutters out for you. They're full of leaves," Emmett said.

"Yes, I have a ladder. But I don't know if you should be climbing up on things." She thought of babysitting her nephew when he was a toddler, how all-consuming it was to keep a little boy from climbing too high, choking, running into the street, or poking his eye out somehow. She didn't want to treat Emmett like a child, but any diversion from potential danger felt like a proper move.

"Worried I'll jump off?"

"No, I—"

"Well...it's not so high up there. Wouldn't do me any good, really," he said, turning to look at her.

"Stop it. It's not that. You just don't have to do so much. You cook and do dishes...you're a cat rescuer. I mean, wow."

"Joel used to clean them out?" he asked, giving his attention back to the gutters.

"I guess. I never really paid attention to stuff like that. I hadn't noticed they needed cleaning out," she said, stepping over to look up with him.

"The rain shouldn't be pouring off the side. It should be running smoothly through and out. Over here." Emmett pointed with his cigarette hand. "That's why it feels like we're inside a car wash when we're in the house. Because your gutters need cleaning out."

"Oops. I didn't know that. I kind of like the sound it makes," she said. She liked the sound it made falling on the hood of her slicker, too. She watched the rainwater spill out of the gutters, listened to the dulcet drip-drip-dripping. "Supposed to ease up in the morning...sure...maybe you could do it then? I'll pay you in breakfast and coffee?"

Coping mechanisms: cigarettes, fresh air, finding cats in the rain, listening to the baseball game, cleaning out gutters.

"Right on," Emmett said. He smoked and got quiet as the baseball game stretched into the seventh inning.

~

By the time Tallie's power was restored, the Giants had won the World Series. She and Emmett had come inside, hung up their wet things. Tallie put a towel beneath the coatrack to catch the rainwater. She opened her laptop and ordered her vitamins, donated to the nonprofit against sex slavery she'd thought about earlier. She put the kettle on while Emmett and his backpack went to the bathroom.

He'd left the backpack inside when he'd gone out on the porch. Jackpot. Tallie had unzipped it quietly in the dark, shoved her hand in, felt around, making sure there wasn't some violent evil inside. She touched the little ring box he'd shown her. Something else wrapped in paper—a book? Books? Another small box or book and some clothes—cotton, denim, wool. Plastic bottles. She couldn't see a thing, just felt around. Lifted the backpack with one hand to see how heavy it was—not too heavy, not too light. She put it down quick, in case he came inside.

Tallie was right about his energy—that lilac puff. She stood in her living room chewing her thumb, looking down the hallway, picturing Emmett behind her bathroom door with that backpack. He didn't have a gun or a severed head in there. It was mostly soft things; she knew that. But she still jumped and slapped her hand to her heart when the teakettle surprised her, screaming from the kitchen.

EMMETT

From: JoelFoster1979@gmail.com
To: Talliecat007@gmail.com
Subject: Re: i still care about you too

Yes Tallie, I am trying. Finally. And I appreciate you saying it, because I really am. And you're right. I should've treated you better—my parents remind me of that a lot. They're not letting me off easy, just so you know. You've asked tough questions, but I will try my best.

My love for Odette is different, but I don't know if I can explain it. It was a surprise. I do want to be a good man. I'm trying to be a better man. If what you're asking is whether or not I love her more than I love you, the answer is NO. It's just different. And I fucked it up with you. I am trying not to fuck it up with her.

It feels very strange to be a father and I don't think it has sunk all the way in yet. I can probably answer this question a little better down the road. I can tell you I love my daughter fiercely even though at this point she just sleeps and cries. And yeah, I mean it feels weird to have a baby with a woman who isn't you. I always thought it'd be you. Wanted it to be you. We tried so hard. You know all this.

126

You sound different and I mean it in a good way! I truly don't know where we go from here, if anywhere, but I'm so glad you reached out. I'm so glad, Tallie. And I haven't texted or talked to Lionel much since the divorce and am not sure if it's okay for me to contact him anymore... I know he's still pissed at me, but if you wouldn't mind telling him I miss him. And he'll always be my brother... even if he hates me.

I'm getting emotional writing this, so I'll stop. But if you don't mind, I do have a question for you. Are you seeing anyone? (Is that too weird to ask?) I'm asking because if you ARE seeing someone, I hope he treats you right. I hope he's the complete opposite of me.

Hope to hear from you soon,
J

~

"*Funny Girl*? You said this was your favorite?" Emmett asked Tallie, slipping the DVD case off the shelf and holding it up.

"Definitely."

"Do you want to watch it?"

"It's pretty long."

"I don't mind if you don't. Seems relaxing," he said, flipping it over. "I'm guessing it's funny?" He smiled, looking at her.

"You're clever," she said. "You were upset earlier, when the lights went out. You're feeling better?"

"I feel like being quiet, watching this, if that's okay. I'm really comfortable here."

"It's *hygge*. You've heard of it? The Danish word? It's about making things cozy, comforting. It's like an American fad now, but sort of a way of life for some people. Making things as comfy as possible... it's what I do—" Tallie stopped and changed the expression on her face, like an engine slowing, then revving back up. "I use the idea of it in my classroom."

"I've never heard of it, but I feel it here. It's overwhelming. And I mean that as a compliment," Emmett said.

"I accept it."

(The jumping candlelight cuts through the rising tea-mug steam. The steam looks like cartoon smoke. Six tea lights in a half-moon on the table. The walls of Tallie's living room are the color of creamed coffee.)

~

They started *Funny Girl*, and Tallie picked up her knitting and began slipping the needles and yarn through her fingers. Fast. She barely glanced at it, knitting around and around, scooting small neon-colored plastic markers across the cord connecting the needles when she got to them. Emmett watched, appreciating how soothing and hypnotic it was. She mouthed along with parts of the dialogue—the songs, too. He enjoyed it for a while but soon found he couldn't focus. He hated that he'd contacted Joel, the subterfuge of it. If Tallie got something out of the emails she couldn't have gotten otherwise, when he left her, he wouldn't feel so guilty. Even when he did dumb shit, his tender conscience was a crutch. It'd plagued him his whole life. He took on other people's emotions, absorbed them without wanting to, like an abandoned sponge.

"Y'know earlier when you were talking about how it feels for Joel to get something he wanted so much...his baby...I'm sure part of it does feel wrong and weird for him. Doing it without you, since he always thought it *would* be you," Emmett said.

If what he said surprised Tallie, she didn't let on. Instead, she kept her face plain, shrugged.

"What's something small about him you miss? Christine would drink from my water bottle. I'd leave it somewhere and come back to a pink lipstick print on it that tasted like strawberries or cherries. I miss that."

Tallie put down her knitting and paused the movie.

"A sweet memory. Thank you for sharing it with me," she said, crossing her legs on the couch.

"I don't really talk about this stuff to anyone," he said.

"That's why I mean it when I say thank you for sharing it with me."

"You're easy to talk to. I'm sure people tell you that all the time."

"I've heard it before, yes," Tallie said.

Barbra Streisand was frozen on the TV screen—a silent witness to their conversation.

"It's okay if I mention something I *don't* miss about him first?" she asked.

"Such a rebel."

"I am." She smiled at him. "Joel was obsessed with the news and would get constant notifications on his phone. Wanted to keep CNN on all day long. Drove me mad! I stopped keeping up with the news after he moved out. I hate it."

"Understood," Emmett said. Another reason to love Tallie—she hated the news as much as he did.

"A *little* thing I miss about him is that he would sometimes leave his bag of chips on the side of the couch when he was done instead of putting it back in the pantry. It used to annoy me, but I found myself missing it once he was gone. I'd put a bag of chips there myself, to feel like he was here. And this is embarrassing, but his...lunulae...the, um, half-moons on his fingernails. They're really pretty. He has really nice hands. It sounds so ridiculous to say aloud now," she said.

"Don't be embarrassed, please. And it doesn't sound ridiculous to me," he reassured her.

Not much surprised Emmett, and not much sounded ridiculous to him, either. He had his own nights when he'd stayed up, wrecked and crying. The longest nights of his life. Nights he'd slept with Christine's T-shirts on her side of the bed, hoping to wake up next to her. Nights he'd sat alone in the chair in his living room, rocking and rocking, thinking of Brenna, Brenna's eyes, Brenna's voice. Brenna had been real; he knew it. But where had she gone? There were wide cracks in his sanity, something he'd been so sure of *before*.

After had devoured *before*, leaving him crumpled.

"Some big things I miss about him are...how funny he is and honestly, his body...ugh, I was just so physically attracted to him it almost made me sick. And...I also miss sharing sadness. Now, lucky me, I get it all to myself," Tallie said. "We spent a lot of time alone together. Entire weekends in this house, only us. I guess that's why I find myself thinking...was I making all that up? Where the hell did it go?"

"You weren't making it up."

Tallie scrunched her face, then straightened it. "What's something big you miss about Christine?" she asked, pulling her hair over her shoulder.

"Her messy aliveness. She really went for it, y'know? So full of life and couldn't get enough of even the things she hated. She really rocket-burned out instead of simply fading away," he said, the answer breaking through quickly, requiring almost no brain energy from him at all.

"That's beautiful. *Tragic* and beautiful."

"Well, yeah...that's a perfect way of describing her."

He let his mind drift, and Tallie seemed to do the same, both of them transfixed by the quiet and the weight of the conversation and Barbra's face on the TV screen. When she spoke again, Tallie asked Emmett to tell her something he loved about himself.

"I'm good in the kitchen," he said.

"That you are. What else?"

"Not a proper answer?"

"No! I was only wondering what else you'd say."

"Um...I'm a hard worker. I don't half-ass things. Except my bridge jump...yeah, I guess I half-assed that, but it wasn't *all* my fault. You're partly to blame, you'll have to admit," he said, smiling at her. She looked uncomfortable, but he kept smiling. Kept smiling and smiling until she finally smiled back. "There we go," he said.

"I didn't like that joke."

"Sorry. But yeah. I'm normally pretty emotionally resilient. An easy heart. I can usually deal with a lot...more. I have before."

"Easy heart. I can see that in you, but we all have our weak moments, for sure."

"What's something you really love about *you*?" he asked.

She took her time and thought about it before answering. "Well...I'm patient and rarely rude to anyone. And I try to look for good things in people, even when I'm hurting."

"And that's why you didn't kill your ex-husband in his sleep?"

"Exactly why. And when I do get lonely, I spend a lot of time with Lionel and his family," Tallie said.

"How many kids does your brother have?"

"One. A boy. He's six. I'm knitting this sweet little sweater for him." Tallie held up her yarn and needles before grabbing her phone. She swiped through and held it out, showing Emmett a photo of a little brown boy grinning, missing teeth. "His name is River...and I don't want that name to trigger anything for you because of the bridge and yesterday. It's okay for me to keep going?"

"Yes. And no one else is like you, by the way," Emmett said, taking the phone from her, looking closely at the photo of River— the little boy whose picture was stuck to the fridge more than once. "He's super cute," he said, feeling as if his heart had been wrenched open, scooped out.

"You haven't mentioned any siblings. You don't have them?"

They were surrounded by candle flickers. The house went wavy and shimmering, like they were being consumed. *Deuteronomy 4:24; Hebrews 12:29.* God as a consuming fire. And the devil, always there, too. Confusing him, telling him to give up, to let go, that there is only one way out. The constant grappling. Dissociation again—the swirly, conflicting feeling of floating gravity. No matter how fast or far he ran from it, it caught up to him. He stood, closed his eyes.

"Are you feeling okay?" Tallie asked.

"Sometimes I get dizzy." He lifted his weighty eyelids, focused on her.

"I'll get you a glass of water," she said, walking to the kitchen.

"I'm making too much trouble for you." He followed behind her.

"You aren't. I *want* to help you, but you have to let me. Are you on antidepressants? They can cause dizziness. You should sit. I'll make some more tea," she said. She handed him the water and went to the table, pulling out a chair for him. She put the kettle back on.

(*The chair is quieter than expected as it slides. The walnut wood of the chair matches the walnut wood of the table exactly. There are four chairs. The kitchen tile: gray sunbursts on white. The sunbursts are connected by thin gray lines. Tallie's breath smells like tea.*)

"I'm not on antidepressants," he said, sitting. His heart beat as if he'd been running. The edges of the world curved in closer, dimmed. Tallie sat, too.

"Have you *ever* been on antidepressants?"

"Not really."

"Dizzy spells are the worst."

"No, I don't have siblings. I'm an only child."

"Are you sure you don't want me to take you to the hospital? We could go if you're not feeling well," Tallie said.

"I don't need to go to the hospital, Miss Tallie, thank you. Will you hand me my backpack, please?"

"You don't mind me getting it?"

"No. Will you get it for me, please?" he asked, putting his head in his hands.

TALLIE

She found his backpack next to the couch. Pam had perched herself upon it. Tallie apologized for having to disrupt the cat's napping area and petted her head. She handled his backpack gently, placed it on the floor at his feet in the kitchen.

"I'll show you what's in here. It's not scary. Just stuff," he said, unzipping the front pocket and pulling out an unlabeled orange plastic bottle rattling with pills. "Allergy medicine and beta-blockers. The beta-blockers settle my heart, my adrenaline. It's a low dose, but they can make me dizzy." He took a small, round orange pill with his water.

Medication: antihistamines, beta-blockers. Antidepressants, maybe?

"Of course," she said, knowing beta-blockers blocked norepinephrine as well as adrenaline and were also prescribed for anxiety and stage fright, relaxing the automatic fight-or-flight response. She didn't treat any clients who relied on beta-blockers alone for anxiety management, but at least Emmett had something.

Tallie made two fresh mugs of tea as Emmett put the items on her kitchen table, the things she'd felt but not seen. The fuzzy blue snow hat she'd bought him at the outlet mall. A black lighter, a soft pack of cigarettes. A pair of oatmeal-colored wool socks rolled into a neat thick ball. One pair of white boxer shorts. A navy-blue pocket T-shirt folded into a pair of dark denim. The diamond wedding ring in its ring box. A bag containing a travel toothbrush and toothpaste, a plastic tube of deodorant. An unopened unscented bar of soap. A clean white washcloth, a clean black towel. The snaky cord and chunky thunk of his phone charger. An old plum-red copy of the New Testament—the size of a deck of cards—with a scrap of paper torn from a children's coloring book sticking out. A brick-size manila envelope. A pair of citron fabric butterfly wings with elastic shoulder loops.

"Can I?" Tallie asked, sitting and holding her hand out.

"Yes," Emmett said. "Unremarkable, like I said. And I have that Kershaw knife I keep clipped to my jeans if you want to take it from me. So you're not scared."

"I'm not scared," Tallie said. Could she levitate from sincerity? She picked the items up, inspected them as if she were an archaeologist, attempting to glean everything she could from his culture and the time period in which he lived. She felt closer to him immediately, seeing and touching more of his stuff, as if his secrets had taken physical form. When she got to the envelope, she peeked inside and gasped. What had felt like a book wasn't a book.

"Emmett, how much money is in here?"

"Thousands, around ten."

"Okay, wow. And you had the nerve to ask me if I was afraid you'd rob me blind. Aren't you scared to walk around with all this money?"

"I don't care about the money. I was going to leave it on the bridge anyway for someone to find, hopefully put to good use," he said. "And I'd like to give you more, for everything you've done for me." He began peeling off hundred-dollar bills, a couple of twenties.

"I don't want you to give it to me. I mean it. Stop," she said, putting her hand on his. He stacked the money for her neatly and pushed it to the edge of the table. It wasn't entirely weird for someone considering suicide to drain their bank account or whatever he'd done; saving money quickly lost its importance next to matters of life and death. But she still asked, "You won't tell me where you got this?" She touched the envelope with the tip of her finger.

"Not illegally. I promise," he said.

"Why are you walking around with it?"

"I don't know."

"You don't know?" Tallie raised her eyebrows. She sat back in her chair, frustrated. Leaned forward, frustrated. Drank her tea, frustrated.

"Look, I know how this sounds, but it's not dirty money, and it's mine. I saved it, that's all," he said.

"And the clothes, the toiletries? You had all this stuff? Why'd you let me think you didn't?" She touched the plastic inside his toiletries bag, the travel-size items she loved to buy before vacation.

"I don't have pajamas or anything as comfortable as what you gave me. I didn't intend to mislead you."

"Do you have an ID?" Tallie asked, scanning the table and looking inside his backpack.

"Not on me," he said.

"But you have a license?"

"Yes."

"Not with you?"

"No, not with me," Emmett said.

"So you told the police officer what, earlier?"

"Exactly what I said. I told him the truth. My name, my Social Security number. They can look that stuff up."

"And what's your name?"

"Emmett."

"Emmett what?" Tallie asked, annoyed.

"Emmett Aaron Baker," he said a little slowly, watching her face. *Client Name: Baker, Emmett Aaron.*

"Emmett Aaron Baker," she repeated, lighting up. There it was.

Her stomach Ferris-wheeled hearing him say his full name, echoing it in its entirety for the first time. She envisioned herself tapping his full name into Google. "I looked up *Emmett* and *Clementine, Kentucky*, and couldn't find anything. What would happen if I looked up *Emmett Aaron Baker*?" she asked.

"Nothing would come up," he said with his eyes stuck to hers.

"You're the *one* ungoogleable man left on earth?"

"I didn't say that. I just don't put myself out there," Emmett said. He took his right hand and raked his hair to the left, off his forehead. A move Tallie loved on men.

"I scanned the list of *America's Most Wanted, Kentucky's Most Wanted*, and a few more," she confessed.

"Good. Sure you did. But you didn't see me," he said confidently.

"Right. I did not."

They drank their tea in silence. The rain fell across her windows like the car wash Emmett had compared it to. She imagined him clapping the ladder against her house, cleaning out the gutters. She imagined telling Lionel. He would've noticed they were full next time he stopped by when it was raining. Lionel would've looked up and told her in his booming alpha-male, king-of-the-mountain, big-brother voice, "Either I can do it or you need to have someone come clean out your gutters." She was proud of herself for taking care of it before Lionel could fuss at her.

"And these?" she asked, touching the butterfly wings.

"I'm not ready to talk about those. Or this," he said, pointing to the coloring-book paper—a treasure from a child.

"What about this?" She lifted the little Bible.

"My grandfather's, given to him by his parents on the day he was born," he said, opening to show her the inscription written inside.

To Samuel. Welcome to Earth. March 29, 1933.

"You were raised religious?"

"Baptist," he said.

"Me, too."

For someone who'd felt such intense emotion the day before and who had wanted to end his life, Emmett had an aggressive calm about him. Whatever sent him to the bridge must've really been *truly* unbearable. Thinking of what it could have been was like staring into a too-bright light without blinking. Tallie's eyes watered.

"Does it bother you, talking about God? About religion?"

"Not really," he said.

"So yesterday you said, 'What if there's no God'... Is that what you believe?"

"I think God is there, but indifferent."

"Feels too cruel to me. Him being there, but not caring. I can't believe in that kind of God," she said.

"But when things get dark and hopeless... that's exactly what it feels like."

Tallie took in his response. She knew healing—*if* and *when* it happened—happened in increments, the same sneaky way the days got longer and shorter. Barely noticeable at times, slow. Tallie had been treading water of her own, in that estuary where sadness spilled out into healing and joy. Believing in God came easy for her, even in her worst moments. Even when she sat there and listened to her clients tell her their secrets—the hidden, terrifying demons some people kept locked away for so long that when they finally did talk about them, it was as if a cloud of black death wanted to swallow them whole. She'd seen people come out at the other end of that darkness. She knew God was real.

When people were really messed up, most of them wanted to do better, only they didn't know how. So they showed up in her office, simply wanting to learn more about themselves and how to live in this world. She wasn't exactly labeled a Christian therapist, but with their permission, sometimes she liked to mention to her Christian clients that the Bible talked about all sorts of people—a lot of terrible, confused, miserable people. Murderers, thieves, you name it—Jesus was the *only* perfect one, and He surrounded Himself with imperfect people. The Bible was full of surprises and unlikely heroes, people who made mistakes. And even when she didn't want to, she thought often of Odette's tremulous voice echoing in the apartment stairwell after Tallie had driven over there and confronted her not long after Joel had moved out. Tallie had stared at Odette's vulpine face, her mouth frozen in a little rose twist. "I'm sorry. Everyone makes mistakes," Odette had said.

It was something Tallie always told her clients, reassuring them that she'd made a lot of mistakes, too. Being a human was hard, and life was proof—there was no escaping it. "You're human, and you have to reconcile that with yourself somehow. Forgive yourself. Allow yourself to feel everything deeply, to grow and learn," she'd say.

"But what do you really believe, Emmett? Deep in your spirit, without thinking."

"I believe in God...but I think He's forgotten about me."

A chill skipped across Tallie's bones like a rock on water, but her house was too warm. She got up to lift the kitchen window as rain spattered at the screen. The ledge dampened; the humidity and smell of soggy leaves hemmed them in.

"Well, He didn't forget about you on the bridge yesterday. He held you in His hand and didn't let you go. And He won't...even when it feels like He's not there...He is."

Emmett said nothing.

"And this, is this important to you?" Tallie asked, holding his backpack up with two fingers like it was a wet skunk.

"No. I want it to disappear."

EMMETT

The rain was letting up. Tallie opened the back door and pointed to the gas grill she said had belonged to Joel.

"Never been used. Can't we put it in there and light it up like a barbecue?" she asked.

(There is a yellow-orange orb of light—like fire caught in a jam jar—behind the frosted glass next to Tallie's face. Pretty, glow. She holds the long lighter in her hand, flicks it.)

Tallie had gone to her bedroom and returned with a stack of her wedding photos. She'd shown him the one on top: her in a garden in a long lace dress standing next to a tuxedoed Joel, looking over at him as he smiled for the camera. She'd shoved the photos down into Emmett's empty backpack.

"Do you want to talk about why you want this gone?" she asked.

"Not really. I don't need it anymore, that's all. Do you—"

"No. And I have another backpack I can give you," she said, always thinking ahead. Tallie probably made a to-do list every morning and never ran out of anything, never forgot to pay a bill. Probably had never been late returning a library book in her entire life.

"And you promise you'll stop carrying around a huge amount of cash?" she asked, lifting the lid of the grill. It yawned open, revealing more black.

"Yes, ma'am," he said. He set the backpack on the metal rack.

"Cool it with the ma'am."

"My bad."

"Should we say a few words? I'll start. Goodbye and good riddance," Tallie said.

"Goodbye, backpack. I loved you once, but not anymore. You're dirty, and I need a new one. But know this: I will never forget you," Emmett said, lowering his head and clasping his hands in front of him. He closed his eyes, then opened one to peek at Tallie so she'd know it was more than okay to chuckle along with him, and she did.

"Amen," Tallie said. She turned on the gas, clicked the flame to the green fabric, and they watched it catch. And go.

~

Emmett and Christine had needed new supplies for the first trip they took together. It was spring, and they'd been serious since their first date, at the end of summer. They'd driven from his place to Red River Gorge, about two hours north. He'd hiked part of the Appalachian Trail with his youth group in high school, had a hiking pack. He needed a new, smaller backpack, too. He and Christine had gone to the big camping store, thirty minutes outside of town. He held up a black bag, and Christine commented that black backpacks made her sad. He held up a tangerine bag, and she said it was too annoying, too alert. When Emmett held up the deep green one that would later burn in Tallie's grill, Christine said it was just right.

Christine, his brown-haired Goldilocks.

~

April, two weeks out from the full pink moon. At their campsite, Emmett made crispy salmon and cannellini beans in cumin tomatoes. After eating, they smoked a bowl of Kentucky green by the firelight under the endless black sky. It wasn't until they'd crawled into their tent, sated and laughing, that Emmett realized he'd forgotten the most important camping item he meant to bring: condoms. They always used them, no exceptions. "Birth control pills make me completely crazy. I can't take them," Christine had warned him in the past.

"I'm so sorry. This was supposed to be our first romantic weekend away, and I blew it," he said to her as she lay there naked in his sleeping bag, a spring zephyr raising the scent from between her legs. He'd once walked past a bowl of ripened nectarines at work, and their jabby musk had smelled just like her.

"You're being so dramatic about this. It's okay," she said.

"I just wanted everything to be perfect, so we could escape town . . . for a night. Your family—"

"Look. My family sucks. There are *literally* KKK members in it. And my dad has always hated your dad. We both know this! Fuck all of them, okay? We don't need them," she said.

"They're still your family; there's nothing you can do about that."

"My dad said he'd stop giving me money if I didn't break up with you, and he knows I won't do it. Here I am, with you! Where I want to be. We don't *need* them. We don't need anyone."

"I'm sorry I forgot the condoms."

"I'm not," she said, pulling him on top of her, guiding him inside.

And when she told him she was pregnant, without hesitating he'd gotten on one knee on the dock behind the restaurant and promised to buy a ring as soon as he could. Two days after that, Emmett put on his pressed white shirt and brown jeans, and they went to the courthouse with Hunter and Savannah in tow, got married, walked out into the springtime sunshine as one flesh. Christine's hair was pulled over her shoulder, braided loose with sweet pea blossoms. She wore a petal of a dress, the peachy color so tender and unassuming it made him want to cry.

~

"Damn, it feels dangerously good to destroy things," Tallie said out on the deck, satisfied.

"You're sure you don't mind? I can give you money for the grill."

"Apparently you can give me money for almost everything."

Emmett smiled before a deep sadness moved through him. "I'm heading out early Sunday morning. Just so you know," he said. It had begun raining again in steady drips as he and Tallie stepped into the kitchen. She went to her bedroom and returned with the black backpack she said he could have. He thanked her and took it, began filling it up, thinking of Christine saying black backpacks made her sad. *Are you sad now, Christine? Please say no.*

"Where will you go? Back to Clementine?" she asked.

"I know it would make you feel better if I told you I was going back to Clementine, but I don't know what I'm going to do."

"Your parents would be elated to see you, to know you're okay."

"How do you know that?"

"Do your parents have any mental health issues...if you don't mind me asking?"

"No. I mean, not that I know of," he said.

"Anxiety, depression?"

Emmett shook his head.

"Well...they're your parents, and you're their only child. That's how I know they'd be elated to see you."

"But not all families are warm and loving. Some are *extraordinarily* anemic. Not everyone's parents are so great. Some are really terrible," he said.

"Are yours terrible, Emmett?"

"No, but a *lot* of them are," he said, zipping up his newly filled backpack, setting it in the kitchen corner.

"Will you tell me about them? What are they like?"

He told her his dad worked for an agriculture and farming insurance company and was looking forward to retiring soon and that his mom was a damn good cook. He told her his parents weren't perfect, but his mom was close. His dad had barely missed the Vietnam draft and was a new generation of man. He'd never laid a hand on Emmett to hurt him, making him a rarity in the country town where they grew up, where most kids were raised going out to pick their own whipping switches from the trees in the yard. He told Tallie his parents were quiet and private, and they'd only wanted one child. That they'd happily welcomed Christine into their lives as their daughter-in-law and they'd grieved alongside him when she died.

Tallie asked if Christine's family was anemic, and Emmett nodded.

"Well, *your* family sounds loving and kind. Trust me, they do not want to lose you. They don't even want to think they've lost you. I'd be elated to see my *cats* alive if I thought they were dead," Tallie said.

Emmett stood with his hands in the pockets of those gray sweatpants that weren't his. Tallie had offered to throw them in the dryer since he'd gotten the knees a bit wet cat hunting, but he didn't mind. They were close to dry now. He leaned against the counter as Pam pawed into the kitchen and meowed up at them.

"She's hungry," Tallie said, going into the pantry and pulling out a crinkly bag of cat food, beckoning the orange one.

"I'm glad your cats are alive," he said, hoping to end the conversation.

"Do you know how to play gin rummy?" she asked him after feeding the cats and opening the kitchen drawer. She held up a deck of cards.

"Sure do."

Tallie asked Emmett if he wanted to play cards for a little bit before they finished *Funny Girl*, and then she asked him what he thought about chocolate chip cookies. And what if they added pumpkin?

"That's rhetorical, right?" he asked.

"It would be *so* wrong and rude to October to make them without pumpkin," Tallie said.

~

They worked together to make the dough from scratch, Emmett eventually taking over completely with the stirring and scooping. With the cookies in the oven, he and Tallie played gin rummy. She asked him if he'd gone to college, and he told her no. She asked him if his mom had been the one to teach him how to cook so well, and he told her yes, he'd grown up cooking with his mom, grandparents, and uncles, and he loved to eat, so it only made sense he'd know how to cook, too.

The pumpkin chocolate chip cookies were perfectly gooey, both of them eating two and leaving nothing but tiny crumbs on the plates next to their newly refilled mugs of tea. Tallie went and retrieved the fuzzy red hat she'd gotten at the outlet mall and instructed him to get his fuzzy blue one out of his new backpack. They put them on and played a couple of hands of five-card draw, switching hats on every new deal and using the loose cigarettes from his soft pack as chips. Tallie's straight flush beat his full house on the last hand.

Playing cards at Tallie's table reminded him of the nights he and Hunter and the rest of his restaurant buddies would drink too many beers and play poker in one of their basements, smoking and eating and laughing, sometimes until the sun came up. Emmett was a terrible gambler, afraid of losing too much, of giving something away he should've kept. On the crickety summer nights after he and Christine were married, the guys would come over and play at their place. They'd set up in the garage so no one would smoke in the house, allowing Christine and the baby inside her the time and space to get their rest. Emmett plus Christine plus eternal summers and both the good and the bad that came with them—they fought often and hard but forgave each other just as quickly. Emmett remained increasingly optimistic about their forever, caught in the net of the blissful *before*, happy about the unexpected joy they'd been gifted and leaning deep into the wonder.

TALLIE

Barbra Streisand as Fanny Brice, belting "My Man" onstage. Hands raised, bathed in black, diamond earrings swinging like earthquaked chandeliers. The punchy power in her vulnerability had always bowled Tallie over, especially after her divorce, when she realized how strong she actually was. Even when she thought she couldn't push through, she turned around and saw that, somehow, she had. She thought she and Joel were forever, and she'd been astronomically wrong about it. At first, she'd been so fucking jealous of Joel's new life she thought it'd kill her. Literally.

It had felt unbearable, and yet she'd borne it.

She reached for a tissue and wiped her eyes. "Sorry. It always makes me cry," she said.

"Crying doesn't make me uncomfortable. I'm totally okay with emotionalism," he said, smiling and parroting back some of her own words from the night before.

"Ha, ha."

"*Funny Girl* took a heavy turn, didn't it? I liked it. I liked the movie."

She'd wondered if he'd doze off toward the end, but he hadn't; he watched intently, like he might be quizzed afterward.

"Good," she said, smiling before sniffing, blowing her nose. And after some quiet, "All right. I'm properly worn out, and it's very late. I'm going to bed. Do you think you'll be able to sleep?"

"Yes. I'll go to bed, too...on the couch. I'll go to *couch*," he said, patting the space next to him.

"Do you need anything tonight?"

"No. Thank you."

She scooped up Jim, and Pam followed them into the kitchen. "And the dizziness?" she asked, loud enough for him to hear her from the couch.

"It's better now."

"What about the dimming, detached feeling you had earlier? That's better, too?"

"Did I say anything aloud about feeling like that? I honestly can't remember."

"No, but you got the look," she said, setting the cat on the counter as she filled her water bottle and picking him up again when she was finished. "I can tell when my anxious...students get the look."

Family history of mental illness: none.

Symptoms: panic attack, depersonalization, dissociation, dizziness.

"I'm feeling better," he said.

"Good. Good night, Emmett."

"Good night. Good night, kittens."

Tallie switched off the lamp, leaving on the hall light like she had the night before, but she left her bedroom door unlocked this time. Simply closed it and put her ear to the wood, listened. Kept it there, mouthed his name. *It's happening. Remember this. This is the wildest thing I've ever done,* she thought, holding her breath like a prayer.

She emerged from her bathroom dewy and clean-faced. She googled *Emmett Aaron Baker* and found nothing.

Nico texted see you tmrw, mooi, and she considered responding with there is a man i do not know on my couch and you will meet him tmrw, but i don't know what it means. i am relearning even my own heart, but simply sent him yes pls, mooi before putting her phone in the nightstand drawer.

She was supine under her cool sheet and weighted blanket, feeling guilty and awful and *was she really doing this but*. Put her hand between her legs because it was quieter than her vibrator buzz. Tallie let herself go and thought about the unlocked door separating her from Emmett out there on her couch. Thought about him finding her in that position, her hand beneath the blanket moving around like a busy mouse. She imagined his strong tiger body standing by the bed, watching her close her eyes and turn her head to bite the pillow. Imagined Joel, jealous, watching her. Nico, too. She thought about the sext Nico had sent her a month ago: i have a lesson this afternoon, but tonight…i want to make you come. He'd done exactly that, more than once. She thought about how good Nico made her feel and how good Emmett could make her feel if she'd ask him, if she'd let him.

Tallie was a tightly tied knot that needed to come undone. She imagined all he wasn't telling her—his danger and darkness and secrets and the *what-ifs*—whipping like wind, snapping like thunder. An unstoppable storm. Her desire and his force and the mystery wrapping around it, revving up and swirling, knock-knock-knocking harderharderharder against her bedroom door until that gasping mouth of the world tugged loose and split wide open. Swallowed her up.

PART THREE

SATURDAY

EMMETT

Emmett was on the couch, curled like a comma, sleeping. He'd thought about Tallie behind her locked bedroom door as he drifted off, hoping she'd appear to him in a dreamy, sugar-spun haze where he was a different man with a different life. No *before*, no *after*. But instead, he dreamed the power went out again. He'd had his eyes on Christine and Brenna, their faces eclipsed, then illuminated by glows of sunlight and moonlight, swapped out for the lamp in Tallie's living room. The dream clicked to an unending cone of darkness. Christine and Brenna were gone, wisped into black. Emmett screamed for them at first, then forgot their names. Couldn't scream them anymore. He said, *I'm sorry, I'm sorry, I'm sorry*. Chanted it, rocking himself in a cold, concrete corner. Alone. The only man in the world, left behind, pulling at his hair. *I'm sorry, I'm sorry, I'm sorry.*

"*I'm so—*" He woke himself up saying it in the quiet of Tallie's house. Frenetic flashes of black, white, and red with his eyes closed. Eyes open and crying, he saw Tallie standing over him with her hands held out, like she was preparing to catch him if he jumped into her arms. Once she saw he was awake, she turned on the lamp. She sat by his head and touched it, the tuft of hair at his temple. She put her hand on his, asked if he was okay.

"I'm sorry," he said, pressing the heels of his hands to his eyes.

151

"That's what you kept saying over and over...'I'm sorry' pretty loud, not yelling...but it woke me up. Is this a recurring dream? Do you remember what was happening? Do you want a glass of water?" Tallie said.

Emmett looked at the clock: *4:13.* The cats were now on the couch next to them, purring and rubbing their heads against Emmett, begging to be petted. He sat up, obliged. Tallie didn't wait for his water answer. She went into the kitchen, got a glass for him. He took it, still trying to surface from the deep sleep he'd been swimming in.

"I'm sorry," he said again after he'd drunk the water, set the glass on the table.

"You don't have to apologize. I want to help you. Do you need anything?" She sat beside him, offered him her hand. Palm up, she set it on his thigh.

(Tallie looks concerned. She has her thumbs through the thumbholes of her long-sleeved shirt. Her big brown eyes are now behind a pair of lavender crystal cat's-eye glasses.)

"It was about my wife."

"I'm so sorry, Emmett."

He'd been relieved when he slept well the previous night. No nightmares, no screaming. His brain had been far too exhausted. He was embarrassed he'd had a nightmare in Tallie's house, somehow cursing their cozy bubble and ruining the *hygge* she'd been talking about. He was sure nightmares weren't allowed to be a part of *hygge,* but he couldn't stop them. No matter what he did or where he went, his blood and bones remembered. All he could offer up was a pitiful *I'm sorry,* whether it was whispered or hollered or whether he was in his own bed or on Tallie's couch. Suicide wasn't *hygge,* either, and if Tallie weren't there next to him, that was the only thing that would've been on his mind, no question.

But she *was* there. And she kept her hand on his thigh, and Emmett put his hand in hers.

(The room smells faintly like pumpkins and sugar. The couch is soft, so soft, almost painfully soft, like moss. Tallie's hand is warm, and she is breathing slowly, deliberately. The trees tattoo the roof with rainwater.)

~

Emmett got up early, before Tallie. He went to the bathroom, changed into his jeans and flannel shirt, brushed his teeth as quietly as he could. He filled a bottle from Tallie's cabinet with tap water and found his way out to her garage. He stood with his back to the wall, eyes closed, listening only to his breathing before lifting the ladder. Finding and flicking the switch to open the garage door.

The clouds had reluctantly revealed a gray-white hint of sunlight, a break in the rain again. Emmett clapped the ladder against the house and began scooping out the wet leaves from Tallie's gutters. He scooped and slapped them down onto her grass and bushes. Scoop and slap, scoop and slap. He got so in the zone that he was genuinely startled when he heard a woman's voice below him, saying hello.

"I'm Tallie's mom, Judith," the woman said, smiled.

Emmett looked down at her, at the pumpkin and bucket of wine-dark chrysanthemums in her arms.

"Hi," he said, before politely asking her how she was. She stood at the bottom of the ladder, told him she was fine.

"Tallie's so smart to get you up there cleaning out those gutters. Feels like the rain will never end, although I guess technically it did, for a little bit. It's supposed to start up again this afternoon, I heard. Y'know her husband used to clean the gutters out, but now they're divorced. Her *ex*-husband," Judith spilled, her brain-to-mouth gutters clearly cleaned out.

Emmett came down the ladder.

"She may still be sleeping, Miss Judith," he said with his feet on the ground. "Can I get those for you?" He took the bucket of

153

flowers, walked them up the steps to the porch, and put them there. Judith followed him with the pumpkin, which he also took from her and put on the steps with the other ones.

"Thank you so much. What's your name?"

"My name's Emmett," he said, drying his hand on his jeans before holding it out for her. Judith took it and shook.

"Nice to meet you, Emmett."

He told her the front door was unlocked before he went to the ladder, moved it, climbed up, continued the wet scoop-and-slap. In his periphery, Judith took a long look at him before disappearing inside.

~

When Emmett finished cleaning out the gutters and bagging the leaves, he washed his hands in the sink of Tallie's laundry room. When he emerged in the hallway, Tallie was standing by the couch, folding her knitted blankets. Judith's voice lifted up from the kitchen. Emmett wasn't sure how Tallie wanted to play this. He was fine with Judith thinking he was a random handyman, stopping by on Halloween morning to clean out Tallie's gutters. He could walk in there, let Tallie pretend to pay him, leave, go up the road, find a distraction until Judith left. Then he remembered that he'd left the couch half looking like a bed, left the pillow there on the edge, the blankets strewn and looping like soft cursive. And there was no work truck in the driveway he could claim was his, but Tallie could take care of it, tell her mom whatever she wanted.

"Thanks for cleaning out the gutters, Emmett," Tallie said with a completely normal amount of earnestness that gave him no clue what she was truly thinking.

"My pleasure. No problem."

"You've met my mama," Tallie said as Judith stepped into the living room with a mug of coffee, both cats trailing behind her.

"You look so familiar to me, Emmett. Are you from Louisville?" Judith asked.

"No, ma'am. I'm from Clementine."

"Clementine. Clementine? That's—" Judith sat on the couch, tucked her feet beneath her.

"Southeastern Kentucky," Emmett finished, nodded.

"Emmett, do you want a cup of coffee?" Tallie asked.

"Uh...yes. Yes, please," he said as Tallie headed to the kitchen. He followed her, passing Judith flipping through a magazine, drinking her coffee next to the cats. She smiled up at him.

Tallie mouthed good morning to Emmett once they were alone in the kitchen. He touched her shoulder, leaned down to whisper in her ear. Her hair smelled like his: *orange blossom and neroli, a lemon tree by the ocean.*

"Do you want me to act like I'm only here to clean out your gutters?"

Tallie put surprise on her face, shook her head.

"She'll assume you're some secret new boyfriend I haven't told her about. It's kind of exciting," she whispered, smiling and lifting her shoulders in a precious, childlike way. She poured his coffee, handed him the mug.

"Your secret new boyfriend who sleeps on the couch?"

"I know it's weird, but trust me...this is how she works."

"So it's okay if I make breakfast? Boyfriends make breakfast," he said, still whispering.

"Yes, they do," Tallie said.

"Apologies again...about last night."

"No need. You're feeling okay this morning?"

"I'm okay."

"You're sure?"

"I'm okay," he said again.

Emmett stepped into the kitchen doorway and asked Judith how she liked her eggs.

155

~

Tallie and Judith were on the couch, and Emmett was in the kitchen, finishing up breakfast. In addition to the eggs, he fried bacon, put orange slices in a bowl, made eight biscuits from scratch.

"Wow, you're kidding me. Look at this," Judith said as she sat at the table. Emmett had plated their food, placed Judith's over-easy eggs and everything else in front of the chair. He'd put Tallie's scrambled eggs and the rest of her breakfast next to it and took a seat across from them, ready to follow Tallie's lead about who he was and what he was doing there.

"Emmett is a *stunning* cook. Seriously. He made steaks last night, and it was the *most* delicious dinner I've ever eaten in my life. I'm still upset about it," Tallie said.

"Lovely! What brings you to Louisville?" Judith asked.

"Tallie Clark," Emmett said, letting his lips curl. He knew Tallie would appreciate it.

"My, how sweet is that?" was Judith's response.

Tallie beamed, took bites of her food.

"She's one of the kindest people I've ever met. And I mean it," he said.

"She's a good girl. I'm very proud of her," Judith said.

"I can only imagine," Emmett agreed.

"How long have you two been dating?"

"Mama...I'll tell you everything later. Let's enjoy breakfast," Tallie said.

"Well, you're young and handsome...just what Tallie needs. Most women could use one of you around!" Judith said, laughing and wagging a finger at him.

Emmett smiled and said thank you.

"Mama, stop."

"Oh, hush," Judith said.

(*Judith is wearing a striped turtleneck and small gold hoop earrings. A pearl ring on her right middle finger. Her hair is gray, pulled into a low bun. Judith and Tallie have the same nose, the same mouth. Judith touches Tallie a lot, pets her like a tender baby animal—her hair, her arm, her cheek.)*

Judith talked and talked. She told Emmett how she'd quit smoking and felt like she'd lost part of her personality. She was so addicted to nicotine gum that she wondered if she should start smoking again. She told stories about Tallie as a little girl, how naturally smart, kind, and curious she was, how she devoured books. Grounding her from reading was the only way Judith could punish her. She thought Tallie would be a writer or a librarian. Judith told Emmett when Tallie was little, she'd say "Goodbye! I'm going to the moon!" before she walked outside at night.

She bragged on Tallie's brother, Lionel, how he'd made an obscene amount of money working in finance, how she didn't really understand the way most of it went down, but he played with other people's money and somehow that ended up making him a lot of money, too. Lionel traveled back and forth between Louisville and New York City, and even though Lionel and his wife had a nanny, sometimes Judith stepped in to look after her grandson, River. And River continued to be such a blessing to their family, especially after all those years of Tallie unsuccessfully trying to get pregnant.

Emmett watched Tallie's face melt like ice cream.

"She's hands-down one of the strongest people I know," Emmett said, looking into Tallie's eyes.

"Yes, she is." Judith nodded in agreement and finished her biscuit. "And she knows how to make everyone feel real special. She's always been like that."

"That's the truest thing I've heard all day. And . . . yeah, we're excited about the big bash tonight," Emmett said. He watched Tallie lower her eyes in relief at the subject change.

"Tallie told you I only go every *other* year?" Judith asked him.

"No, I didn't know that," he said.

Judith continued talking. Explained that she and Tallie's dad, Gus, alternated years so Lionel wouldn't have to worry about them arguing. She didn't get along with Gus or Tallie's stepmother. She'd recently broken up with a man she'd dated for three years. Tallie chimed in to say she'd gotten to know and love him, missed him already. Judith told a couple of stories about Tallie not liking her boyfriends in the past, especially when they turned out to be assholes. She said Tallie had a strong God-given radar for people and energies.

They finished their breakfast while she talked, Tallie jumping in only to keep Judith from going too into detail about family and marriage drama. And Tallie had stopped Judith completely when she began talking about how Joel had them all fooled.

"Let's talk about something else, Mama," she'd said.

"Fine. Well, that's a long way of saying I won't be at my own son's Halloween party tonight. I'm playing bunco with my knitting girlfriends instead," Judith finished.

"Tallie told me she made those blankets on the couch. I'm sure she learned from the best," Emmett said.

Judith smiled before telling him he was too kind.

~

Tallie's mother stayed for an hour after breakfast before saying she'd be moving along.

"You really do look so familiar to me. I can't get over it. Maybe you remind me of an old movie star. Maybe we met in another life?" she asked, noisily popping a rectangle pillow of nicotine gum from its foil.

"Maybe we did," Emmett replied.

Tallie thanked her for the mums and the pumpkin. Judith told them to have a great time at the Halloween party. Tallie said she'd call her tomorrow and let her know how it went. And before she left, Judith hugged Tallie, and she hugged Emmett, too. Tightly, as if he were her own. He returned it.

158

"That's my mama," Tallie said, curtsying in front of him.

"It was nice to meet her. I didn't know how much you wanted her knowing about me."

"You were perfect. And by lunchtime everyone in my family and everyone in her neighborhood will know your name, what you look like, where you're from, and that you spent the night here last night."

"And that doesn't...freak you out at all?" he asked.

"For me to be on the side of her good, positive gossip for once? Not really," Tallie said.

Emmett smiled, and not one time when Judith was there did he think about dying. The bridge had gifted him the supernatural ability to recognize the smallest moments of light, effervescent with relief. Pretending to be the man Tallie wanted him to be smoothed his mind into a gleaming blank. He could pretend to be someone else who was pretending to be someone else. The cracked husk of his heart inside another and another, ad infinitum. Evidence of how he'd closed himself off out of necessity. Grief. Guilt. And fear.

Scrabbling every day since was the most exhausting thing he'd ever done. Survival was the reason she wouldn't be able to find him online, the reason it took him an extra breath to recognize his name in her mouth. He could've been from Clementine, but he wasn't. His name could've been Emmett Aaron Baker, but it wasn't. Tallie had easily believed his lies, and he wished the telling had magicked them true.

TALLIE

When Tallie had been alone in the house with her mom, she told her not to mention anything about her being a therapist. No TLC discussions. And for as much as her mom loved to talk, she loved having secrets with Tallie even more. It really hadn't concerned her, her mom stopping by, surprising her and Emmett like that. Immature as it might've been, Tallie liked how it made her seem mysterious, like she wasn't the vanilla wide-open book everyone seemed to think she was. And things with her mom certainly could've gone worse. Once she started talking, there was nothing to do to stop it. At a young age, both Tallie and Lionel had learned to hold their breath and ride it out.

Tallie was used to making excuses for her mother. ("She didn't mean it that way. She comes off rude sometimes, but she has a heart of gold.") Her whole life, Tallie had suffered through her mom telling her things she should've kept to herself. From remarking on her new stretch marks as she bloomed into a teenager to trying to persuade her to take part of the blame when it came to Joel's affair. ("How were things in the bedroom for you two? Were you closed off? Did you give him any signals that this sort of thing would be okay?") Tallie became a therapist instead of going to one, and she knew well enough how deeply a trained mental health professional could analyze that decision. She automatically put everyone else's feelings and situations in front of her own because she was raised by a self-absorbed mother. Judith had a way of making Tallie feel as if her life or problems would never be as important as Judith's own. Tallie promised herself if she adopted a baby, she'd never make the same mistake. She was an easy forgiver but had realized early on that she and her mom would always have a complicated relationship. She didn't know one woman who didn't have a complicated relationship with their mother, and that was at least one thing keeping her therapy practice in business—in fact, she'd never met a client yet who wasn't able to talk at loquacious length about their mama.

~

With her mother gone, Tallie sat at her kitchen table watching Emmett unload the dishwasher, then load it back up with their breakfast plates. She'd tried to stop him, but he told her it was therapeutic and that it really did make him feel better.

"It was probably therapeutic to burn your backpack in the grill last night," she said. "It was for me...the wedding pictures."

"Absolutely."

Her orange cat made himself known, hopped up on the counter. Tallie stood, picked him up, and held him like a baby because he loved it. She petted his head.

"Want to know something else that's hard for me to process?" Tallie asked Emmett after they'd been quiet for several minutes. Before he could answer, she continued talking. "I wonder who all knew about Joel's affair. *Everyone* at the museum? All his friends? All her friends? Was I the *only* one who didn't know? It's all so embarrassing."

"You aren't the one who should be embarrassed. That's on him," Emmett said.

"That's what I would burn if I could. Those obsessive, embarrassed feelings! But...okay! I know you're not big on therapy or support groups, but there's this concept I heard about that I think could be helpful for you. For both of us!" she said. She wanted him to know she'd been not only hearing him but also *listening* to him.

"Oh, really?" he asked from the sink with a light in his voice that relieved her. Like he'd flicked a lamp on in his throat.

"First, let me ask you this. What are some things worth living for? What makes you happy?"

"Suicidal the day before yesterday, making a list of things worth living for today...hmm."

"Ah, joie de vivre," Tallie said, putting the cat down.

"Um...days like this...the rain and nowhere to be. I love those days. And I don't know...but yeah, that moment you realize you're falling in love with someone who loves you back. That's a good moment. And first kisses, first everything, really," Emmett said. "Another easy one is the knockout of a home run on opening day," he said, clicking his tongue to mimic the hollow sound. He turned to her, leaned against the counter. "And honestly? One time I had this peach at the lake...this *perfect* peach...when I bit into it, it bit me back. Second week in June some years ago. That peach...that peach alone is probably worth living for."

"Wow. These are the best answers. I'm truly impressed."

"I told you I'm trying to impress you. Glad it's working."

"Stop it. Okay, so I asked because I heard someone mention 'cleaning off your table.' Like, you imagine taking off the shit that weighs you down and start simple. What would you put back on your table after you cleaned it off? What are the things you would keep? Like, for example, I would take my infertility off the table. In the past I had every pregnant woman in this neighborhood memorized. How far along she was, how big she was getting. Everywhere I went, it seemed like there were at least ten pregnant women there or women with newborns. I'd take that and those feelings off the table and Joel's affair, his new life. But I would keep this house. I *love* this house. I don't know how I would've survived my divorce without this house. My shelter...it's protected me in more ways than one," Tallie said.

She told him Aisha called Fox Commons *Tallieville* and often stopped by with wine so they could do face masks and watch *Masterpiece* or marathon trashy reality TV. She talked about how Lionel, Zora, and River came over for dinner often and how her dad and stepmother visited, too, but usually Tallie drove the thirty minutes to their farmhouse to see them. Only her mother liked to pop in unannounced.

"And in the spring and summer, I have peonies and black-eyed Susans, sunflowers and hostas, salvia and hyacinths in the garden. There's a pair of pale blue hydrangea bushes back there the size of small hatchbacks...hot pink knockout roses circling the birdbath...Oh! And I like looking out the window and watching the squirrels eat. Sometimes I'll be eating, too, and I like to think, look at us! Just little creatures, sharing a meal together!" Tallie said, remembering the last time she'd done that. Such a small, sweet light of pure joy.

Emmett was turned away from her, loading the utensils into their skinny dishwasher baskets.

"That's pretty damn cute. And I do love this house," he said, his voice ghosting into the wide-open appliance.

"So...what's something you would put back on your table?"

"Peace."

"When's a time in your life you had peace?"

He turned to her and crossed his arms, put both hands under his armpits, his thumbs stuck up flat against his shirt. Tallie noticed the biceps she either hadn't seen before or had ignored.

"Probably before I got married," he said, kept his eyes on Tallie.

"Oh, no. I hate to hear that."

"My wife was so beautiful, and I loved her deeply...every part of her. She had a sweet heart, too, but she wasn't a peaceful person, and we didn't have a peaceful marriage. She was dangerous at times...difficult...restless. Grew up having a lot to deal with. Our relationship was hard, to say the least, but I was wild about her. Pure madness. I will never get over her. She was my ace...my whole heart. Still is," he said with an unquiet intensity that rocketed through the air and seemed to blow back her kitchen curtains. Tallie let it settle before speaking again.

"You light up when you talk about her. Through the pain and the blushes...you do. I can see it pouring out."

The corner of Emmett's mouth lifted. He raked at his hair. His face: like hard rain when the sun was shining.

"But you fought a lot?" she asked.

"Yes, we did."

"Understandable. You were so young. How bad did your fights get?"

"Sometimes I'd have to hold her to get her to calm down, and it worked, but she hated it."

"Hold her like how? Show me," she said.

Tallie stood and faced him with her arms at her sides. Emmett lifted her hands and put each of them on her opposite shoulder. He hugged her tightly; she tried to move but couldn't. She tried harder, to no avail. When the fear snuck in, she told herself, *It's happening. I'm trusting him to do this. I'm trusting him to do this.*

"You're strong," she said into his shirt, after squirming some more before giving up. He let her go. The blood rush of relief.

"I didn't want to hurt you," he said.

"You didn't hurt me," Tallie reassured him. Breathing hard, she brushed her hair from her face and stepped back. "Um...do you have *any* sort of relationship with Christine's family?"

"Not even a little bit."

"And your relationships with your previous girlfriends' families?

How were those? Bad breakups can ruin all that, I know," she said, leaving him plenty of room to bring up Brenna or whomever he wanted to discuss.

"They were all fine, I guess. Until they weren't."

"I keep asking you to talk about everything because I want to help, if I can. I know it's been a hard few days for you on top of the fact you're still grieving. And for some, that never goes away. People like to say time makes it easier, but that's true only for *some* people. All this to say I appreciate you letting me keep an eye on you this weekend, Emmett," she said.

"You always focus on how everyone else is doing, so maybe I'm keeping an eye on you, too."

His words, that truth, made her dizzy. After her divorce, she'd begun thinking of herself as a piece in an art museum—she had to be handled a certain way in the right environment or she'd be ruined. She hadn't been able to say this aloud to anyone, but it was as if Emmett had listened to all she hadn't said and somehow knew. She hugged him, comforted by his body heat in that white shirt, those muscles she'd admired earlier, his strong arms now pressed to the sides of her neck. *I'm trusting him to do this.* And as she imagined him restraining her like that, hugging her and squeezing and never stopping, she relaxed into him more.

"You're my friend now, you know that? I like you. We've shared heart energy so we can never be true strangers again," she said against his ear.

"Good. I'm glad to hear it. And I like you, too," he said against hers.

∼

Tallie had put on jeans and a comfy oversize black turtleneck sweater after she showered. She'd done her three-minute face of makeup, pulled half her hair up in a messy-on-purpose bun, and left the rest loose to curl and kink in the humid autumn air. When she came out of the bathroom, she found Emmett scrolling through his phone on the couch with her cats purring beside him.

"They're going to miss you when you leave tomorrow," she said.

He put his phone in his pocket, stood. "They're my buddies," he said, leaning over to pet them one more time.

Tallie expounded on her knowledge of therapy pets, going over to stand in front of the cats, getting on her knees before them, petting their heads, scratching the base of their tails.

"Might be something to think about. There's been so much scientific research done on therapy animals if you want to read up about it. They've started using dogs in courtrooms to soothe anxious people on the stand. Did you have pets growing up?" she asked.

"I had an orange cat named Ginny, after my grandmother. And a big, sweet mutt named Moe."

She suggested they go for a walk through Fox Commons to one of the restaurants for lunch before they got ready for the Halloween party. Tallie put on her wellies and rain slicker. Emmett picked up his flannel shirt from the couch, and as she watched him slip his arms inside, she wondered if their kitchen hug had lasted too long.

~

Tallie pointed to one of the golf carts as it made its way up the street.

"I have one of those. Oh, you saw it in the garage. Lionel bought it for me when I moved in, but I prefer to walk most of the time," she said.

She'd tried to talk Lionel out of it, telling him she'd buy one for herself later, but he'd insisted, assuring her it was *the* way to travel around the posh neighborhood. Her golf cart was myrtle green with cream vinyl and a canopy. She enjoyed driving it and would occasionally scoot herself to the farmer's market or the bakery in it. Or to the coffee shop to read or poke around on her laptop and scroll through beauty blogs and pin recipes, fashion, and home decorating ideas to her Pinterest boards. In the summer, she and Aisha would drive it to the gelato shop and to the amphitheater to watch the sun set over the lake or to hear free live music on Wednesday nights. Lionel had gotten *TLC* detailed on the side in leaning white cursive. She liked how the wind felt on her face, how it blew her hair back when she was driving it. But at times she'd felt lonely in it, not having a husband anymore or a boyfriend or a child to fill the passenger seat. It annoyed her that the positive *sisters are doin' it for themselves* articles and *girl power* anthems she read and listened to so often didn't reach out and touch every shadowy, thorny corner of her anxieties and insecurities.

"I'll tell you what...on Thursday, I didn't picture myself walking around this fancy neighborhood, hanging out with a woman. I feel like I'm living someone else's life," Emmett said.

"That's depersonalizing. It's *not* someone else's life, it's yours. And I'm glad you're here," Tallie said, touching his arm.

"I don't know how I'm going to make it through the winter," he said after they'd walked a bit more.

"I don't know how I'm going to make it through the winter, either. No one does. None of us know what's going to happen one day to the next in this life. We just...keep going," she said, surprising herself by being so bare with him. She could've tried to pretend like the winter would be no problem for her, that she was translucently optimistic about her future. She'd gotten used to pretending with people who didn't know her well—and her family, too, when she didn't feel like discussing it. It was easier to act like she'd always be fine, but she knew better. Even people without a history of mental illness had to go to great lengths to protect their mental health.

Taking Friday off from appointments was one of the self-care boxes Tallie checked. In the past few months, there had been a rising energy to Tallie's diligence about her own mind and feelings. She'd sometimes write the letters *m* and *h* on her hand in black ink, a reminder to recognize the need for protecting her mental health.

She thought of her good and bad days as Morse code messages— every little bit recorded in her bones—wanting to honor the time and energy it took for them to be translated and transcribed.

"*Everyone* needs someone to trust, someone to talk to. It sounds like you've been doing all this emotional work on your own, which is so hard it can feel impossible. I could help you find a therapist if you'd give it a try. You can look at it as adding tools to your toolbox. We all have a toolbox," she said.

"Ah, a toolbox. So there's a hardware store down here somewhere?" he asked, looking around.

"You're—"

"Oh, yeah? I'm what?"

"Wow," she said, smiling and shaking her head.

Another golf cart passed them, the sound zipping over the wet road like a record needle on vinyl. Tallie waved, and the man in the cart waved back, a neighbor she recognized but had never actually spoken to.

Tallie took Emmett's hand as they continued walking. Not inter-locking fingers but holding his hand as if they were grade-school friends, making a connection: a red rover chain blocking out the rest of the world, if only for a moment. She imagined the neighbors whispering to one another about how they'd seen her dressed like Paddington Bear, holding hands with a young man on Halloween. They'd gossip about how Tallie and her new beau had stopped in front of the trattoria and Thai noodle shop before ultimately decid-ing on the Irish pub across the street. How the green bulbs framing the sign shone on the wet sidewalk and eerily flickered the gloss of their rainwear—those two ambling aliens aglow.

EMMETT

He'd been Emmett since Thursday evening, and he would continue being Emmett to Tallie, everyone he would meet at the Halloween party, and anyone else he came across. His real name was too recognizable. And although Tallie had been the first person to use the word *striking* directly to him, he was all too aware that he had a unique, memorable face. He imagined it plastered on posters around his hometown. Wouldn't his family put up MISSING posters, even when they thought he was dead? Wouldn't they still be looking for his body so they could put him to a proper rest? What picture would they use? One of him smiling next to Christine, Christine cropped away? One of him holding hands with Brenna, Brenna snipped out? One of him from the restaurant, tired and smoking in his kitchen whites? One of him on the church camping trip, wearing his back-pack, glancing over at the camera a moment before he knew the pic would be taken? He'd always stood out in his little town: his hair, his freckles, the unmistakable mix of blackness from his father's side with his mother's whiteness. Christine's dad, Mike, had said the word *quadroon* in front of him once, as if it were a word he used or heard every day and not an obscene word written in pale pencil in a slave auctioneer's ledger, next to a dollar amount and *sold*.

People often told him he looked familiar, and he could read the surprise and horror on the pitying faces of the ones who knew *why* they recognized him. As if he'd morphed into Francisco Goya's *Saturn Devouring His Son* or the hellscape in Hieronymus Bosch's *Last Judgment*—those terrifying paintings that revealed something new and fearsome every time they were examined. Francis Bacon's *Three Studies for a Crucifixion*—wriggled, bloody flesh devouring itself. Emmett had spent hours, weeks, months with that art history book in the library. Flipping, absorbing, memorizing, wanting to be emptied out and filled up with something else. *Anything* else. It didn't matter what.

~

While Tallie was in her bedroom getting ready for lunch, Emmett was on the couch, composing what he knew would be his last email to Joel.

From: talliecat007@gmail.com
To: joelfoster1979@gmail.com
Subject: Re: i still care about you too

joel,

i don't mind telling lionel you mentioned him. you know how lionel is. i'm going to his halloween party with a date, so the answer to your question about whether or not i'm seeing someone is yes. i am. it's pretty new. i just met him recently. he's a chef. my mom met him for the first time this morning when she stopped by. she talked his ear off, of course, but he did a great job of listening to her. he's quiet anyway, so it worked. it's too early to say what'll happen with us, but i really like him. a lot. he watches funny girl with me and does the dishes.

you know the end of funny girl always makes me cry, but now it makes me wonder what would've happened if i'd fought harder to stick it out with you. all that country-song shit about standing by your man. maybe if i'd had an affair of my own to even it out? although the baby trumps it all, right? clearly you win. is that how this works?

speaking of…i can't stop thinking about adopting a baby. maybe soon? i have the money and the stability and it feels like the right time. at last. cue etta james.

i had no way of knowing if i could be happy alone again! and being happy is one of those things that feels phonier and phonier the more you talk about it, but…i feel like if i squint, i can see it. and i need that hope. the hope alone is enough for me.

but i do wonder who knew about your affair. everyone at the art museum? all of your friends? all of hers? maybe none of it matters anymore. i don't know. at least i don't have to put the chips back in the pantry for you now, right? that's your new wife's job.

there's no need for you to be in a rush to write me back. i think this quick reconnection has been good for both of us and honestly, i wish you well. the point is, by the grace of god, i forgive you. and i will be here, squinting.

truly,
tallie

∾

"Tell me about your grandmother Ginny," Tallie had said to him after they'd gotten their water with lemon at the Irish pub.

He told Tallie his grandmother's real name, Virginia. But he left out the part about her living on Emmett Lane for most of his life. He told her she'd given him his gold cross necklace and that Ginny died seven years ago. He talked about her house—her kitchen, the pigs and chickens she kept in her backyard, the beehives and fresh honey.

"My mom's parents were great, too, by the way. They're both gone now. Married for sixty-five years," he said.

"I never met either of my grandfathers because they died before I was born, but my grandmothers were pretty great, too."

"Tell me about them."

"I asked you first."

"I asked you second."

Tallie scrunched her nose up at him. "My dad's mom was a quilter and a visiting nurse. Made the best pound cake in the entire world. My mom's mom worked at the greyhound racetrack. She smelled like violets and drank her bourbon straight," she said.

"My kind of people," Emmett said. "Did they live here? You spent a lot of time with them?"

Tallie nodded. "Lionel and I spent most of my childhood summers at my maternal grandmother's house with my cousins while my parents worked. She lived in the West End. Okay, seriously, I'm done! Now, you."

"So yeah. My grandmother Ginny and her sisters were beekeepers, which was equal parts fun and terrifying," he said. The pub waitress set down one brown wicker basket of Irish soda bread, another filled with sourdough. She slid softened shamrock-foil rectangles of butter across the table and asked if they'd need more time.

"I'll have the fish and chips, please. And so will he if he likes fish and chips," Tallie said to the waitress. "Do you like fish and chips? They have the best. It's my favorite," Tallie said to him, not needing to look at the laminated menu flashing and catching green light as she handed it over.

"I'll take the fish and chips," Emmett said, loving how easy Tallie had made it for him.

(The waitress's name is Kelly. Her name tag has a shamrock on it. She's wearing slip-on sneakers. Green. Tallie is pretty and red-lipped at

her side. Some of her hair is down. She put on makeup, dressed up a little. "Tunnel of Love" by Bruce Springsteen is playing. An American bar... even an Irish pub... isn't an American bar if they don't play at least one Bruce Springsteen song a day.)

"Beekeepers! I love it," Tallie said across from him. She opened her eyes wide, put her napkin in her lap, and got her knife out. While she buttered her bread, Emmett talked, buttered his own.

"Virginia is my grandmother who taught me how to play gin rummy. We called it *Ginny* rummy. She was my father's mother," he said. "She and my grandfather Samuel had a scandalous inter-racial relationship. It's his Bible in my backpack. He gave it to my grandmother, and she left it to me."

Tallie listened and ate while he talked.

He told her about his grandfather's family owning the main grocery store in town. How his grandmother sold honey to him. How they fell in love, got death threats. How somebody had attempted to burn the grocery store down.

"Yeah. All that good stuff. This, of course, is southeastern Kentucky late '40s, early '50s. They wanted to get married but obviously couldn't. And then my grandfather was sent to Korea." He told her his grandfather was killed in 1953 in the Battle of Pork Chop Hill at about the same time his grandmother found out she was pregnant with his dad.

"My grandmother wrote him a letter and told him but wasn't sure if it got to him. She didn't know if he ever found out she was pregnant," Emmett said truthfully.

For all the lies he'd told, finally telling more of the truth was calming, like unclenching a tight fist. Emmett's grandmother had kept Samuel's obituary behind clingy photo-album film. He and his dad had gone to the big public library to read the grocery-store-fire news article on microfiche. Emmett had leaned in close, staring at his grandfather's face, the tenderness in his eyes. He looked at it for so long that his vision blurred, lost to the gray.

"So sad and fascinating. All of this. I want to hear everything. Your family history is like a movie I want to watch *and* a book I want to read, Emmett," Tallie said, rapt. His fake name had hopped from her mouth like a cricket.

He imagined his real name smoking from her lips, floating up and away. Some other time, some other place, he'd be real into Tallie. She was so damn sweet and really cared about people. So often, the dark cloud that followed him threatened to wipe him out entirely, making it hard to think ahead more than a matter of days. But. Tallie was the kind of person to make him believe in Monday morning.

Emmett relaxed in the booth as she studied his face like a treasure map. Why couldn't he stop telling her things? He kept talking and talking. Told her about how hippie-peaceful his maternal grandparents were amid the hot, bubbling ignorance in his hometown. And more about Christine's family and how it was well-known small-town lore that Christine's dad had pined for Emmett's mom when they were younger and used to tell everyone he was going to marry her someday.

"He was borderline obsessed with my mom before she married my dad. Even named his boat after her. More than once he cornered and tried to kiss her, but my uncles did a pretty good job of chasing him off most of the time. The biggest fight my dad and Christine's dad ever had was when they were in high school and my dad caught her dad spray-painting his brand-new car. Her dad got out a bright orange *n-i-g* before my dad clocked him," Emmett said.

"Sheesh," Tallie said.

"Yeah. Just a lot of really stupid stuff. Christine's dad always thought my mom should be with him. It was messed up that he felt jilted before, but especially after she married my dad...a half-black man. Then, boom, they had me. So Christine being with *me*? Another, even bigger nightmare of her dad's come true," he said, knowing how dramatic it all sounded. It was like a Shakespearean tragedy; his and Christine's families loathed each other, and in a flash, his young bride was dead.

Christine, his Juliet.

"Ugh. How did you and Christine navigate that? I can only imagine how hard it was. No *wonder* you fought so much," Tallie said, pushing her bread plate and knife to the edge of the table, making the waitress's life easier.

Emmett drank his lemon water, let some of the truth fall through the slats in his brain. "Christine and I had a lot of problems, but we don't get to choose our families, and she certainly would've chosen differently if she could've."

"Emmett, it sounds like you have a sweet family. I know how much they love you and how much you love them. I can see it on your face. Please let me contact someone to let them know you're okay."

The waitress brought their food, warning them the plates were hot. Emmett leaned back, promising not to touch his.

"It's not that easy," he said to Tallie once the waitress walked away, leaving them alone again.

"Tell me why not."

"Because there's nothing left for me in that town, and it's better this way, trust me. Besides, when I wrote my parents the letter, I *truly* thought I'd be dead by now, so I'm being completely honest when I tell you I didn't think this far ahead," he said.

He'd wanted to spare his parents the horror of finding his body themselves, so that meant no gun, no pills, no hanging. The hovering possibility of the body his spirit was currently inhabiting dead-floating in the Ohio River was perfectly macabre and fitting for the holiday. He refrained from letting a dark smile of relief slide across his face.

"But this is too important—"

"I can't explain it all; I really can't. Everyone's life gets so tangled up with everyone else's. And everyone has dark secrets they don't want anyone holding up to the light." Emmett stopped and took his time, tried to think of how to put a positive spin on what he was saying because it was what Tallie would do. "But also...there's forgiveness, right? Out there floating in the ether if we can find our breath and catch it?"

"True forgiveness is severely underrated, for both the forgiver and the forgiven. I knew I had to find a way to forgive Joel so I could go on with my life."

"Right. So would you be okay with seeing him again? Or if he reached out to you? What if he walked in here right now?" Emmett asked.

"I...don't know. But I don't think I want to see him? The photos on social media are enough, I guess. Too much," she said.

"And you said he and Lionel *were* friends. How did he react to what Joel did?"

"Lionel would be civil to him now, because that's how Lionel is. But there was a point last winter, before Joel moved away, when he wanted to pretty much kick his ass," Tallie said, digging into her food. "Nope. Enough about me, you sneak. I'm not letting this thing go about your family. I'll ask you again."

"I understand. I'd be doing the same thing you are...if our situations were reversed," he said. He ate a couple of fries, dipped them into the ramekin of tart vinegar. He took some bites of his fish, too. He'd cooked and plated a hundred million orders of fish and chips at his family's lake restaurant, but this lunch was out-of-this-world delicious. Had food tasted better since Thursday evening, or was he imagining it? Deciding to stay alive for a few more days had done wonders for his appetite and taste buds.

"And so what would you do now, if you were me?"

"This is delicious."

"You're not changing the subject this time, by the way."

"Yes, ma'am," he said. She glared at him. "Yes, *Tallie*," he said, correcting himself. "If I were you, I would enjoy this delicious lunch, go home and get dressed for my brother's dope costume party, and enjoy my evening. That's what I would do."

"Emmett—"

"Happy Halloween?" he said, wry as sandpaper.

"You're taking advantage of your lilac puff. Things would be *completely* different if not for your lilac puff."

He winked at her before speaking again.

"Now, all right. Please tell me who's going to be at this party tonight. I want to hear more about the Tallie Clark kith and kin," he said with his salt-vinegar mouth, rubbing his hands together underneath the table.

"Well, you know my mom isn't coming. She was clear about that," Tallie said.

The waitress refilled their waters. A man at the bar turned and looked out the window beside them, leaving his eyes on Emmett for too long before swiveling around. Did he recognize him? Would the man say something to someone? *It wouldn't matter. Remember, nothing matters*, Emmett's brain chanted, forcing him to listen.

(The man at the bar is wearing a white pocket T-shirt that is too tight around his stomach. The woman next to him is wearing a pointy witch hat—felt, black. They have sausages, fries, and beers in front of them; they've ordered the same thing. The woman is drinking her beer. She's wearing a white T-shirt, too. She puts salt on her fries. Someone at the end of the bar is speaking loudly into a phone. "Tell him I'll call him later," he says. He laughs. Someone else in the back of the restaurant is laughing, too. The cash register dings.)

The man at the bar turned away from him and looked at the other window, not paying any attention to Emmett. He'd considered someone possibly recognizing him at the Halloween party but knew people wouldn't be paying close attention to him. Instead, they'd be drinking and dancing and whatever else, lost in the costumes.

"And my dad and his wife will be there . . . they've been married since I was in high school. I wasn't needing any bit of a stepmom, but I love her and we get along fine. My dad's name is Augustus, but everyone calls him Gus, and my stepmom's name is Glory—"

"No Gus, no Glory," Emmett said.

"Most people get a kick out of that," she said. "Okay, let's see...bunch of Lionel's friends and our cousins. My best friend since elementary school, Aisha, usually comes with me, but she's at a yoga retreat in Lake Tahoe this weekend. And some of my other girlfriends show up a lot of the time," Tallie said, counting people off on her fingers.

"You and Joel used to go together? He's a Halloween guy?"

Tallie flattened her hand in the air, tilted it back and forth—the universal hand signal for "so-so."

"Every year except last year because we were separated," she said.

"This is the first time you've ever taken another dude?"

"Dude," Tallie said, laughing. "Sorry, I just don't think of you as a *dude*. Not like, some *dude*."

"Some guy, some man, some date," he said, definitely flirting, but only a little.

"I've been dating or married to Joel since day one of Lionel's costume parties. Although this guy I dated in college and off and on after...Nico Tate...he's the one I was dating a bit when I met Joel...we started hanging out again sometimes...he told me he would be there tonight," she said, eating. Drinking.

"So is he going to be pissed you're bringing me?" Emmett asked, thinking of the pictures he saw of her on Nico's Facebook page. Embarrassment tingled his ears, remembering them.

"If he is, it'll be news to me. I mean, at one point...Nico wanted to get married, but I didn't. Or couldn't. Or wouldn't. He was busy playing a lot of tennis, professionally for a bit. I'm not quite sure what happened between us. We were together, then we weren't. He married his childhood sweetheart, but they got divorced...and honestly? Sometimes I think I made the wrong choice not marrying him back when I had the chance. Waiting and finding Joel, marrying him instead. Then I feel awful for thinking it, which is ridiculous because I obviously don't owe Joel any loyalty at this point. So yeah, it's a nonstop loop up here," she ended, pointing to her head.

"All right, but hear me out . . . you *could've* been Tallie Tate."

"Ha! No. I wouldn't have changed my name. I'm dying Tallie Clark."

"Not anytime soon, I hope."

"Right you are," she said. "And besides, I'm never getting married again."

"Me neither."

They looked at each other, still and quiet in the noisy, crowded pub.

"Well, tell me if you need me to give you space tonight if your boy Nico Tate is there. Men can get weird," Emmett said.

"Ain't that the truth? And nice try, but I'm not letting you off the hook completely about talking to your family. I won't bug you anymore about it tonight, though. Not until tomorrow. Deal?"

"Deal," he said, wiping his hand on his napkin and offering it across the table for her to shake.

∼

When they were finished at the pub, they went over to the gelato shop. Tallie: stracciatella and basil. Emmett: butter pecan and black cherry. He paid for lunch and the gelato, too; they walked through Fox Commons with their little cups, pale ping-pong scoops.

(The storefronts and homes are decorated with pumpkins, scarecrows, and leaf garlands, strings of purple lights wrapped around the wrought-iron banisters and porch swings. Orange and yellow and rich wine-colored everything with acorns and walnuts underfoot, like storybook illustrations.)

There were plenty of nice neighborhoods in his hometown, but there wasn't anything like Fox Commons. It was much more than a neighborhood: it was a fully operating city within a city. Clean and safe. The kind of place where people lived and worked, and if and when something terrible happened there, they'd probably look earnestly into the news camera and say, *We never imagined this could happen here.*

The neighborhood kids were dressed in their Halloween best. They passed a buzzing group of tiny robots, a gaggle of princesses, countless superheroes, a trio of mummies, several covens of little witches. There were plenty of food trucks over by the lake—kettle corn, s'mores, and caramel apples, too. And a small hay maze was set up with people snaking inside, defiant under the heavy gunpowder skies that seemed mere seconds away from exploding. A little girl wearing butterfly wings ran past, reminding him of the butterfly wings wilted and resting in his new backpack at Tallie's place. Another little girl squealed at something behind them, startling Tallie, who threw up her hands and turned around before laughing.

"She scared me! Pregaming for tonight," she said. "Oh! And there's lots of food at this party. Plenty. Which reminds me, I need to stop by the bakery for a cake. It's Lionel's favorite."

Since Tallie didn't take his hand, he didn't want to seem too forward by initiating it. The warmth of touch comforted him; he hadn't realized quite how much he'd missed it. She walked close, occasionally touching his shoulder to guide him to look at something she wanted him to see—a small black dog dressed as a flower, a big brown dog dressed as a pirate, pint-size twin boys dressed as skunks. And he knew she was trying to steer him away from the house with the yard filled with fake tombstones. The silly pun-names, the skeleton hands shoving up through the leaves. If people weren't actively grieving, they'd probably never think about how hard Halloween could be on those who were. So much death. The constant reminders of where everyone ended up, never leaving them alone for even a second.

"Let's go. These tombstones...I hate these things." Tallie tugged his sleeve.

She took his hand as they walked to the bakery for a pumpkin spice cake with white buttercream frosting. While she was inside,

Emmett went across the street to the farmer's market, lifted a bouquet of sunflowers from its water bucket, dripped it over to the cash register. When she stepped onto the sidewalk with the cake, he took it from her, trading for the flowers.

"Aw, what for?" she asked, smiling.

"For you. And for Van Gogh."

"Oh, yes, our sweet Vincent. Thank you, Emmett," she said and hugged the flowers to her chest.

A fresh round of rain had sent the costumed kids and their parents scattering, golf carts slicking across the asphalt. Emmett and Tallie—hands held, hoods up—took their time walking to her house. Past the lit-up porches and pumpkins, orange welcome mats and Halloween wreaths. Tallie waved and said hello to her neighbors. They were friendly to Emmett, too, everyone, smiling and busy and *it's Halloween* happy.

~

From: JoelFoster1979@gmail.com
To: Talliecat007@gmail.com
Subject: Re: i still care about you too

Tallie,

I don't feel like I've won. No, that's not how this works. And thanks for answering my question of whether or not you're seeing someone. Thanks for not making me feel like a fool for asking. (He sounds perfectly lab-created for you, btw.)

Yeah so...I want to tell you a couple things and then we can take some time off emailing, yes. If that's what you want. Again, I want to say I appreciate you for reaching out. And I know it's not all about me but, it really has made me feel better.

I want to confess something. Something I assume Lionel hasn't told you.

Lionel found out about Odette and me first. He was fucking pissed and I truly thought he was going to kick my ass. Lionel can be scary. I begged him to let me tell you myself, but I was a coward and I didn't...you found out on your own because you're not stupid. The only reason Lionel didn't tell you himself was because we were in the middle of our fifth IVF cycle. He said it would stress you out too much, knowing. He found out because a mutual friend of ours from the art museum told him. And I promise I didn't know this person knew. Odette and I...well it's not like we were openly flirting at work. Like I said, I never set out for any of this to happen.

I know you look up to Lionel and think his life is perfect, but I know some things...

He'll hate me forever for telling you this but he confessed to me that early in their marriage, he stepped out on Zora. It was one time, when he was still half-living in NYC...a woman up there. He and Zora had only been married for a year. He confessed to her and he said their relationship has been stronger ever since. He learned his lesson and didn't lose Zora in the process. I swore I wouldn't say anything, so here I am breaking that promise. But the way he told me made me feel like maybe he was telling me...to encourage me into thinking if he and Zora could stay together and work something like that out, maybe you and I could too. When I moved out of the house and into Odette's...I still held out hope you and I could...make it work somehow. I wanted to. I feel like maybe we were both considering finding a way to stay together...but everything happened so fast...and then...Odette told me she was pregnant.

I felt like it was okay to tell you this now because...well, because you really do sound happy and healed and like you've moved on. And I don't want to keep any more secrets from you. Odette and I have been going to counseling and I'm learning how to be more open and honest. Therapy is essential to you/your life...and I know how much you tried to talk me into it...I'm just sorry it took all this for me to finally go.

Another thing I want to tell you is that I haven't changed my Facebook password on purpose. I know you log in, I know you check it. I can see when it happens. Is it weird I like that we have the secret connection? We aren't connected anywhere else...I didn't know if we'd ever speak again...and then you emailed me.

I hope you do adopt a baby if it's what you want. And I don't care how corny it sounds...I hope you have the best life and that you get *everything* you've ever wanted. No one deserves it more. You'll be an AMAZING mother. You deserve all the love and best things the world has to offer. And my inbox is open to you. No worries if this is the last of our emails, but understand I am deeply (grievingly) sorry for hurting you/us like this. I know these words can never be enough. You're the complete opposite of broken. And your forgiveness means the world to me.

J

~

He took a shower, not able to get Joel's email out of his head. End communication with Joel. It was stupid, and it was over. Now Emmett knew things Tallie didn't, and he wouldn't tell a soul. He hated knowing her brother's secret and that he'd kept things from her; her face lit up when she talked about Lionel, even when she was fussing about him.

Emmett turned the shower water up as hot as it would go in an attempt to wash away his sins, got out smelling like Tallie again. He'd taken his small bag of toiletries into the bathroom and bent over to drink water from the faucet after he put a beta-blocker on his tongue. Emmett flossed and brushed his teeth with his own travel toothbrush and toothpaste, used his own woodsy-smelling deodorant to remind him he'd be leaving Tallie's soon. He put on the navy-blue suit Tallie had hung on the bathroom door. She told him she'd considered returning it but forgot. Thought of donating it instead but never got around to it. So it'd stayed in a zipped bag in the back of her closet alongside her coats and dresses like some sort of dark spirit. A harbinger of exactly what, she said she didn't know. "Maybe tonight," she'd said, wiggling her fingers in a supposed-to-be-spooky way that made him smile.

The suit was expensive and slim, a bit tight around Emmett's waist and a little short in the leg. The jacket sleeves stopped perfectly at his wrists but snatched too much when he held his arms out or up. He looked at his reflection in the full-length mirror on the back of the bathroom door and held his arms straight up above him, like an upside-down diver who would make the tiniest Olympic gold-winning splash. Tallie had given him a white dress shirt and a gas-blue tie, a pair of thin navy-blue socks with small ice-blue polka dots on them. Emmett smoothed his hair and beard, leaned forward, and stared at himself for so long he began depersonalizing. To stop it, he closed his eyes and kept them closed.

Tallie knocked on the door. His heart kicked hard, and he was thankful the beta-blocker would start working soon enough and soften it. He'd always been overly sensitive to his heartbeats, recognizing the smallest of normal electrical adjustments it made throughout the day.

"How's it look?" she asked.

"You tell me," Emmett said as he opened the door, his heart marching like an entire troop of soldiers.

"Oh, wow, it works! Suited and booted! It looks great on you!" Tallie said brightly from the hallway. She reached behind her to flick the switch. The bulbs on the ceiling cast wide angles on the walls and the slip of floor beneath their feet. Their bodies painted dramatic shadows in the corners like the darkness and light of a Caravaggio painting. She looked him up and down, stopping at his face to make eye contact and smile.

Emmett took her in. Steel-gray suit jacket and tight matching skirt that stopped at the knee. Pantyhose and a pair of black heels almost bringing her nose-to-nose with him. Scully was full-time sexy. Tallie in that suit in front of him? Equally irresistible.

(Happy and pretty in her pencil skirt. Creamy black makeup on her eyes, flicking up at the corners. Her lips are glossy and auburn. Wolf whistle.)

"You look *really* nice. Um, is that your pencil skirt? It's the same color as a pencil. Is that why it's called a pencil skirt?" he asked.

Tallie laughed at him after thanking him for the compliment.

"What? I'm wrong?" he asked, chuckling along. He really had no clue what a pencil skirt was, and apparently she wasn't going to tell him.

"Men are ridiculous," she said, patting his shoulder. She handed him the Mulder FBI badge they'd gotten from the Halloween store. He clipped it on to match hers. "Mulder and Scully wear trench coats a lot, and tonight would be a perfect night for a trench coat, but alas, I do not have two."

"These badges will do the trick," he said, holding his badge out so it was parallel to the floor. Mulder's upside-down face looked back at him.

"Ready?"

"Hold on," he said. He unclasped his necklace. "Scully wears a cross."

"Oh, no. Are you sure? It's precious to you, and I wouldn't want anything to happen to it."

"No worries," he said, stepping behind her. She held her hair up for him; he did the clasp. The gold cross flickered like candlelight and dangled just below the hollow of her neck, above the unbuttoned top buttons of her white-as-death blouse.

TALLIE

After they stopped at the coffee shop for a pumpkin spice latte for herself and a black coffee for Emmett, Tallie drove to Lionel's house with Emmett in her passenger seat. The cake was on the floor in the back; her car smelled like an October dream. Algebraic crackles of light flashed Emmett's face and hers as they drove the wet roads all lit up with streetlamps. The sun had set gold, and she drove deliberately slow, wary of trick-or-treaters in the autumnal darkness.

"My brother's house is wild," Tallie said to him. She had the radio turned down low; Counting Crows faded into Fiona Apple. "He had it built by this waterfall that's part of the design, and it powers...something. It's so over-the-top and strange. It's modeled after the Frank Lloyd Wright in Pennsylvania. The Fallingwater house," she finished, seeing Emmett's impressed face in the light. "I don't mean to sound braggy."

"You don't sound braggy."

"And if at any point you need to talk or you feel anxious tonight, please let me know. What's most important is your mental health," she said.

"And yours. I'm not the only person in the world."

"I know, but it's okay if we focus on you."

"I appreciate it, but I'm okay. Right now, I'm okay."

"You're sure? Because crowds and unfamiliar spaces can—"

"Tallie, I'm okay," he said.

She drove through the open gate leading to Lionel's street, over-flowing with cars parked on the sides and in the grass. Costumed partygoers walked on the edge of the road. Two skeletons wearing puffy white wigs, every member of the Village People, a hot-pink Care Bear, and Mario and Luigi.

"I usually park up here, and we can walk over the back way. There's a gate, but I know the code. And a bridge...a wooden bridge," Tallie said, speaking carefully. She glanced at him, wanting to be extra sensitive, in case hearing the word *bridge* could trigger an impulse.

"Your brother's house has a gate and a bridge?" Emmett asked.

"I'm telling you, it's like one of Gatsby's parties," she said, slowing to a crawl because of the people and parked cars. The rain had stopped, but the rivulets still slipped through the grass and across the pavement, catching in her headlights as they spilled to the sewers, fleeting.

"Have you two always been close?"

"He's five years older, and he never let me hang out with him when we were kids. Unless his friends were busy, then he would. But I had to promise not to tell anyone he played with my Barbies. He said he'd kill me if I did, and at the time I one hundred percent believed he would've done it. He has a *very* strong personality. I'm making him sound like an asshole, and he's really not! He's just...well, you'll see," she said. "He graduated college summa cum laude and went off to New York and came back like Scrooge McDuck, swimming through a gigantic pile of gold coins. He's one of those guys who knows *everybody* and is good at *everything. Everyone* loves him. All my girlfriends have had crushes on him at one point or another—even my best friend, Aisha, and she's a lesbian half the time!" Tallie laughed. "I guess all of it could make me jealous.

Maybe it would if I were a man. He can be difficult, but so can I. I love being his sister. His energy is gold. It's always been gold."

"So's yours."

"That's what you think?"

"Yes. And I like how you make your brother sound. Simpatico. Larger than life," Emmett said through the dark of the car.

~

Lionel's place was encircled by the forest on his property, and Tallie knew the secret spot where she could park her car. She and Emmett would be able to walk over the bridge leading to the enormous patio with two huge fire pits flanking it and a heated infinity pool in the middle that seemed to spill out into the grass like an illusion. In season, the bridge was surrounded by a copse of fecund apple and pear trees and a bright patch of wildflowers that attracted myriad hummingbirds and bees. It was a genuine certified wildlife nature preserve and sanctuary. They had a gardener, but Tallie loved getting her hands dirty with Zora and River. In the spring, they planted rows and rows of sunflowers, although oftentimes the deer would get to them before long—the big sunny blossoms appearing in the afternoon, disappearing overnight.

She turned down a gravel road with a mohawk of leaves in the middle. The ride was bumpy and louder than the smooth street—popping rocks, wetness sucking at the tires. She stopped the car once they got to the edge of the bridge. There was a wide-bowl clearing under the sky. The landscaping lights leading to the bridge shone like little spaceships across the leafy black. Tallie smoothed her skirt after getting out of the car. She went in the backseat for the cake, which Emmett insisted on carrying. He also insisted on putting her car keys in his pocket, so she did him one better and gave him her lip gloss, too, so she could leave her purse in the trunk. He slipped it into the inside pocket of his suit jacket, and Tallie wished she had that on a short video loop the same way she'd wanted one of him shaking the cigarette from the soft pack.

"Li usually has a big screen set up outside with a movie playing on it. Last year it was *Psycho*," Tallie said after punching in the gate code. Her heels crunched up the wooden steps of the bridge. Emmett was right behind her, and she reached for his hand.

The quiet that ribboned through the darkness was slowly eclipsed as they got closer. Floody creek water gurgled over rocks below. Peppy chatter and music from the house rose like a heat shimmer, getting louder as they crossed the bridge out there alone. Emmett was fetching in that suit. Tallie imagined the two of them stopping, Emmett taking her in his arms, kissing her neck, her mouth, gently putting her earlobe between his teeth. She held the vision of him wet on the metal bridge over the river against the man in that suit next to her on the wooden bridge. Two completely different bridges, two completely different men. Two jagged, mysterious halves of a whole. The zapping was back—her heart, her body, her blood   like a mad scientist's creation humming with life and green lightning.

"Ta-daa!" she said, motioning her free hand toward Lionel's house. Gray stone, glass, and more gray stone and more glass sprawled out and up and over in front of them. A small rolling knot of costumed people hung on the hill to their left, next to a bricked fire pit. A pumpkin-carving station was set up not far from that, and another, bigger crowd spilled into the yard, down the rocky pathway leading to more gardens. No one seemed to mind the mud. Orange and purple lanterns floated atop the infinity pool. One woman wearing not much more than glitter stood near the edge of it with gigantic angel wings sprouting from her shoulder blades, casting two wing shadows on the glowy water. A movie Tallie loved was playing on the large projection screen. She pointed and turned to Emmett.

"*Donnie Darko.*"

"Aha. And wow, damn," he said, fully taking in the scene before looking at her.

"It's extra."

"I feel underdressed."

"No. You're perfect."

They walked across the patio, Tallie saying hello and waving to the people she recognized. She spotted Zora, dressed in full Athena-goddess-of-wisdom regalia, standing by one of the tall glass doors, drinking champagne from a flute. Zora, looking every bit the former Miss Kentucky she was, wore two armfuls of chattering gold bangle bracelets and a thin gold headband of leaves. Her black curls hung loose and wild around her face, over her bare brown shoulders. When she saw Tallie, she smiled and put both hands in the air.

"Lulaaah!" Zora squealed.

"Zoraaaa!" Tallie squealed back, going to her and hugging her. "Aren't you cold?"

"We must suffer for beauty, girlfriend. And *who*, oh, *who*, is this? Emmett?" Zora asked, looking at him.

"I see you've talked to my mother. Yes, Zora, this is my friend Emmett. Emmett, this is my beautiful and lovely sister-in-law, Zora."

"Nice to meet you," Emmett said, putting out his hand once Tallie and Zora finished hugging.

"Girl, now, you *know* Judith texted me *everything*. A pleasure to meet you, Emmett. Any friend of Tallulah's is more than welcome here," Zora said, ignoring his hand and hugging him instead. Zora was putting her flirty, sweet voice on top of her slightly slurred and starry champagne voice.

"Where's Li? He wouldn't tell me his costume. I brought his favorite cake," Tallie said, scanning the crowd behind her and what little she could see inside.

"Oh, you'll see him in there! And you're—" She squinted at Tallie's FBI badge; Emmett's, too. "Mulder and Scully! Cute!" she said, waving at people behind them: an Elvis, two people dressed as panda bears, and a zookeeper followed by a person in a peacock costume plumed with blue, purple, and black feathers.

"Where's my nephew? River's with your parents?" Tallie asked.

"Yes! He's a dinosaur. They took him trick-or-treating with his cousins. He's so cute you'll die. I'll show you a million pictures later. Go, go! Put the cake down, get some food! Crush a cup of wine! Enjoy the night! Happy Halloween! Find me later!" Zora said, exclamation-pointing at them.

~

As soon as they got into the kitchen, Tallie put the cake with the rest of the food. Emmett was next to her smelling deliciously woodsy, looking up and around at what he could see of the house from where he stood. "Want to do a tour first? Probably the easiest way to find Lionel anyway."

"Okay," Emmett agreed. She saw him eye the champagne.

"Sure you feel okay having one?" Tallie asked, holding up a small green bottle and a fun, twisty straw for him.

"Thank you."

"Me, too," she said, getting one for herself. "And if we want, we can sleep here. A lot of people stay over . . . if they drink too much is what I mean . . ." She stopped, conflicted. Emmett wasn't her client, and she wasn't responsible for him. He was a grown man; he could have a drink. He could handle it, she'd seen him. But she also knew how fragile his headspace had been on Thursday evening. Okay. She decided to press Pause on taking mental therapy notes about him for the night, and they'd have one drink—two at most.

"Got it," he said.

She spotted one of her clients across the room dressed as Wednesday Addams. She and her clients had a rule of ignoring one another whenever they crossed paths in public. Tallie always felt like a spy when she did it. They made eye contact and looked away. *Clark, Tallie Clark.* Tallie watched her when she wasn't looking, attempting to see if she was with the man she'd shown Tallie a photo of, the man she discussed with a pinched red face every therapy session. And she was. Of course she was.

Tallie turned and bumped into a friend from college; they'd recently reconnected in barre class.

"Hey, girl. You look cute. Are your legs still sore from Tuesday's class? Mine are! Is that normal? Who are you dressed up as?" her friend asked, rapid-fire. Happily buzzed.

"Scully. From *The X-Files*. You're Bella Swan?" Tallie asked after taking in the brunette wig, brown jacket, backpack, and long gray cabled mittens she was wearing. "That's your Edward?" Tallie asked after looking behind her and finding a bloody-fanged vampire in a gray peacoat with the collar popped. He was talking to a guy dressed as the poop emoji.

"Yes, it is. And whoa, I saw Nicodemus Tate around here somewhere! His name is so great...like some kind of prince or something. No, a king! Nico*demus* Tate," her friend said, letting Nico's name linger on her tongue for a moment before glancing around wildly like a chicken. "He asked if I'd seen you. You guys aren't dating again, right? Oh. Shit. Sorry," she said to Emmett.

"You're fine." Tallie put her hand on her shoulder. "No, Nico and I aren't dating. But this is Emmett, my Mulder," she said. Tallie had felt a twitch of *something* hearing Nico's name and knowing he was in the house—like she was a guitar and someone had flicked one of her strings.

"Gotcha. Whew. Girl, Emmett's cute," her friend said, holding her hand to her mouth and whispering the last part although on no planet would Emmett not be able to hear her. "Nice to meet you, Emmett. It's good to see you both. Maybe I'll text you tomorrow and let you know if my legs are still sore. Maybe she broke us. She kicked our *ass*. That's still sore, too!" she said, waving at them before rejoining her vampire love.

"Okay, are you overwhelmed?" Tallie asked Emmett when they were alone.

"I'm enjoying myself."

"Perfect," she said, opening her bottle of champagne, slipping in the straw. Emmett skipped the straw but opened his bottle and drank from it. She took his hand again, happy this was a new habit they'd sunk their teeth into.

∼

Tallie and Emmett walked down the hallway and up the stairs, taking their time, stepping aside for a jockey in neon carrying a near-life-size cardboard horse cutout, a man in a three-piece pumpkin suit, and a Little Bo-Peep, complete with shepherd's crook and her two costumed sheep. Tallie pointed to the photos on Lionel's wide cream-colored wall, drinking and describing them to Emmett.

Lionel, Zora, and River backed by the Pacific Ocean, the Atlantic, Lake Michigan. River bundled up in a teddy-bear costume. Lionel holding baby River up, up, up in the infinity pool water. Zora, ready-to-pop pregnant with River.

Tallie paused at the photo of Zora, remembering how cute she was waddling around that monster of a house. How Zora would take Tallie's hand and place it on her belly so she could feel her nephew thump-flop around in there like a fish.

Tallie's dad and Lionel in Yellowstone. Lionel, Zora, and River in Atlanta. Lionel and Zora in Vancouver at the 2010 Winter Olympics. Lionel and his best friend at the 2014 FIFA World Cup. Lionel, Zora, and River sitting next to a pile of leaves. Lionel, Zora, and River and a snowman, waving at the camera. Lionel and Tallie and their parents at Lionel and Zora's wedding.

Nico and Tallie had gone together to that wedding all those years ago, and Nico had been stoked when Tallie caught the bouquet. There'd been some overlap between those first few dates with Joel and a reconnect with Nico. Joel had been at the wedding, too, and he and Tallie had shared a drunksy slow dance to a Louis Armstrong and Ella Fitzgerald duet. She and Nico went back to his place and had sex in the kitchen. He slicked the hem of her dress up around her waist and unzipped himself—his suit pants sliding down slowly, pooling around his feet like an inkblot.

She knew all the stories behind the photos on Lionel's wall. She'd even noticed a year ago when Lionel replaced a picture of him and Joel—sweaty after one of their soccer matches—with one of Tallie and Zora in the kitchen, posing like supermodels.

~

"Way too many bedrooms up here. I mean, who's sleeping in these bedrooms?" Tallie said, drinking her champagne. She and Emmett had made it to the third floor of Lionel's house after stopping to chat with a few more people Tallie knew. On the top floor: four bedrooms, two bathrooms, an office the size of a public library, and a library the size of a small city. At least one amorous couple had hijacked the biggest bedroom at the end of the hallway; a tube sock hung limp and phallic on the doorknob.

"I saw Tinker Bell and a werewolf go in there. Although I didn't know adults needed to do the tube-sock thing. We get it. It's overkill, really. Now, *that's* braggy," Emmett said quietly, thumbing toward the door.

"Wow, you're right. It *is* braggy," Tallie said, laughing.

They wandered lazily, taking everything in. Still no sign of Lionel, but there was plenty to see. Tallie peeked into one bedroom with the door open. A couple dressed as a fork and spoon kissed against the wall. A Bride of Frankenstein sat on the bed, scrolling through her phone before looking up and giving Tallie a smile that she returned. In another bedroom, two of Tallie's cousins, dressed as salt and pepper shakers, waved to her. She asked them if they knew the fork and spoon and they exploded into laughter, telling her she was the fourth person to ask them that.

"*Fork* person to ask us that," her cousin said before laughing again. Tallie giggled, patting them both on the head.

"Have you seen my brother?" she asked.

"Not yet. What's his costume?" her cousin asked.

"He never tells me," Tallie said. Emmett stood quietly, listening.

"Lionel is withholding. He's been like that since he was a boy," her cousin said.

"Don't I know it? And this is Emmett," Tallie said, touching his shoulder.

"Aunt Judy told us *all* about Emmett. Well, Aunt Judy told Mama, and Mama told us," her cousin said, motioning to his sister standing next to him.

"Nice to meet you both," Emmett said.

One cousin winked, the other waved before Tallie and Emmett went across the hallway to nose around. That bedroom ceiling was covered with orange and silver balloons trailing slick, curly ribbons. They found a small group of costumed partyers, a rainbow strobe light, a phone on the bed with trippy electronica beeping from it. Lionel's best friend, Ben, dressed as LeBron James, was laughing and dancing with a woman in an owl costume. He waved to Tallie, and she waved back.

∼

The second-floor landing was astir with a gob of women in beaded flapper dresses. Tallie stared in wonder before looking down over the balcony and turning, literally bumping into Nico, not immediately recognizing him in costume.

"Hey!" he said, his voice giving him away. And if it hadn't, his eyes would've—that unmistakable cerulean blinking at her from his pale greenish-yellow face. He was wearing tattered pants, and the T-shirt underneath his blazer read THE MONSTER'S NAME IS NOT FRANKENSTEIN. Was the Bride of Frankenstein his date? Something that felt like jealousy prickled Tallie's armpits; she'd lied to herself when she thought she wouldn't feel it. She was an electric guitar now, and someone had plugged her in, started shredding.

"Hey! Hi! Nico! There you are!" she said, looking at the fake bloodied-plastic bolts stabbing out of his neck.

"What's up, Scully? You look stunning," he said, showing all his teeth. One of Tallie's favorite things about Nico: the sharky shock of his full smile.

"Oh! Thank you," she said. "Um yeah, Nico, this is Emmett. He's Mulder." *Nicodemus. Nico, Nico, Nico.* It was a great pleasure seeing him after one non-Nico month.

"Nice to meet you, man," Nico said, shaking Emmett's hand. Emmett smiled politely, drank his champagne.

"Have you seen Lionel?"

"Not yet. I think some friends of mine came up this way," he said.

"Are you looking for a Bride of Frankenstein?" Tallie asked.

"Nope. Should I be?"

"There's one up there. I thought maybe she was yours," she said, with relief ticking and cooling.

"She's definitely not mine," Nico said and smiled again like he could eat her up in one bite.

"Okay, well, there's also Tinker Bell and a werewolf in the bedroom, the twins from *The Shining*, superheroes in the library, maybe a piece of toast, too," Tallie recalled.

"Superheroes! That's them. I'll catch up with you later, *lieve schat*?" he asked, looking at her, calling her *dear treasure* like always. Nico's mother was from the Netherlands. He was a polyglot, and Tallie especially loved hearing the Dutch walk up the stairs of his throat and stomp out.

"Yes. Come find me later!" she said, feeling hot. She waved and Nico continued up the stairs.

"So that's your man," Emmett said before taking another pull of champagne.

"What? Oh. No. I mean in *college*, yes, but not um...anymore."

"You're blushing. You look like you just got plucked."

"What?! I don't even know what that means. Quit it."

They walked down the second-floor hallway, where through the crowd, she recognized her brother by his height and how his body moved. He was standing in the corner, tall and hairy in a fully masked Bigfoot costume that looked straight off a Hollywood backlot. The kind of expensive, realistic Bigfoot costume pranksters bought and donned so their friends could film them walking through the woods in order to sell the footage to sensationalists.

BIGFOOT SPOTTED AGAIN, THIS TIME IN KENTUCKY!

Small orange bulbs twinkled and drooped across the ceiling, glimmered from the open bedrooms. When they got to him, Lionel reached into the cooler on the floor, slooshed around in the ice, and pulled his Bigfoot hand out. He shoved a glowing pony of beer at Emmett, awash in pumpkin light. He'd finished his champagne, and Lionel took the bottle from him, clinking it into a small recycling box. It was classic, perfect-timing, *larger-than-life* Lionel, anticipating Emmett having an empty bottle although he'd never met him and being responsible enough to make sure he recycled the glass. Her brother was cosmically unreal.

"Li, this is Emmett," Tallie said, hugging her brother around his furry waist. Lionel hugged Tallie back, squeezing her until she squeaked. He reached up and snatched his mask off, held it in his hand like an Old Testament king who'd just decapitated a traitor. His handsome face was a little sweaty, smiling.

"Emmett, I'm Lionel Clark, Lulah's big brother. Welcome to my home. Welcome," he said, wrapping his arms around Emmett and patting his back.

"Nice to meet you, Lionel. I've heard so many awesome things about you," Emmett said.

"Well, same, because our mom called this afternoon and told me she had breakfast with you two. And that you were cleaning out

Lulah's gutters. Thank you, Emmett. I was going to say something to you about it," Lionel said, looking at Tallie.

"Of course, no problem," Emmett said.

Tallie walked around Lionel, petting his costume.

"It's got Chewbacca vibes, right?" Lionel said. "And you two are *X-Files*! I dig it. You both look great. I've just been chilling up here by the cooler, spying on people walking around looking for me."

"There's a Tinker Bell and a werewolf totally boning in one of your bedrooms upstairs. And Nico's here," Tallie said.

"Nico Tate? Are you...y'know what...all right, then," Lionel said. Tallie shook her head and smiled at him. "Happy Halloween, right?"

"Happy Halloween!" Tallie said, giggling a bit.

"So Emmett, you're from Clementine?"

"I am," Emmett said.

"Well, I'm glad you're here. And I'm glad you're taking good care of my sister," he said, putting Tallie in a mild headlock, giving her a gentle noogie.

"Li, stop. You're messing up my Scully-ness!" Lionel released her, and she punched his arm. "Are Dad and Glory here?" Tallie asked, refluffing her hair.

"Yeah, Dad texted me. They should be down there somewhere," he said. "Hey, let me know if y'all need anything. Make yourself at home."

Tallie finished the rest of her champagne, and Lionel took the bottle from her before reaching into the cooler and handing her a drippy pony of penny-colored beer.

"Oh, I love you," she said to him.

"I love you, too, Sis."

Tallie and Emmett walked down the long twinkling hallway, pulsing like a bloody vein leading away from her brother: the heart. She turned to see him pulling his Bigfoot mask onto his head, secreting himself again.

EMMETT

(There is a small art gallery on the first floor of Lionel's house. Most people would probably call it a hallway, but it's wildly spacious, lined with framed paintings. Two large Goldscheider vases frame the doorway like centurions. A golden Brâncuși-like sculpture on a table casts its shadow on the shiny hardwood. A Brâncuși recently bagged over fifty-seven million at auction. Everything in the house is moneyed, dripping with it like the waterfall splashing beneath the large living-room window.)

Since he'd left his phone at Tallie's, Emmett had no access to his emails, but he was still thinking about them. It was all he could think about when he met Lionel for the first time upstairs. It was all he could think about when Zora welcomed them in. On sight, Emmett had decided that Lionel wasn't a douchey finance bro or an asshole. He was generous and kind, not worried about his house and expensive art collection getting trashed by drunken people in elaborate costumes. Emmett had liked him immediately, and Lionel and Tallie really did seem to click on and glow around each other.

The party was catered, but partygoers had also brought a bounty of cakes, cookies, pies, fruit. It wasn't quite bacchanalian, or at least not *yet*, but the atmosphere whished, as if anything could happen.

Everything in excess—the wine, the food, the house that grew before Emmett's eyes anytime he moved around inside the wide expanse of it.

(Costumed people fill the kitchen, milling in and out of the three pairs of tall glass doors leading to open air. Drinking. Dancing. Mingling. Eating. Revelers swig bubbly gin with tropical-green wedges of lime. Clink bourbon. Chug beers. Slush their glasses full of red or white from the wine spheres, bob for apples in the sink. A rotating cast of bodies octopussing—arms reaching out for marshmallow-chocolate squares, salted nuts, stinky cheese, and figs. Limp hands made alive and desirous over and over like The Creation of Adam.*)*

He and Tallie filled their plates with spicy chicken wings and steak kebabs with green peppers, tomatoes, and mushrooms. Fries, jalapeño poppers, and sweet piquant peppers. Olives stuffed with herbed goat cheese. A man in a yellow hat carrying a copper bucket of champagne bottles scooted past them with a white-faced capuchin monkey on his shoulder. The monkey squeaked, looked Emmett in the eyes, opened his little mouth wide; Emmett stared back at it, opened his mouth, too.

"Hey, man," he said, smiling at the monkey before he disappeared.

"Dang it. I totally forgot to tell you about the Man with the Yellow Hat and his Curious George! He's here every year," Tallie said. She laughed and held her hand over her mouth, finished chewing before motioning across the room. "I want you to meet my dad and stepmom," she said, lifting her hand at the couple walking toward them dressed as Shaft and Foxy Brown. "Hi, Daddy," she said, hugging him. "Glory, you look so pretty."

"Thank you, Tallie," Glory said, stepping back to give her a spin.

"Y'all, this is my friend Emmett. Emmett, this is my dad, Gus, and my stepmom, Glory," Tallie said, nudging him forward.

Emmett said hi to them, shaking their hands.

"You two really do look great. The *Shaft* theme song should've started playing when you walked over," he said.

Gus nodded and laughed. "It was definitely playing in my mind, hence the swagger."

"Who are y'all?" Glory asked, leaning forward to see Tallie's FBI badge. "Oh, the alien show that scares me," she said, recognizing it. "Even the theme song creeps me out."

"I'm Scully; he's Mulder."

Emmett drank from his almost-empty beer bottle and didn't even mind the small talk with Tallie's family. She was so happy, talking to everyone. He told Gus and Glory where he was from and that Tallie was the reason he was in Louisville, the same thing he'd told Judith that morning. Although it was a lie, it didn't *feel* like one anymore. Now he couldn't imagine Louisville without Tallie and didn't want to. Gus and Glory talked about being born and raised in Louisville and how much they loved to travel. They'd recently returned from Greece and had plans to visit again the following spring.

"Where's my son?" Gus asked, looking around.

"He was upstairs in a Bigfoot costume, but don't tell him I told you," Tallie said.

"Deal. We'll find him and scoot. You know I'm an early bird," Glory said, before touching Tallie's face and saying, "*You* look so pretty. And it was nice to meet you, Emmett."

"Nice to meet you, too," Emmett said before they walked away.

~

He and Tallie finished their plump little beers. Zora and some women were dancing nearby on the patio to a Tears for Fears song blaring from the outside speakers, and Tallie stepped out to join them. *Donnie Darko* had ended and restarted, playing silently on the projection screen by the pool. Emmett had seen the movie many times before, oddly comforted by how it was funny, unsettling, and so like a comic book all at once. He walked closer to the doors, leaned over to see the screen. Straight ahead, Tallie was talking to three women dressed in sequined frocks—the Supremes. Their dresses caught the light, sent it scattering onto the other costumes and flashing across the window glass.

He spotted Bigfoot in the distance, shadowing across the leaves, walking alone with smooth, long strides before disappearing into the trees. Having lost sight of Lionel, Emmett refocused on Tallie talking to her friends. His Scully, delighted and popping glossy olives from her plate. He adjusted his tie, his FBI badge, took another bite of his food. Watched the projection screen—Jake Gyllenhaal and Jena Malone in a darkened theater next to the metal-faced rabbit. He glanced inside the house at the couch in the living room and saw a woman in an intense red dress with her eyes closed, slack as a dying rose. He stared to make sure she was breathing. She wasn't. Emmett's adrenaline flared hot, and he walked toward her. As soon as he got there, her eyes opened. She shot up, laughing loudly and pointing at someone across the room, never giving Emmett a thought. A balloon pop went off like a gunshot in the kitchen, startling him again.

"Shit," Emmett said to himself. He finished his last bite of food and put his plate in the kitchen before walking outside and standing against the door.

"Hey, man," Lionel said, stepping next to Emmett and putting his Bigfoot mask on the ground. Zora had spun across the patio and was dancing with a group of women, all of them dressed like Greek goddesses. Emmett saw Gandalf and the hobbits Tallie had told him about in the grass. Gandalf was tromping through the leaves, holding his staff to the sky, pretending to cast a spell. A couple of the hobbits cartwheeled.

"Your house is *truly* out of this world," Emmett said. Tallie looked over, and he gave her an *I'm okay* smile.

"Thank you. It's extra, I know. But I couldn't help myself." Lionel laughed lightly. Emmett's own laugh caught him by surprise, and he leaned into it. "So you and Lulah...how's that going? My mom said you make delicious eggs . . . biscuits, too," Lionel said, playfully leaning, knocking Emmett's shoulder with his own.

"Your sister is unlike anyone I've ever met. She outshines everything," Emmett said to Lionel, looking right at him.

Lionel was finishing up a piece of the pumpkin spice cake Tallie had brought for him. He was only a couple of inches taller than Emmett but seemed to tower over him in his Bigfoot costume.

"Where'd you two meet?"

"At the coffee shop on Rose," Emmett said. He'd fill Tallie in later. In all her talking, that was a question Judith hadn't asked over breakfast.

"Gotcha. That's her favorite one."

Tallie flashed past them like a butterfly, holding on to the hand of a woman dressed as a unicorn. The two of them stopped not far from Emmett and Lionel. Tallie and the unicorn wiggled their hips, dancing to the New Wave sound track piping up and out into the October night sky with its half-full moon. That moon Emmett thought he'd never see again, whether it was blocked by concrete or clouds or rain or his life, ending.

A tight circle of people across the patio lit a joint, and the wind carried the smell over. The good-stink of weed smoke reminded him of camping trips. High school and trees. The afterglow of sore feet and burning eyes, late nights at the lake restaurant, the moonlight on the glassy black water. All the moons he'd lived under. Seeing the consistently ever-changing moon felt like a gift. He gazed up at it like he was seeing it for the first time as Lionel began talking about some businesses he'd invested in downtown, near the coffee shop.

When Emmett noticed Tallie looking at him again, he winked at her. He knew they were pretending; he hadn't forgotten. He thought he'd heard someone say his real name when they were on the third floor, and his face flushed. A guy in a Han Solo costume was staring at him in the kitchen, and he imagined him pointing, asking him what he was doing there. But Tallie could *almost* make him think what they were pretending was real. She'd ramped up her flirting, barely stood beside him for more than thirty seconds without touching him or holding his hand. He watched her dance, his cross hanging around her neck.

"Dancing Queen" by ABBA came on, and Lionel hollered, "This is for you, Lulah!" before turning to Emmett and adding, "You know this is her jam." Tallie—the dancing queen—blew Lionel a kiss through the air. "Maybe I've seen you there...at the coffee shop on Rose. I know I've seen you *somewhere*," Lionel said.

"You seem familiar to me, too," Emmett lied. He waited a moment before asking Lionel about the house. What year it was built, how long it took. He was relieved when Lionel launched into the details. Emmett pulled a cigarette from his inside pocket, offered one to Lionel, who took it. They lit them, smoked. Emmett leaned, watching Tallie dance to Pet Shop Boys, Donna Summer, Oingo Boingo. Zora reappeared with the other goddesses, and Tallie got lost somewhere in the middle. People popped up to talk to Lionel, to remark on his costume. People asked Emmett who he was dressed as before they saw his *X-Files* badge. One guy said nothing, only whistled the first six notes of the spooky theme song as he passed. Lionel introduced him to a couple more of his and Tallie's cousins, usually opting to call him Tallie's *boyfriend*, at which Emmett just smiled.

(Lionel is handsome, charming, and hilarious. Possibly the most confident man on earth, as if he's never been told no. Not even once.)

"Joel was my friend. They met through me. So I still have some guilt about how that went down," Lionel said when it was just the two of them. Emmett could've blown his mind and repeated what Joel had confessed in the email, but instead he blinked. Nodded.

"Well, she has nothing but glowing things to say about you. She's proud of you. It's not your fault Joel's a dick."

Lionel laughed. "I'm glad she's back out there. I'm glad she brought you tonight. Your chemistry is more than obvious."

"I'm crazy about her," Emmett said, spotting Tallie in the crowd.

Slow and intoxicating: "Don't Dream It's Over" by Crowded House soared from the speakers as she walked toward him. When she got there, she threw her head back and held out her hand, pulled him toward her. They walked next to the pool, where everyone was dancing. When Emmett looked at Lionel again, Lionel lifted his cake plate to them in cheers.

"I love this song so much," Tallie said, putting her arms around his neck.

"I told your brother we met at the coffee shop," Emmett whispered into her ear.

"Good boy," she said into his. "You feeling okay?"

"I am," he said, with his arms around her waist.

"By the way, the unicorn said you looked familiar, too. I told her lots of people say that to you. We'll have to scour the internet for your celebrity doppelgänger later."

Tallie reached into the inside pocket of his suit jacket, took out her lip gloss, put it on, and returned it where she'd found it. They looked at each other, their faces so close with the night-blue music lifting, spilling out across the stars. If only the sky would open and zoom them up.

"You look handsome," she said.

"You're *striking*. You're lightning."

"Sweet Emmett," she said. *Emmett.* He needed to tell her the truth. "Tallie—"

The air popped above them; a rocket shot across the sky. Tallie gasped and looked up. Emmett, startled by the sound at first, relaxed upon seeing a chandelier of glitter against the black. Fireworks. And maybe it happened all at once. Maybe he leaned down to her. Or had she gotten on her tiptoes? At first, the kiss was chaste, kindergarten-sweet. Was this pretending? But when Emmett pulled her closer, the music got louder. The kiss swelled. Their kiss: surprising, dark crush like a jewel wrapped in velvet. Their kiss: a real but different, better version of Klimt's. Emmett opened his mouth a little to let her in, keeping his hand on the small of her back, pressing her body against his. He pulled away, turned his head, put his mouth on hers until she stopped and looked at him, bit her bottom lip.

They kissed again; her mouth was liquor, starry and sweet. How long had it been since he'd kissed a woman? He felt lust-crazy with his mouth on hers. His charged Halloween heart: Fuseli's *The Nightmare.* Caravaggio's *The Incredulity of Saint Thomas.* What if he never stopped feeling this way? Could they freeze time, kiss forever? What if they stopped only when someone tapped them on the shoulder because the sun had come up? How had he managed to think God had forgotten about him when he was kissing and holding Tallie like this as proof of hope?

Tallie put her hand on the back of his head, lightly brushed her fingers through the hair that fell against his neck. He was burning like the fireworks above them. Like a star, afraid he'd poof to smoke and disappear if she ever stopped.

Please don't stop. Goodbye! I'm going to the moon!

The crowd outside erupted into applause when the fireworks were over. Emmett heard Zora holler for everyone to step inside for the costume contest, and he felt the scrum of revelers shift. Tallie kissed him and kissed him and kissed him with her greedy champagne mouth. Emmett returned her kisses with equal fervor—like a man on his last day—and stopped only when his eyes-closed darkness sparked with a peculiar flurry of light.

Only Emmett, Tallie, and Lionel in syzygy, *aligned like an eclipse,* on the nearly empty patio. Lionel, at least twenty feet away, standing alone in his masked Bigfoot costume. Lionel, nowhere near the pool, far too close to the blazing fire pit. Lionel, the right side of his body, violently torched. Lionel, consumed with fulgent orange flame. Lionel, Lionel, burning bright.

PART FOUR

SUNDAY

TALLIE

Emmett pressed his palm to Tallie's shoulder, moving her aside. The concerned look on his face caused her to turn around, just in time to see him run across the patio and take off his suit jacket. Slow motion. Volcanic flames blooming. Fast-forwarded. Emmett—quick—pushed and swept Lionel's leg with his foot to make him fall away from the fire pit before throwing himself on top of him and wrapping the jacket around Lionel's costumed body. Lionel. Lionel was on fire.

Emmett was all over him, patting hard. They rolled together. Ha! They'd planned this while she was dancing with her girlfriends. This was a prank, part of Lionel's costume. Last year, it was Houdini and the water tank. This year, Bigfoot on fire. Bravo, boys.

They were no longer alone on the patio. Costumed bodies clumped around the fire pit where she was standing, not knowing how she got there. A man dressed like a hippie did the peace sign and said the party was totally rad. He laughed and the hippie woman next to him whooped and laughed, too.

"Is this part of his costume?" someone slurred.

Zora's glass fell against the stone, and she flashed by in a blurry white zip, dropping to her knees next to Emmett and Lionel.

209

Emmett had taken off Lionel's unburned mask and had his knife out, carefully cutting parts of the furry fabric away from Lionel's body. The sounds coming from Lionel's mouth were feral. Whole-bodied. Horrific.

Not a prank.

Tallie's mouth locked in a voiceless scream as she watched Emmett carefully raise Lionel's legs and place them lengthwise along a concrete planter he'd knocked over. He put his face close to Lionel's and talked to him.

"I called 911!" someone shouted.

"Hey, Lionel. Lionel, look at me. You're all right. You're going to be okay. EMS is on the way," Emmett said.

Zora was crying, screeching. "Oh, my God! Lionel! Shouldn't we get it completely off him?"

"No. It could make it worse where he's burned. I'm cutting away the unburned parts to cool him down. Let them do the rest. What's important now is to keep him calm. They'll be here. They're on the way. It's okay now. The scary part is over," Emmett said, unshaken.

"What can I do? How can I help?" a man in a bee costume bent down and asked.

"Okay, okay. Go out to the street and direct the ambulance here," Tallie said to him, speaking for the first time since it all happened. The bee flung his bobbing antennae in the leaves and ran. The heat whipped through the cool air. Someone threw a bucket of pool water on the fire pit, then another, until it finally fell dark. The back of Tallie's hair splashed cold on her neck.

"Li, are you okay?" Zora asked, from her knees.

Emmett touched her shoulder. "He'll be okay."

"Are *you* okay?" she asked him. Emmett was nodding as soon as she opened her mouth.

Lionel hissed and groaned, mumbled incoherently. Emmett touched his face, talked to him in a measured, soothing voice, like he was a small child. Tallie was scared to look at his body again; she could smell the burning flesh. She sat down next to them and echoed Emmett in words and movement. Looking only at Lionel's face and talking to him, reassuring him they'd called for help. She told him how much she loved him and that he'd be okay. Lionel's best friend, Ben, was next to them doing the same thing until a siren pinched the air and whirling red lights dizzied streaks across the sea of trees encircling the house.

"Hey, Li. Li, look at me, man. Help is here already, and God sees us. He's not going to let anything else happen to you. This was it. We'll be right here with you," Emmett said.

"Li, you'll be okay. Don't move. Just don't move, okay?" Tallie said, repeating it like a charm. Zora did the same. Emmett put his hand flat on Lionel's chest and kept his mouth close to Lionel's ear. Tallie watched Emmett's whispering mouth move. Lionel grunted, sucked in a deep breath, sobbed it out. Tallie hadn't seen her brother cry since they were kids. Seeing Lionel cry scared her more than anything else. She shivered on her stockinged knees next to Emmett. The ground tilted beneath them, didn't it?

"Help is here, Li. Help is here," she said to him. Was he nodding? "Don't move."

"Hold still," Emmett said.

"Li," Zora said through tears.

The costumed crowd was silent now save for crying and reverent whispers. Someone had turned off the music. The glowing water licked the swimming pool, ticked like a slowed clock. The projection screen flickered blue.

"Dear God, please, please, please let him be okay," Tallie prayed aloud, standing once the EMTs jingled up and clanked through the leaves, the night grass, onto the stone.

∼

Once Emmett and Tallie were at her car, she got her phone from her purse in the trunk and called her parents, told them what had happened, what hospital they were following the ambulance to. Emmett was driving. Tallie had taken his face in her hands and made him stare into her eyes, double-checking to see if he was too impaired. "I'm fine, Tallie. Tallie, I'm good," he'd said, loosening his tie and slipping it out of the collar. He'd tossed it in the backseat before starting the engine and putting the car in reverse. Zora's brother and sister were staying behind at the house to keep an eye on things. The partygoers who were okay to drive had stuffed themselves into cars, disappearing into the night. The too-drunk or too-stoned ones who weren't passed out were left wandering around the house in a daze. The world was so loud again—engines and slamming car doors and tires slicking the wet pavement—the sharp shift in mood still vibrating the air. They followed the ambulance down Lionel's street, turning onto the main road and gunning up the highway ramp.

"Do you really think he'll be okay?" Tallie asked. She was shaking. She'd started when Lionel caught fire and hadn't stopped.

"Yes," he said calmly and nodded.

"You...you just *sprang* to action. How'd you know what to do?"

"It's important to get the person on the ground. Our natural impulse is to remain standing or to run, which makes everything worse."

"Shit. Thank you," Tallie said. "Are your hands okay?" She took his right hand in hers, turned it over. Emmett winced and returned it to the steering wheel. His clothes clutched a fiery funk she could taste.

"We're almost there. He'll be fine. It'll be okay."

~

At the hospital, Zora was with Lionel, and everyone else sat in the waiting room. Tallie's parents and stepmother walked through the automatic doors at the same time.

"Zora's back there with him," Tallie said as she went to them.

"But he was awake? Talking to you?" her dad asked. He and Glory stood there in jogging suits, squeaky sneakers, and raincoats.

"Right after it happened, he was talking to Emmett. Emmett put his jacket around him and got him on the ground. He put the fire out," Tallie said, pointing toward Emmett, who was sitting in a chair by the wall. He was leaning forward with his elbows on his knees, his tender hands curved in *c*'s, straight out in front of him. Tallie had begged him to let a doctor look at his hands, but he'd refused. His palms were red and raw. She'd gone across the street to the twenty-four-hour drugstore and gotten aloe, antibiotic ointment, and gauze. Talked him into letting her tend and wrap his hands herself as they waited.

"So Lionel's okay? Is Emmett okay? Is anyone else hurt?" her mom asked, furiously chewing her nicotine gum.

"We're waiting to hear more. Everyone else is fine," Tallie said. Her parents and Glory followed her to the chair where Emmett was sitting.

"How long has he been back there?" her mom asked over Glory, who had opened her mouth to say something.

"We've been here for twenty minutes," Tallie said.

"He'll be okay," Glory said with faith. Her dad put his hand on her back, and Judith turned to Tallie and rolled her eyes.

Being at the hospital was bad enough without having to play referee between her mom and Glory when Glory wasn't even participating. Tallie sat between them, leaving Emmett on the edge of the aisle next to her mother, who was now talking to him, telling him he was a hero.

"No, ma'am." Emmett shook his head with that bridge-hollow look in his eyes.

"Mama?" Tallie said, hoping she'd shut up. Emmett had rolled up his sleeves, revealing hot pink splotches on his forearms. She asked him if he needed anything for them. More gauze, aloe? He shook his head.

"Tonight has made me start smoking again. I'll be back," her mom said, standing and grabbing her purse. Tallie watched her walk out the automatic doors. There were a couple of costumed people in the waiting room. A little boy dressed like Spider-Man holding what appeared to be a broken arm and a little girl in a banana costume, sleeping on her mother's shoulder. A man wearing a polar bear suit sat flipping through a magazine, the bear head in its own chair beside him.

Tallie's dad leaned forward and touched her knee. "I'm sure he'll be fine. He's tough," he said. "And thank you, Emmett. For helping him."

"No need to thank me, Mr. Clark."

The waiting-room televisions flashed an episode of *Law & Order: SVU* that Tallie had seen a hundred times. Glory pulled her knitting out of her bag, and Tallie asked her about it. It was a nice distraction. She listened to Glory talk about the dishcloth pattern she was using, how she'd found a sale on cotton yarn instead of ordering it from her usual place. The details were comfortably mind-numbing. Ben sat across from them in his LeBron James costume with his arm around the owl woman from the party. Popeye and Olive Oyl sat beside them, friends of Lionel and Zora.

~

"*Lieve schat*, are you all right?" Nico asked when he showed up, not long after Tallie's parents. He'd ditched his blazer and bloody bolts but was still greenish-yellow-faced, standing there in his THE MONSTER'S NAME IS NOT FRANKENSTEIN T-shirt, scratching at his head. "Is Li okay?"

Tallie hugged him, told him what she knew.

"Chips," Nico said quietly, frowning. It sounded like *ships*, and he said it oftentimes instead of *shit* because he'd grown up hearing his Dutch mother say it. Nico slacked his shoulders and let out his breath. He looked at Emmett. "Is *he* okay?"

"Burned his hands a bit," she said. Emmett had his head back, his eyes closed.

"Your boyfriend?" Nico asked close to her ear.

"He's my friend...a new friend," Tallie said, thinking about the kissing. Madness. How had everything happened so fast?

"Well, do you need me to stay here with you? Do anything? Have you eaten? I could grab you something. Where's Aisha?" he asked, looking around as if she'd appear at the mention of her name.

"Lake Tahoe. She'll be back tomorrow. Today," Tallie said, realizing it was Sunday. "I'm fine. I'll get some food. Thank you. I'll text you later."

"You're sure?"

"I'm sure. Go home and sleep," she said, hugging him. He said goodbye and took her face in his hands, kissed her forehead before walking away.

~

Tallie was quiet sitting next to Emmett, in case he was sleeping. She closed her eyes and slipped her heels off, let her head lean on the wall. Was Lionel alive? She opened her eyes in panic, looked at Emmett, still beside her. She glanced at the flashing television before letting the wallpaper pattern blur and come back into focus. Is this how it happened? The family cautiously hopeful but worried, waiting in those chairs until the doctor or surgeon came through the doors with a mournful look on their face, warning of bad news? Tallie closed her eyes again, tried to concentrate on breathing to quell her seasick stomach. Lionel couldn't die. Lionel wouldn't die. But what if Lionel died? Poor Zora. Poor River. Her parents, his friends. All of them. People really did die from things like this. Freak accidents killed more people than Tallie cared to think about. Lives gone in an instant, unexpected last heartbeats happening every terrifying waking moment.

Lionel had been in New York City on 9/11, and for those three hours that morning when Tallie couldn't get hold of him, she'd attended his funeral in her mind. And several years back, Lionel had been in a snowmobile accident during a work trip to Green Bay. Judith had called Tallie and said "Lionel's hurt," and Tallie's brain had done the anxious work of putting him in the ground before her mom could tell her that he'd only had a small fracture in his wrist. The thought of losing her big brother was overwhelming. How would any of them go on without him? She was crying again, attempting to hide it but couldn't, and waved her dad and Glory off before they could make a fuss over her. She put her head in her hands. Shook. She felt Emmett's warm hand on her back, and, besides knowing Lionel was okay, it was the only other thing she needed in the world in that moment.

She let herself cry, caught her breath, and leaned her head against the wall again. Would she fall asleep? Did she? She wasn't sure how much time had gone by when she opened her eyes to see the scary doors slide open.

Emmett stood. Tallie got to her feet and touched the cool wall to counter the asleep-to-suddenly-awake dizziness. Her dad and Glory creaked in their chairs. They watched in silence as Zora, wilted, stepped into the waiting room in her Athena costume, the white fabric ethereally floating her across the floor—a ghosting that could be a sign Lionel didn't make it.

When did the walls go liquid?

Tallie looked over at her dad and Glory. Where was her mother? Was her mother really going to miss this? She needed to fucking be here. Tallie made eye contact with Zora.

"Lionel's . . . okay. Or will be. But he won't be in his own room for a few hours. So honestly, y'all should go change and get some rest and come back in a little bit," she said to them. "And thank you for saving him, Emmett. I didn't see it, but someone told me what you did," Zora said, going to him and hugging tight.

"He's awake? Talking? He's okay?" Tallie flipped the words out quickly. She couldn't remember the last time it'd felt so good to cry. Emmett put his arm around her shoulder. Her dad and Glory joined the circle they were standing in and expressed breathy relief at Zora's news.

"He's knocked out now because of the medicine. He was in so much pain. That was beyond scary," Zora said, crying, too.

Her mom returned from outside with a ripe cloud of smoke clinging to her. The anger Tallie had felt toward her mother, thinking she'd miss some awful announcement about Lionel, melted away. *Lionel was okay.*

Her mom stepped closer to Zora, who shared the news again.

Lionel was okay.

"I'll stay here. Y'all need food? Something to drink? I'll go downstairs to get it," her mom said.

"Could you bring me crackers? And tea?" Zora said. She told them she'd called her parents and River was safe and sound, sleeping at their place. "What time is it?"

"Almost two," Emmett said, looking at the clock. Tallie could *feel* it—she always felt like a skinned, raw version of herself in the middle of the night.

"We're supposed to set the clocks back an hour tonight," she mumbled, remembering. Everything was stretched and pliable, like taffy. Even time didn't make sense anymore.

"Please go get some rest," Zora said.

Her dad and Glory said they were going to the diner across the street for coffee.

"He looks at you like he's in love with you," Tallie's mom said to her when she hugged her.

"Who, Nico?" Tallie whispered. Her mom had always liked Nico, but she'd been out smoking when he'd stopped by. She hadn't seen him.

"No," her mom said. When she pulled away, she nodded her head toward Emmett.

"That's enough. I'll see you soon, Mama," Tallie said before Judith went down the hallway.

"We'll be back. Soon. Tell Lionel that. Tell him we love him," Tallie said to Zora, hugging her.

"I will," Zora said. "He loves you. He loves you so much. Like you wouldn't *believe* how much a guy could love his baby sister," she said to Emmett.

"I love *him* so much. I don't know what I'd do without him," Tallie said and wiped her eyes, took a deep, shaky breath. "And please call me if my mother gets out of hand," she added with a whisper.

"I will, I promise," Zora said. "See you in a little bit."

~

At her house, Tallie and Emmett stood in the hallway outside the bathroom.

"Here—I don't want to lose it. Thank you for letting me wear it," she said, reaching behind her, unclasping his necklace. Emmett was unbuttoning his shirt. "Wait. I'll help you. Really, you should be careful with your hands. You should probably take ibuprofen, too. Does that work for burns? Works for any pain, right?" she said. She got behind him and clasped the necklace around his neck. She stood in front of him and began unbuttoning his shirt for him, his arms lank at his side. The smoky smell coming from him was so intense it could've set off an alarm.

"My hands are fine. They're just tender."

"Emmett, will you let me do this?" she said, her frustration spilling over. She'd scheduled the weekend off to take care of herself and ended up taking care of everyone else. Again! She was tired. So tired.

"Yes. I will let you do this."

Tallie was on the verge of tears, unbuttoning one of his buttons and then another as he stood there quietly, not moving, his back now against the wall. Her cats were in the hallway with them, squinty and blinking in the light.

"You're so *fucking* stubborn," she said. Hungry, exhausted, worried. It felt good to curse at him, to let it out.

"I know I am," he said, nodding.

"It's fucking *annoying*."

"I know it is, but I like when you boss me around."

She was careful pulling the sleeve off his left arm, careful turning him and pulling the entire shirt off his right. And when he was facing her, standing there in his white T-shirt, she reached for the hem and pulled it over his head. Slowly. His skin blushed like a mild sunburn. Once he was shirtless—nothing but his gold cross around his neck—she gently pressed herself to his bare chest and kissed him, breathing in deeply. He shared her breath. His bandaged hands went to the sides of her face, the gauze like feathers.

"We didn't get to talk about the kissing," she said, kissing and pulling away. Emmett was quiet, kissing her neck. "And it's confusing, I know, because it's Sunday. It's officially Sunday now, and you're leaving today. And something's up with you, I know it. Everything you won't tell me...you close up and I can't get it out of you and we barely know each other. You didn't even flinch when my brother caught *fire*!" she said, eyes closed, head turned to the ceiling, Emmett still kissing her neck, her earlobe.

"Is this okay?" he asked before kissing her mouth more aggressively. She nodded.

"Is this okay?" he asked, unzipping her skirt. She said yes.

"Is this okay?" he asked, getting on his knees in front of her, pulling her skirt down. One black-stockinged foot stepping out of the circle it made was her yes.

"Is this okay?" he asked, looking up at her. "Tell me this is okay."

"I like when you boss me around, too."

"Good girl."

He tugged at the strip of lace between her legs, moving it aside.

The black lace she hadn't worn since Joel left; the lace that matched the top of the thigh-highs clipped to her garter belt. Tallie heard *lieve schat* and *Nico, Nico, Nico* in her head, telling her Joel didn't have the only cock in the world when she said yes to Emmett. Emmett had one, too; of course he did. This Emmett Aaron Baker— genuflecting before her as if she were a goddess—hooked her knee over his shoulder.

EMMETT

(Two fluffy decorative pillows on Tallie's bed, one long king-size pillow, a knitted blanket on top of a butter-colored comforter. Nightstand: her glasses, a squat lamp, two bobby pins, a black elastic hair band, a flat tube of hand lotion, an empty glass, Mythology: Timeless Tales of Gods and Heroes *by Edith Hamilton. The top of her dresser: two candles, a small tube of lip balm, dried roses poking from a slim bottle, a pale green milk-glass dish covered in earrings, airy necklaces hanging from the long neck of the lamp, a black-and-white photo-booth strip of her and Nico Tate, glass bottles of perfume—circle, rectangle, square.)*

Tallie sat on the bed in her black lace, unbuttoning, unzipping his pants. The intimacy of being in her bedroom rushing, flooding his veins. A riotous, overwhelming shrine to femininity, as if a pink puff of powder would smack him from overhead and knock him out. Above her nightstand lamp: Courbet's *L'Origine du monde*, Klimt's *Frau bei der Selbstbefriedigung*.

"Is that you?" Emmett said, looking at the erotic postcards, then at her, lifting an eyebrow.

"It *was* last night . . . and . . . I thought about you," she said, falling back, her hands covering her face. The end of the sentence almost lost to the muffle.

"While I...was on the couch?" he asked, having stepped out of his pants. Emmett had held his thoughts captive, never allowing himself to imagine Tallie fantasizing about him, slamming the door on his own fantasies about her before too much could tumble out. Her telling him she'd touched herself thinking of him was a fat, blinding rip in the space-time continuum. The wind howled deep inside him, the icy black. Lightning flashed the shadows. He lay next to her in his underwear, every cell throbbing.

"Oof, I can't believe I told you," she said from behind her hands. "I'm not being myself. I'm acting like someone else. It's tonight...this weekend...everything's making me feel crazy."

"Now *you're* depersonalizing. You're not crazy." His hands ached as he placed them on his bare stomach.

"What else do you think about me?" she asked. They stared at her ceiling—whipped egg whites and sugar.

"I kept myself from thinking about a lot of things. But now since you told me that, and after the hallway, I'm thinking about other...things," he said, tenderly readjusting himself with his wrists, still hot and smarting. His mouth tasted like Tallie, like sweet and salty fruit. Honey, too. What women tasted like. And even in the moments when he'd doubted the existence of God, he'd remember how God had made women taste. Proof alone.

If an artist had been scritching briskly in the darkness—capturing them like the Klimt—they would've drawn Tallie's bedroom, lit by one lamp. M. C. Escher's *Drawing Hands* come alive, penciling Emmett watching Tallie boldly shed her lace while simultaneously limning Tallie with one hand, touching herself, wet with both of them. Tallie putting her finger between his lips, into his mouth. Tallie reaching between his legs. Emmett, at the same time, hungrily kissing her mouth and breasts. Pushing his face against her. The taste of her on his tongue again and again until the crest. Tallie, scrabbling at the comforter beneath her, writhing in a rasped blur. Tallie breathless, sitting up in a fuss and carefully placing his arms above his head before licking a warm trail down his chest. Tallie sliding beneath the elastic of his underwear and taking them off, greedily destroying him. Tallie's body and hair and redolence pouring all over him like water, him inside and on top of and underneath her. And the artist, now finished, blowing the spent scratchings across the paper before wiping it clean. Leaning back and looking at it, completely sated. Chuffed.

~

The alarm Tallie had set busily buzzed on her nightstand, waking them. They'd slept in her bed together, naked and touching. Flash to separate showers and Emmett making cheesy eggs and toast in her kitchen. Zora had texted, letting them know Lionel was in his own room now. They could see him but there was no rush; he would be sleeping for a while. Emmett had dressed in his own clothes, had his new black backpack waiting by the door. The yellow-white line of sunrise stretched across the navy of Tallie's window.

Tallie had rebandaged his hands after his shower, and he didn't think of suicide then. He didn't think of suicide when they were wrapped in her blanket as they shared their post-orgasms cigarette on her deck in the rainy dark, either. He'd put Tallie's sheets in the washing machine and started a load; he'd scrubbed the fire off him, smelled like her soap and his own deodorant. If he *had* to, he could go back home, surprise his parents with his existence. Let them know he was okay before leaving again, finding someone, something, somewhere to start new. He didn't allow himself to think the someone could be Tallie. They'd begun so broken. He'd tell her everything before he left. He'd go to the hospital to see Lionel, maybe have lunch with her, but after that he'd head out. If she didn't try to stop him, he'd leave.

He envisioned himself walking to the bridge and continuing to walk. To walk across it and turn around, walk across it again. Never wanting to jump, not once looking down at the Ohio and wishing he were in that glorious free fall, the wind whistling his ears. Or he could walk in the opposite direction and hitch a ride out, the same way he got to Louisville. Walking and thumbing down truckers, not worried about what could happen to him, because it didn't matter. People had no control over what happened to them anyway. Everything was kismet.

~

(The happy sunflowers vased on the kitchen counter. A ceramic rooster: cream, green, and red. Silver hoop earrings next to a bright blue mug, a short fat spoon. A scalloped-glass sugar bowl.)

Tallie was wet-haired and blushing in her glasses, standing in front of him drinking the coffee he'd made for her. The steam fogged her lenses as she apologized.

"For what?" he asked.

"For crossing a line...whether you think so or not...I *feel* like I crossed a line with you, and that wasn't my intent. You're working through a lot of shit...a lot of shit you haven't told me about, and so am I...and then Lionel and last night—"

"I'm a grown man, Tallie. Please don't talk to me like I'm not," he said. Maybe because she was a teacher and so used to talking to kids, it came naturally to her, but he'd had enough of it.

"I'm sorry. I don't mean to. This is just an extraordinary weekend, and I'm trying to honor it. That's all," she said. She stared into her coffee as if there were an answer in her mug to a question she hadn't asked aloud yet.

"I don't think there was a line in the first place, so how did we cross it? Who made the rules? How can we know if we're following them or not?"

"I don't know. I don't know anything, Emmett. I just didn't want you to think I was, like...trying to take advantage of...anything."

"Ridiculous. I could say the same thing, couldn't I? Because I definitely don't want you to think I was trying to take advantage of anything, either."

"I don't feel that way at all."

"Neither do I. Are you upset with me?"

"No! I'm not upset with you! Are you upset with *me*?" she asked.

"Do I seem upset with you? Did I seem upset in your bedroom?"

"Did *I* seem upset in my bedroom?"

"Okay, well, we could do this all morning," he said, smiling at the absurdity of their circled conversation.

"You're sure you want to come to the hospital with me? I want you to," she asked.

"Of course I do. I'd like to know Lionel is okay. And I'll leave later today."

"Going?"

"To my parents'. I sold my house."

"You changed your mind about going back there?"

"I guess. I'll stop by, but that doesn't mean I'm staying."

"Right. Well, thank you for making breakfast with your poor hands," she said, putting her plate in the sink. They'd eaten sleepily, standing at the counter.

"Will you take a picture of yourself for me? You look pretty," Emmett said.

"Wow." Tallie covered her face, shy. "Thank you. And enough of that."

"So yes?" he asked, lifting her phone off the counter and handing it to her. She held her mug, tilted her head a little, smiled, took the photo. Then took a picture of them together like puppied teenagers, their heads touching. "Send it to me?"

"You have to give me your number."

"Obviously," he said before smirking and telling her. He imagined the turned-off phone in his backpack receiving the message, saving it for later.

Tallie put their coffees in travel mugs, and Emmett's heart clicked as he prepared to leave her house for the last time. He got on his knees to stroke the cats with the part of his hands that stung the least, to tell them thanks for letting him hang out with them over the weekend.

~

Tallie stopped on the porch and abruptly said, "Yeah, I don't own a gun. I only told you that on Thursday so you wouldn't mess with me."

"Well, I believed you. And maybe you should get one. People are crazy," Emmett told her. He used his energy to focus on not tearing up as he followed her off the porch, taking one last look at the gutters he'd cleaned and the cheery pumpkins on her steps, like little suns.

~

Holidays were difficult, but Christine had loved decorating for Halloween, draping their shrubs in fake spiderwebs and putting pumpkins on the porch. And she'd loved their house from the moment they'd seen it. The color: honeybee yellow.

She called it their Honeybee House, wanting to name it after his grandmother's beekeeper occupation, the same way the characters in the old-timey books she liked to read named their vast estates. "Let's go back to the Honeybee House," she'd said when they were out in the world and she'd had enough. Emmett held the image of their Honeybee House in his mind and put Tallie's house right there beside it.

~

Zora, no longer in her Halloween costume, sat in the hospital hall-way, texting. After greeting Tallie and Emmett, she launched into the details, telling them where Lionel's second- and third-degree burns were. His arm, torso, and leg. There would be more than one skin-graft surgery in his future. He'd been admitted to a room in the burn unit with a two-visitor-maximum rule; Gus and Glory were in there with him.

"It's less than fifteen percent of his body, and apparently fifteen percent is the scary number, so that's a relief. He's still knocked out," Zora said, taking a deep breath.

"Oh, wow. Thank You, Jesus," Tallie said.

"My parents are bringing River by later."

"I can hang out with him if you need me to," Tallie said.

"River would love that. You know he's crazy about Auntie Lulah," Zora said before turning to Emmett and adding, "Lionel was asking if you were okay."

"*Me?*" Emmett asked.

Zora nodded. "He worried you'd gotten burned trying to help him."

Tallie touched his elbow and nudged, lifting one of his hands up.

"His hands...a little. He won't let a doctor look at them," Tallie said.

"I'm okay," he said.

"He appreciates what you did for him. We all do," Zora said, tearing up. She stood and hugged Emmett, melting in his arms like sweet powder.

(*Zora is shorter than Tallie, but not by much. They are both taller than Christine was. There is a lot of beeping in a hospital. A lot of announcements. Intercom clicks. Someone calls for Dr. Dorman. Someone's phone chimes; another's whooshes.*)

"He's a good man," Emmett said confidently into Zora's storm of hair. Emmett had known men, both good and bad, who'd made terrible mistakes in their lives, in their marriages. He truly believed

Lionel was one of the good ones. He felt a radiating tenderness toward the women of the world for having to deal with all of it, a tenderness toward Zora as she nodded against his shoulder. "You have a beautiful family," he said.

Zora sniffed and blew her nose. "I hope you're around to meet River."

"I hope so, too," Emmett said.

"Gus and Glory will be back there for a bit. I'll let you know when he wakes up," Zora said.

~

Members of Tallie's family came and went. Outside for fresh air, to the cafeteria for coffee and tea and snacks, or to the canteen area humming with glowing vending machines. Tallie's parents avoided each other. Judith left and returned with her friend Connie, the two of them stepping outside to the benched smoking oasis in the middle of the parking lot, away from the hospital entrance. Tallie's stepmother, Glory, had left to go home and get some rest. Gus sat in the crowded waiting room talking quietly with Tallie's uncle. The TV flashed car and lawyer and medicine commercials, turned down low. The mood was respectful of the hospital and its surroundings, but there was an air of hope and relief within the Clark family, with everyone knowing Lionel's burns weren't life-threatening. Emmett wanted to wait for Lionel to wake up before he left, so he could say goodbye to him and see with his own eyes that he was lucid and okay.

~

The more of Tallie's family Emmett met, the more he felt welcomed by them. He talked and laughed with her dad and uncle; he listened to her mother let out everything that had ever been on her mind.

The more he hung around the hospital, the more he didn't want to leave. And the worse he felt about contacting Joel and keeping up that ruse. The betrayal weighed on him heavier and heavier. Emmett and Tallie had been inseparable since Lionel's party; Emmett hadn't even stepped outside to smoke alone.

~

Emmett and Tallie left the hospital to get chili dogs and apple cider slushies from a fall festival at a nearby church. They lunched on the trunk of her car, under the kind of forever-blue swimming pool sky and orange-gold light only autumn allowed. His brain was still processing what had happened in her bedroom, what it did and didn't mean. But knowing goodbye was coming soon, he kissed her—soft and slow—their slushie-cold mouths warming sweet.

~

"Last night was like our own episode of *X-Files.* So surreal," Tallie said as they walked through the parking lot of the hospital. She tugged at the sleeve of his flannel shirt and stopped him, the afternoon sun glinting off everything like diamonds.

"The entire weekend, really. Even before all this. Woman meets strange man on bridge who could be an alien. Or maybe *she's* the alien?"

"Glitches in the electrical grids."

"Mos def. And not to mention cryptozoology," Emmett said.

Tallie looked confused.

"Well, Bigfoot, of course, and I'm pretty sure I saw a chupacabra, too. Also a fairy and a werewolf. If they spawn, what's that make?" he asked.

Tallie laughed. "A fae-wolf? A were-airy?"

"Wolfairy," he said, lifting his chin and smiling.

"Lovely. And we're *both* the aliens. To be continued...right, Mulder?" she said.

"Definitely to be continued, Scully."

"So...about that...you promise you'll call me? Or text me and let me know you're okay tonight? I know you want to leave, but I'll worry. You know how much I'll worry...and I'd like to see you again," she added with a seriousness that spread to him as he considered the timing of telling her the truth.

"I'd like to see you again, too. I don't want you to worry."

"Come on, seriously, won't you let me take you?"

"You've done enough, and I appreciate it, but I'm a big boy. I can take care of this," he said. He wrapped his arm around her, pulled her in for a hug. "I'll text or call, I promise. You're the one and only person in the world who even has my phone number."

~

Lionel was awake and bandaged. Tallie and Emmett stood next to his bed freshly sanitized, in their burn-unit-mandatory yellow gowns and gloves.

"So glad you're okay, man," Lionel said to Emmett upon seeing him.

"Are you kidding me? I'm so glad *you're* okay. I'm thankful I was able to get to you," Emmett said. Lionel reached out his left hand for Emmett, and he took it, gently. His own hands were still calescent and tender, as if they'd been set on high.

"Thank you. I owe you one. As long as you still want to be my friend now that I'm half monster. A mummy," Lionel said, his laugh stumbling out drowsily and medicated.

"You look great. You really do. You're *impossible* to kill," Tallie said, leaning over and touching his face.

Lionel wanted Emmett to tell him what he'd seen, how it all went down.

"I didn't know what was happening, but the light caught my eye,"

230

Emmett said. "Fire holds such a strange light as it moves...flashes bright. That's how I knew something was wrong."

"I couldn't see much with the mask on. I stepped up too close to the pit. I wasn't even drunk. I'd been nursing the same beer for an hour or more. It was warm," Lionel said.

"I, uh, had to get you on the ground so you wouldn't run. So I knocked your leg out from under you and threw my jacket over you to smother the flames," Emmett said. The *almost* of what could've happened to Lionel rose like a wrecking wave. The haunting flashback took its place in line with the other surrealities he'd suffered through. "It was over quick," he added.

Lionel said something Emmett couldn't make out, so he asked him to repeat it.

"Sweep the leg. Like from *Karate Kid*. That's what you did," Lionel said.

Emmett smiled and quoted the "sweep the leg" line from *Karate Kid* back to him verbatim before adding, "Exactly. That's exactly what I did."

"Emmett, you're officially my new best friend. Lulah, please get his info to me so we can talk again once I'm out of this joint," Lionel said, smiling sleepily. His eyes closed before he winced and showed signs of intense discomfort. Tallie went to get the nurse so he could be given more pain medicine.

(Lionel's eyes open, close again. His mouth is a straight line. He frowns. Half of his mouth lifts in a smile that crinkles his eyes. His bedsheet is white. His blanket is white. The wrapping is white. The walls are white. The nurse comes in, dressed in blue. The morphine drip is clear. Soon Tallie will know everything, and this will be over. Drip. Drip. Drip.)

"Of course. You get some sleep. We'll be around. Well, *I* will. Emmett may be leaving," Tallie said when the nurse was finished. She looked at Lionel, then Emmett. "I love you," Tallie said, gently touching his unbandaged hand.

"Love you, Lulah."

"I'll see you soon, Li," Emmett said, wanting it to be true.

"Looking forward to it. See you soon, brother," Lionel mumbled before turning his head and closing his eyes.

~

In the hallway, Tallie stood with her back against the wall, texting. She smiled at her phone and shook her head, texted more. Probably Nico. Emmett had seen firsthand how Nico looked at Tallie: the same way Emmett looked at the moon. He put his hands in his pockets and waited until she was finished.

"Okay. Hey. Emmett, what if you stayed? You don't *have* to leave. You could stay a little longer. Maybe you need more time. Do you think you need more time?" Tallie asked.

Emmett had found himself hoping she'd ask him to stay, although he knew he wouldn't. Shouldn't. He felt so guilty about being a burden and about what he'd done. He'd been gearing himself up to tell her everything before he left, and he'd put an extra beta-blocker in his pocket just in case. He stepped over and took it with a drink from the water fountain. Now it was finally time to tell her, and he didn't want his heart frenetically tap-dancing when he did it.

But when he looked at Tallie, she was wide-eyed. Thunderstruck. As if she already knew what he was going to say. Her brown cheeks flushed with pink; she pushed her glasses up, and her mouth trembled into a snarl.

"What . . . what the *hell* is he doing here?" she asked over Emmett's shoulder.

Emmett turned to see a man walking down the hallway toward them—a man he half recognized, like someone he'd maybe sat next to on a bus ten years ago.

"It's *Joel*. Joel's here. Why the hell is Joel here?" he heard Tallie say, her breath brushing the flannel on his shoulder. Emmett's blood jumped with chill.

TALLIE

Joel was in front of her wearing clothes she'd never seen before—an expensive-looking graphite-colored sweater and slim pants that matched exactly, as if he'd been assigned a uniform. Wine-red nubuck sneakers. A work of minimalist art, this man who'd once been her sun and moon. His panther-black hair was pulled back with a few escaped curly slips of it hemming his face. She'd obsessively hated those photos of his ponytail, but his hair was glorious in real life, and oh, it annoyed her to no end. He stood there with that body she knew so well and a blue, concerned look on his face. There was a moment when she thought he would attempt to hug her, but he didn't reach out. Instead, he stood close to her, *too* close, as if there'd been no disturbance in the frequency of their previously easy intimacy.

Joel gave Emmett a throwaway glance before refocusing on Tallie and quietly saying hey.

"Joel, what are you doing here?" Tallie said. She could smell him—a comfort and a curse—his cool morning shower ritual and the pricey shampoo that left the taste of tart green apples on her tongue.

"I flew in because I heard about Lionel. Ben texted me," Joel said.

"Is he okay? How badly is he burned? Ben texted me again this morning after he left here, said Lionel was doing better?"

"He's...uh...he's okay."

"Fucking relief. He'll make a full recovery?" Joel asked.

"Correct. Second-degree burns on his arm and torso and a huge third-degree burn on his leg...wait...you flew from Billings this morning? Alone?" Tallie asked.

"Yes. Took about five hours to get here. Delayed a little...it was snowing a *ton*...," Joel said. "Whoa, you got glasses."

Tallie looked at him and nodded, then glanced over at the big digital clock on the hallway wall. Almost evening. Even with the extra hour, the day had scurried away from her like a chipmunk.

"Why?"

"Why what?" Joel asked. Casual.

"*Why* are you here?" Tallie asked, raising her voice.

"Because Ben told me Lionel could die!" Joel scoffed, which made her feel childish and ridiculous for asking the question. "I tried calling you. I tried texting you. I emailed you—"

"Joel, I'm sure Ben was drunk and overreacted. And I blocked your number. I haven't checked my email—"

"Pfft...um, wait. Sorry, sorry, I really have to go to the bathroom. Hold on," Joel said, disappearing down the hall and around the corner.

"I don't know what he's talking about. Ben was probably trashed with his owl girlfriend and had no clue what he was saying! I can't believe he's here," Tallie said to Emmett. She stood there, dumbfounded. "Can you *believe* he'd show up?"

Emmett shook his head stiffly.

"After everything...he flies here and comes to the hospital like we're one big happy family? Wow, I don't know what to say. This is too fucking much."

"Are you all right?" Emmett asked.

"Sure, I guess. But nothing's making sense right now," she said.

Emmett nodded and watched her face. She stared at him, silent, her mind spinning *JoelishereJoelshowedupJoelishereJoelshowedup* around and around like a siren.

She turned when she heard footsteps.

"Okay," Joel said, walking toward them again, his voice lifted in a jolt. "Hey, man," he then said to Emmett, extending his hand.

Tallie watched a blush spread across Emmett's cheeks, lighting him up as if he'd been plugged into a live socket. "Hey," he said, holding out his hands to show Joel he couldn't shake his.

"Joel, Emmett, Emmett, Joel. Emmett helped put the fire out. He burned his hands," Tallie said.

"Oh, wow. Oh," Joel said, taking a look at Emmett's hands before tilting his head at him.

"Joel, you never email me."

"What were you talking about before you went to the bathroom?"

"Um, sure I know we don't email a *lot*, but come on…," Joel began with wide eyes.

"Tallie, can I talk to you for a second alone?" Emmett leaned over and said in her ear.

"Of course. We'll be right back," Tallie said to Joel, loving how good it would feel to walk away from him with another man. Joel took a seat in one of the empty chairs lining that section of the hall- way and pulled out his phone. Tallie and Emmett walked around the corner, where they were alone.

"I'm so sorry. You've been so kind to me. This is my fault Joel is here, and I was going to tell you everything, I swear. I was *just* about to tell you when you saw him," Emmett said. He looked away from her and back again, up at the ceiling, down at the floor. As if he were offstage, too nervous to step out. Was he crying? Tallie's brain swirled.

"Emmett, I don't understand. Slow down. I don't understand any- thing you're saying. How in the world is it *your* fault Joel is here? Trust me, this isn't your fault. What do you mean? Are you feeling okay?" she asked. Was he having another episode? He really ought to look into medication, and she'd tell him that as soon as they got through this part. So much was happening that it was probably shorting him out, sending him into overdrive. It was almost sending her into overdrive, too. Her stomach wobbled like gelatin.

"You took my letters, so I talked to Joel. It was a messed-up thing to do, and I'm sorry," he said.

"Your letters?" Tallie said, searching her mind like she'd searched his pockets on Thursday night. "Okay...right. I...yes...I looked at your letters. I should've said something...Uh, what do you mean you talked to Joel? Talked to Joel how? About what?"

Emmett had talked to Joel? *Emmett had talked to Joel.* The sentence was a cipher, impossible to decode.

Joel rounded the corner wagging his finger at them.

"I *knew* I recognized you, man. You're Rye Kipling. From Bloom. I followed all that shit you went through some years back. The *Southeastern Kentucky News* said you were missing. Why'd she say your name was Emmett? Who's Emmett?" Joel asked, lifting his chin.

His words vaporized, caught in her throat. And now it was Tallie who felt on fire.

RYE

Ryland Miller Kipling was born in 1987 in Bloom, Kentucky, an hour south of Clementine. When he was twenty-three, Rye married Eleanor Christina Bloom in the spring. That same year, Christmas Day, they welcomed their daughter, Briar Anna Kipling, into the world. Briar Anna's hair held the same red-gold-blond as Rye's, and their daughter had Eleanor Christina's brown eyes and Cupid's bow. Rye worked long day shifts that stretched into nights at the restaurant on Lake Bloom in order to pay for their home, the Honeybee House.

When they met, Eleanor told him to call her Christine because she was an actress, and Christine Bloom sounded more old-Hollywood to her. "Like someone they would name a perfume after," she'd said. And once Briar Anna began to talk and say her name—she tried as hard as she could, but no matter what, it came out of her mouth as *Brenna*. So they called her that.

Christine was a bit manic and unpredictable, but Rye had found it alluring, never a problem in the first year of their relationship. He had his own mood swings and weirdness, too, like everyone else. But Christine's mental issues spun out after Brenna's birth. Days turned into full weeks when she wouldn't leave their bedroom. Depressive episodes bled into manic episodes that bled back into depressive episodes that spread into their bedroom again, poured across their hallway floor into the living room and kitchen, onto their lawn. Oil spills slicking everything in their life. She'd been diagnosed with borderline personality disorder and bipolar disorder after having Brenna. Christine told him she'd always felt like she had mental issues, but her parents ignored her, told her she'd grow out of them. The Blooms didn't want mental illness staining their perfect family. They suggested that maybe it was Rye who was making her feel so bad.

Rye accompanied her to the psychiatric appointments, leaving Brenna with his parents for the afternoon. He would go and sit next to Christine on the couch if she wanted or he would stay in the waiting room when she asked, staring at his phone or flipping through new and old issues of *Field & Stream*, *Time*, *People*. Christine would emerge from her dialectical behavior therapy gauzy and backlit with hope. And on they'd go, back home to try again. She'd take her medication and it'd work; she'd hate the numbness and stop. The pattern repeated and repeated, a revolving door of progress and setbacks.

There were strings of days when it seemed as if they could get through this. Together. When necessary, Rye would cook every meal or bring food home from the restaurant, clean the house, take care of Brenna when Christine couldn't. And there were times when Christine, clear and happy, was bright-eyed and attentive to Brenna, asking for help when she needed it. If he was the easy heart, she was the wild one—a big, wild heart with big, wild dreams of being a famous actress and playwright. Christine started working at the local theater again.

Before Brenna, she'd won first place in a playwriting contest for her play about a group of high school students with secret superpowers and had been cast as the local playhouse's first female Hamlet. In the two years preceding getting pregnant, she'd finished highly successful runs as Amy in *Little Women*, Violet in *It's a Wonderful Life*, Emily Webb in *Our Town*, and the title character in *The Prime of Miss Jean Brodie*. After going with Hunter and Savannah to see her in *The Prime of Miss Jean Brodie*, Rye had given Christine two bouquets of daisies and told her she was the crème de la crème.

After they'd begun dating, to help her make some money of her own, Rye had persuaded her to try waitressing at his family's restaurant. She was a terrible waitress. So bad that he had to beg her to quit so his mom wouldn't have to fire her. But she was an outstanding actress. Brilliant and affecting and funny, coming alive onstage in a way she didn't anywhere else.

After Brenna, Rye had encouraged her to start auditioning again. When she scored the role of Maggie the Cat in *Cat on a Hot Tin Roof* at the local theater, he helped her run lines, getting fully into it with her—in the living room, in the kitchen, in the bedroom—reading Brick's parts and Mae's, too, in a whiny, high-pitched southern drawl. They'd collapse together on the floor, wine-buzzed, laughing from too much silliness. Those were the best days after Brenna. When previously safe things like having a glass of wine didn't feel so dangerous anymore. She shouldn't have been drinking on her antidepressants, but they welcomed the small rebellion because it made things feel normalish. And it was settled—Brenna was perfect and would be their only child. When she was two years old, Rye got a vasectomy and was laid up on the couch for a weekend, a nubby bag of frozen peas between his legs.

~

One evening a year later, after a bad morning and a worse afternoon, after a blowout over Christine not eating and not taking her meds, Rye suggested maybe she needed to go for a short stay at the psychiatric hospital. He was willing to try *anything* to calm her anxiety, *anything* to lift her from the concrete fog of depression. The seesaw of Christine's moods and emotions dizzied him completely.

"This will never end. It'll never stop. And I'm so tired," he'd told her.

"*You're* so tired? You? What about me? You want to leave me!" she'd said, her ever-present fear of abandonment snaking around them both like a boa constrictor, squeezing and squeezing.

"Christine, I promise I'm not leaving you. I'll be back. I'm just going for a walk," he'd said, holding her still so she couldn't throw anything else. "Please don't yell. Brenna's sleeping."

She squirmed wildly in his arms like she always did. Kicked, demanded to be let go.

"You want me dead. I'm calling the fucking cops!" she screamed before Rye closed the kitchen window.

~

"No. I'm not missing. It's a mistake," Rye said to Joel in the hospital hallway. "Tallie, I'll explain. If I could talk to you alone for a little bit longer." He was pleading with her, his eyes welling. He didn't want to cry there in front of Joel, in front of everyone. He felt the earth dragging him down and leaned against the wall for balance.

Rye had done this to himself. He was the reason Joel was there, and Joel was the one to out him? It was too stupid to be true. Tallie had her hands up close to her chest. And for all the faces she'd made in the past few days, this was one Rye hadn't seen before. So sad she could burst into tears, so angry she could kill him with her bare hands.

"Yeah...if you could excuse us again that would be...awesome," Rye said to Joel, sniffing.

"Tallie, are you all right? Is everything okay?" Joel asked carefully.

"Joel, please just give us a sec," she said.

Joel looked back and forth between them before saying he'd go find a cup of coffee.

Rye watched Joel disappear and asked Tallie if she'd step outside with him. Out the door at the end of the hallway and down flight after flight of stairs, under the darkening Sunday sky, they would be able to breathe. They wouldn't suffocate under the antiseptic and fluorescence. Outside, they could have a chance.

But in the hallway, Tallie didn't say a word as she began moving toward the door, practically running. Rye had to make a deliberate effort to keep up.

"I can't do this." Her tenuous echo bounced around the stairwell.

"Please let me explain," he said behind her.

"I can't do this," she said again. Going down, down, down, finally shoving the door open at the bottom of the stairs, swapping the artificial stairwell light for the sunset.

"Please. Please hear me out," he said. "There is so much I want to tell you. I created a fake email account and wrote Joel, pretending to be you."

"I...I don't understand. What? When? Why?!"

"I don't have a reason. It was Thursday night. I was drunk when I started it, and it was a stupid, stupid thing to do, and I'm sorrier than I can properly express out here like this. I don't have the words, but I'm trying. I'm literally begging you to forgive me."

"This is scaring me. I don't know who you are," she said, stopping to turn around. She'd walked over to the smoking section; fortunately, they were the only ones there.

"You *do*, though. I opened my heart to you in ways I haven't to anyone in a really long time. You saved my life on that bridge. I lied to you when I said I didn't ask for a sign. I did! I asked for a sign, and the sign was you."

Of course he'd asked for a sign when he was on the bridge:

Dear God, if You're there, if You're real, if I shouldn't do this right now, please have someone stop me. Exit original plan. Enter God and Tallie.

"Then the Giants won the World Series...that was another sign," he said.

"I have no clue what you're talking about. Give me a cigarette," she demanded, holding out her hand.

Rye did as he was told, shaking a cigarette from the pack in his pocket and handing her his lighter, too.

(Tallie lights it, smokes, begins pacing. Back and forth and back and forth and back and forth. She's wearing the same sweater she wore to the outlet mall on Friday; she knit it herself. It smells like her house.)

"Please look at me for a second so I can talk to you?"

"Why should I do anything you ask me to do?" she said. Her eyes searched the parking lot. Was she looking for security? Someone to help her? It crushed him, thinking she was afraid of him.

"Tallie, please. I don't want you to be afraid. I'm going to tell you the truth," he said gently. "The only reason I didn't tell you earlier is because I didn't want you feeling sorry for me...googling me and then...acting differently toward me. Once people find out, it changes everything. *Everything.*"

Tallie stepped away from him.

"I really don't understand anything you're saying! This is all so cryptic...I...once people find out *what*?"

"First, I want you to know I didn't do it to *hurt* you. Just to even out the invasion of privacy. I regretted it immediately, but Joel wrote me back, and I thought..."

He would tell her everything, leaving out the part about Lionel finding out about Joel's affair during their last round of IVF and the part about Lionel cheating on Zora. A lot had happened over the weekend, but Rye knew when to keep his mouth shut. He'd take that shit to the grave as a common courtesy. He considered deleting those parts from the email, showing Tallie the rest. Tallie smoked and used her thumb to wipe the tears that spilled from the corners of her eyes.

(Tallie's nose is hot pink again. As the sun goes down, the sky is hot pink, too.)

"What? What invasion of privacy?"

"My letters."

"Wow. I ... wow!"

"They were private, they were mine, and you took them," he said, trying his best to keep his voice from shaking.

"Okay! I shouldn't have done that! But what the hell? You did something this huge because I took your letters?"

"It just ... set everything off, that's all."

"And so you thought, what? I'm so desperate I need a stranger to talk to my ex-husband for me? Did you tell Joel to come here?" Tallie asked. He could feel the energy of her anger rising, pressing against him.

"No—"

"Tell me your real name. Who are you?"

"Ryland Miller Kipling."

"Who's Emmett Aaron Baker?"

"Nobody. I made him up. I'm from Bloom, not Clementine. They're close to each other—"

"What shit did you go through? What's Joel talking about?"

"That's what I want to tell you—"

"Who's Brenna?"

"Is this where you apologize for sneaking the letters from my pockets and reading them?"

"Uh-huh, yeah. I'm sorry about that, but this is a disproportionate response, and you know it. An overreaction, which may be normal for you. I don't know. One of the letters wasn't even finished. The one to Brenna. *Who* is Brenna?"

"Because I forgive you, by the way. I'm not angry with you. I understand why you would think to do that," Rye said.

"Em—Ryland, Rye...whatever. Answer the question or get out of here."

Rye's bottom lip wobbled at how easily she could be rid of him, how easily he could be rid of himself. He blinked and clawed himself from the edge.

"Brenna is my daughter," he said slowly.

"Great. Awesome. So you lied about that, too! You said you didn't have kids!" Tallie spat out.

"I didn't lie. I don't have a kid. Those butterfly wings in my backpack, they were for Halloween three years ago, but I couldn't give them to her because..." He stopped. What he was about to say made his tongue feel as if it were someone else's, even still. "Because...Brenna's dead."

~

All the fighting with Christine—the word *tired* didn't do it justice. He was *exhausted*.

Weary.

Weary enough in their kitchen to loosen his grip on Christine and let her go after she'd threatened to call the cops. He'd turned his phone off, put it on the nightstand. Left in the middle of their row, wandered like a new Adam whom God had left alone without instruction. He went for a long walk through the October evening, first heading down the muddy path leading to the forest behind their house. He walked, breaking through the hedges and continuing onto the sidewalk next to the road that led the truck factory workers to and from the warehouse. He walked and walked and walked, thinking of the reasons he'd fallen in love with Christine, the memories and hope for the future that kept them stuck together. Thinking about how Brenna was such a glowing orb between them, proof of life and light. But Christine needed to take her meds. Had to. He couldn't do this on his own; he needed breaks sometimes, too. He had to stop feeling guilty about it. He was going to tell her that gently when he got back, and eventually, when the dust had settled, he'd have to tell her sternly.

Rye walked, turning around only when the light ended. When he returned to the house, it was full dark and the garage door was closed. Had Christine closed it? Had he? When? And what was that sound? Was the car running? Why was the car running? Had he left the car running? How long had he disappeared to the sky and leaves?

Eleanor Christina, his Ophelia.

He'd snatched the garage door up and choked, realizing. Held his jacket collar over his face and opened the car door, reached across a slumped Christine and turned the engine off. He said her name, couldn't stop saying it. He hollered for Brenna. He hollered for help. And then again. He looked up to see his neighbor holding his phone in the driveway, asking what else he could do. Rye ran inside the house, calling for Brenna. Silence.

And then.

He found her in her bed—tender as a kitten, still and pale and breathless. He covered his crying mouth and sputtered out carrying her. Their Briar Anna, limp and cooling in her nightgown as he gently placed her—and the fleece she was wrapped in—onto the leaves and front grass. He carried Christine's lissome body, placed it beside Brenna's. Desperately choked and coughed and attempted CPR on them. The lights swirled through the eternity-black doom as first responders showed up to help. Christine and Brenna were incontrovertibly beyond. Gone, gone, gone. Christine, who should've lived well past twenty-six; Brenna, who should've outlived him, who would never grow older than three.

The EMTs had to pull him away from them. He was on his hands and knees, sobbing as the rest of the neighbors peeked through their curtains and stepped out into the moonlight.

Eleanor Christina, his Bertha Mason, his wild one in the garage, not the attic. Eleanor Christina, his Sylvia Plath, who forgot the courtesy of sealing off the children's door. Eleanor Christina, his Medea per accidens.

~

Rye talked. Tallie listened, finished her cigarette, kept crying and sniffing. "How do I know any of this is true?" she asked.

"Look it up," Rye said. And Tallie sat on the bench, pulled out her phone with trembling fingers. "R-y-l-a-n-d. K-i-p-l-i-n-g."

Tallie typed and scrolled as Rye lit his own smoke. He sat on the far end of the bench, staring at his boots.

"You were arrested for this? You went to prison for this? Because they thought you killed your wife and daughter?" Tallie asked after a moment of quiet reading. She looked up at him, her deep brown eyes wide and wet under the dusk.

~

At the police station, his story never changed because it was the truth. Rye had told them he'd left Brenna, asleep for the night, in her bedroom—her lavender lamp shade casting light onto the plush orange rug beneath, the gentle chime of her music box still paling the air. He'd walked past her room on the way to their bedroom to get his socks. He'd looked in on her on the way to the front door, where his boots sat waiting. Christine had followed him stomping, and he'd asked her to be quiet again, reminded her Brenna was sleeping. He told Christine he was leaving. He was tired and angry and needed fresh air. He'd gone, just like that, not turning around to look back at the Honeybee House.

And although he didn't say it aloud at the police station, it was something he knew he'd never forgive himself for. Leaving. He should've stayed. He shouldn't have left Christine alone. He shouldn't have left Brenna in that house with Christine so upset.

"She didn't kill Brenna on purpose. Christine was terrible at science. It annoyed her. She had no idea the carbon monoxide could kill Brenna, asleep in the house." Rye had cried when he'd repeated it to the officers in that little room—one of them Christine's cousin.

Bloom, forever swollen with Blooms.

Rye had defended Christine, explaining she was sick but hid it exceptionally well. She hadn't meant to kill Brenna, and he knew that. He never believed she'd *intentionally* kill Brenna.

~

He'd gone to his parents' house, planned funerals, and picked out what to bury his wife and daughter in. Christine: the pale peach dress she'd worn the day they'd gotten married. Brenna: a white Easter dress that had been too big for her in the spring. Rye put on the new suit his mother had gone out and bought for him since he couldn't bring himself to do it. He'd sat there in the front row of the church, staring straight ahead at Christine's full-size casket; Brenna's small one, mercifully blurred in his periphery.

The autopsy reports had shown that Christine and Brenna had both died of asphyxia from carbon monoxide poisoning. There were also alprazolam, clonazepam, and fluoxetine in Christine's system along with alcohol, but the potentially deadly mix of benzodiazepines was, in the end, unnecessary.

Rye knew exactly what had happened when he'd left the house. Annoyed by how much he'd been pushing her to take her meds, Christine had taken them and taken them and taken them, ferrying the pills down her throat on a warm river of red wine before going to the garage.

Manic.

Overkill.

When the autopsy report was released, Rye was arrested, shocked and numb. Still desperately grieving and barely hanging on. The police accused him of drugging Christine, staging her suicide, killing their daughter.

His and Christine's shared laptop had been seized, revealing a damaging Google search for the mix of drugs and wine and *carbon monoxide poisoning* more than a month before. And more searches for *carbon monoxide car garage* and *carbon monoxide death suicide*, *peaceful suicide*, as well as a short video clip from *The Virgin Suicides* in which one of the characters kills herself in the same manner as Christine.

The town of Bloom was rattled, split right down the middle as to whether he was guilty.

~

Rye told Tallie about Miller's, the lake restaurant. How his family had owned it, but not anymore. He told her about falling in love with Christine there and how he'd cooked in the prison cafeteria, because yes, he'd been sentenced to life without parole for the deaths of his wife and daughter. But then his parents had received a phone call from Yolanda Monroe, an attorney from Release, an organization committed to proving the innocence of the wrongfully accused. Yolanda was the daughter of a longtime Miller's patron and had contacted them after hearing Rye's story from her father. She'd been involved in one other suicide-mistaken-for-murder case and told Rye's parents she couldn't get him off her mind. Her obsession turned into Rye's light.

~

Bloom had been named after Christine's family, and they'd worked hard to put Rye away for life. They'd refused to listen to him before, when he'd told them Christine needed help. Things had been bad *before* Brenna, and they'd gotten altogether worse *after*. But

Christine was reticent with almost everyone in her life besides Rye and Savannah. Christine was an actress, onstage and off, and when she was around her family, she played the role of happy new mother, laughing off any concerns that she was spiraling or overwhelmed. Rye stopped covering the extra shifts to stay home with Christine, to watch over her, to keep an extra pair of eyes on Brenna. And Rye's parents had been helpful, stepping in to babysit and loaning them money whenever they could, even when Rye refused. He'd return home to a pack of cigarettes behind the screen door (his dad's calling card) along with a check or cash.

Christine's family pushed forward as if they *truly* believed Rye could be cruel, heartless, and evil enough to kill his family, then attempt to fake Christine's suicide and Brenna's accidental death. How could they? They'd seen how much he'd loved and taken care of Christine and Brenna. They knew little of him, because they hadn't tried, but how could they believe he would do something like that?

Her family was completely devastated with no one to blame but him. They'd softened a bit after Brenna was born, because they found her impossible *not* to love—this beautiful Bloom baby. But they still hated Rye and Christine together. They hated both sides of Rye's family. They'd gotten their own psychiatrist to claim that Christine's diagnoses had been the result of temporary youthful problems and that she'd soon grow out of them. They'd told the jury she'd been getting better, using two old entries from her seldom-kept journal to prove her flickers of hope.

The sun is shining and I feel a lift somewhere deep inside. I am in love and I am loved. I need to remember this.

Today was good! Only a few dark thoughts! I am trying. Excited about auditions and the small, precious things of the world. I saw a butterfly and two bright yellow birds hanging out in the backyard. They matched the Honeybee House. Yellow makes me so happy and SUNSHINE Baby Briar and Rye do too. I wish everything was yellow.

Her mother, her father, her brothers—red-faced and crying—took the stand against Rye during his trial, glaring at him. He couldn't look directly at them; every time he attempted to look up, to hold his head there, the room spun. His neighbors testified that although he was quiet and they didn't know him well, Rye seemed like a decent guy. They testified that they saw him immediately after he found Christine's and Brenna's bodies. A neighbor remembered hearing a hush of leaves shortly before, like someone was walking back home through the yard. Another neighbor said she'd been out walking her dogs and had heard a woman scream the day Christine and Brenna died, but it hadn't worried her until she'd found out what'd happened. Then she remembered that years earlier, night after night, she'd also heard loud arguments coming from their home. Rye knew what those had been: he and Christine, pretending. Running lines from *Cat on a Hot Tin Roof*.

~

Rye fought hard to take the stand and did, against his attorney's wishes. But his attorney assured him that even though the Bloom family had pull in the town named after them, it was still highly unlikely Rye would get convicted on such a lack of evidence.

He looked out at his family. Hunter and Savannah, by then Hunter's wife, were there, too; both of them knew Christine well and believed in him. He could see everyone's stony, sad faces as he answered the questions truthfully, like he'd sworn to God he'd do.

Did he and Christine argue that afternoon? Yes.

Did he and Christine argue often? Yes.

Was he upset by the problems in their marriage? Yes.

Had he ever considered separating? No.

Had he and Christine argued the evening in question? Yes.

Had he turned his phone off that evening, left it at home? Yes.

Had he used their shared computer to research carbon monoxide poisoning? No.

Had he researched fatal drug interactions? No.

Had he drugged Christine, put her in the car, and started the engine before leaving the house? No.

Had he intended to kill his daughter, too, then stage it to look like an accident? No.

Had he killed his wife and daughter out of frustration and because of financial issues? No.

Had he killed his wife and daughter because he'd accidentally gotten her pregnant and felt trapped and rushed into marriage? No.

Did he have life insurance policies on his wife and daughter? Yes.

When had he gotten those? Years ago, when they were first married.

Did he kill his wife and daughter for the life insurance money? No.

Had he killed his wife? No.

Had he killed his daughter? No.

Christine's mom wailed in the courtroom. Christine's dad rubbed her back. His own father was there with his arm around his mother's shoulders as she cried and wiped her eyes. Rye tried not to shake as he cried on the stand.

No. I did not kill my family. I loved my family. I still love my family. I didn't do this. I would never do this, he said after willing himself to take deep breaths and open his eyes.

No more questions, Your Honor.

The extent of his criminal record prior to the trial:

—When he was sixteen, he was busted for underage drinking, loitering, and toilet-papering houses.

—When he was twenty-one, he was arrested during a bar fight, although the charges were later dropped.

In a little town like Bloom, being a quarter black meant being not-white meant being one hundred percent black meant being an Other. A threat to white supremacy. A blight, a usurper. It was what they'd all feared. And Christine wasn't just any white woman; she was a *Bloom*. That was all the evidence that particular jury needed.

Rye was found guilty of two counts of first-degree murder. On the day of sentencing he stood in that small-town courthouse, in front of the seven white women and five white men who had convicted him, maintaining his innocence.

I loved my family deeply. More deeply than anything else I've ever felt. More deeply than the emptiness of the grief I feel now. And I would never harm them. I grieve for Christine's family, for my family. I am so sorry I wasn't there for my family in their final moments. That will haunt me forever. All this will haunt me forever.

He was sent to a maximum-security prison a hundred miles away.

~

There he wrote letters to his parents, and they visited him. So did Hunter and Savannah before they moved to Montana. After that, he and Hunter wrote each other letters, too. Rye read the art history books in the prison library obsessively, disappearing into them, memorizing everything, a deep love ripening. He went to some of the smaller therapy groups and the church meetings and formed a close relationship with one of the preachers, talked to him about Jesus.

His life had turned into some sort of nightmared misunderstanding. Daring to hope was the only thing that'd kept him alive in there. He tried to stay out of trouble when he was locked up. Kept to himself the best he could, was friendly with the guys he could be friendly with. Was nasty to the ones he knew wouldn't respect him otherwise.

~

(The prison guard is wearing different shoes today. No longer scuffed. He said fucking piece of shit today instead of piece of shit. Modified it. Cell mate

is sick. Stomach flu. Today he told me he believed me, that I didn't do this. He told me he was guilty; he killed a man. The sun was out, the air was cold. One hour went quickly. A fight in the cafeteria. Again. The alarm. Again. Meat loaf, potatoes, rolls. Made the potatoes. Good potatoes.)

Rye's obsessive mental cataloging helped him organize a world that no longer made sense. He talked to himself about what he saw and heard and smelled and thought, as if he were a playwright like Christine, forever setting the scene. It was how he kept himself from going mad.

(Never getting out. Making a life here. The walls are pale green. The toilet is stainless steel like a fork. Like a spoon. Like a knife. The clear water in it is low. People shit in front of other people here. Making a life here. There is too much life here. Trapped. There is no life here. The sunlight makes it onto the cold floor in the big room. Slit-up light. I am recording these observations to keep from going insane. I am recording these observations to protect my mental health. I am noticing everything I can to busy my mind, to help myself cope. I am recording these observations to keep from going insane. I am recording these observations to protect my mental health. I am noticing everything I can to busy my mind, to help myself cope. I am recording these observations to keep from going insane. I am recording these observations to protect my mental health. I am noticing everything I can to busy my mind, to help myself cope.)

~

His attorney had mentioned appealing immediately after his trial, but that was what attorneys always said. Rye's parents were righteously heartbroken and infuriated, claiming not only that his counsel had blown the case but that the police had botched it, too. He should've never been arrested on so little evidence. His parents sold the restaurant to cover Rye's sky-high legal fees and spoke with the media often. They worked tirelessly with the Release program. Never gave up.

~

Yolanda Monroe, along with Rye's additional new attorney, argued that his trial was unfair since the jury was biased in Bloom because of the pull and power of the Bloom family. There was no hard evidence Rye had done it, and there had been recently discovered video evidence that supported his alibi—grainy footage from two different security cameras of him walking and wearing what he'd said he'd been wearing. It was proof he'd been out walking for at least two hours before Christine and Brenna died and that he was still walking during their estimated times of death, miles and miles away from their home. Prior to his trial, Rye had begged his old attorney to hunt down video, but he'd been told they didn't need it.

With the help of Release, he was exonerated after it was found that no crime had been committed. Six hundred and ninety-four days after being incarcerated, he was freed.

~

Rye had returned to his hometown, where his wife and daughter were buried next to each other, where the lake restaurant was owned by a new family, where half the people suspected him of murder. He'd let his parents sell the Honeybee House when he was in prison, moved in with them when he got out. He endured the hateful looks and hollers from the people who'd—no matter the evidence—never believe he was innocent. He tried to live there, got a job doing heavy construction working with Hunter's brother. Demolition. Worked extra shifts to keep himself sore and exhausted, because if he was sore and exhausted, life would feel like punishment, and he deserved to be punished forever for walking away from Christine and Brenna.

~

Once he made the decision to end his life, the obsessive observing was like burning everything in a glass jar before he said goodbye. And although suicide had crossed his mind a lot in prison, it wasn't until he got out that he'd realized his freedom hadn't been the answer. He still didn't know what the answer was. Hell, he didn't even know what the question was anymore.

A day before he met Tallie on the bridge, he'd called Hunter, who was executive chef at a ranch restaurant in Big Sky now. He and Savannah had recently had a baby girl, and Hunter had told Rye he wanted to keep a respectful distance because he knew how devastating it would be for Rye to see Hunter and Savannah and their baby girl when Rye no longer had his wife and baby girl there with him. Rye told him he wanted to hear about their daughter and meant it when he said he was happy for them, that they'd be amazing parents.

When he talked to Hunter, he thought it'd be the last time. Tried his best to keep his voice even when he told Hunter to tell Savannah hi and he hoped to see them soon, the next time they left Montana for Kentucky—Christmastime. Instead, Rye pictured them flying in with their baby for his funeral once his body was found, *if* it was found. And he hated himself for having to do that to them— kill himself and bring more darkness into their lives when they'd recently been warmed by so much light.

He'd called his parents and talked to them like normal, too, neither of them asking where he was or what he was doing, because he was a grown man. He told his parents he loved them. Got off the phone, ditched it for his new one, and cried privately before hitching to Sugar Maple, a town seventy-five miles away from Bloom. He'd sold his truck a week before, lying to his parents and saying he was on the hunt for a new one.

Rye caught rides with two more truckers before making it to Louisville and walking aimlessly. Louisville because Christine and Brenna loved the Louisville Zoo, especially the baby elephant. They came as a family to visit at least once a season. And he'd thrown that money in his backpack because when he was released from prison, people had given him the money they'd raised for him when he was inside. There was more of the money; he'd left it at his parents' place, and his suicide letter would've told them exactly where, once they received it in the mail.

He had prayed for life to give him a break. He had prayed for God to give him a sign. He had thought *All this will haunt me forever* before he climbed up on the bridge on Thursday, praying. He didn't want to die, but he had no other option. It was the only way. How else could he make it all stop?

TALLIE

Tallie couldn't help but cry, seeing photos of Christine and Brenna for the first time, photos of Rye with them. His *Eleanor Christina* and *Briar Anna*. Christine was bright-eyed and so cheerleader-pretty that she looked as if nothing bad could ever happen to her. Brenna had Rye's hair, the same splash of cinnamon freckles. She was so small and alive in the photos—in one of them, holding both hands straight up in the air, with her mouth wide open in squeal. Tallie stared at it, half waiting for the picture to make a sound. One of the websites offered a link to the audio of the 911 call Rye's neighbor made, and Tallie caught her breath. Closed that tab on her phone as quickly as she could before it played.

Rye sat and then stood while Tallie looked at his mug shot: a T-shirt the color of peas, his eyes weary, his mouth an arrow. A photo taken the Christmas before Christine and Brenna died: the three of them laughing, wearing antlers on their heads and ugly Christmas sweaters, Brenna on Rye's hip, Christine with her hand on his stomach, looking up at him. A family portrait: Rye playfully smushed between his strawberry-blond mother and his dark-haired father, a wide oak tree flush with green behind them. She stepped away and smoked as she flicked through article after article, photo after photo of his life before she met him.

A kaleidoscope of contradicting feelings spun in her heart, the colored glass of it shattering and revealing a new emotion with every turn. Rye was a wet petal, still grief-stricken and tender; Rye had betrayed her trust and gotten himself involved with Joel out of pettiness. Rye's story was true, and she had pages and pages of news articles and YouTube videos to prove it; Rye had stayed with her in her home and lied about who he was. Rye was gentle and sweet to her at all times, especially when they'd been in her bed together; when they were in her bed together, it was twinned loneliness and she was worried about her brother, dizzied and desperate for a sexual connection and release to numb her.

Rye had saved Lionel.

She felt sorry for Rye; how could she not?

He may have lied about who he was without her picking up on it, but the core of her instincts had been right. She didn't believe he'd killed his wife and daughter, and some would call her a fool, but she didn't doubt her ability to read people's energies just because she didn't pick up Joel's *cheating husband* energy as quickly as she could've. She'd been wrong about Joel, but she'd never been wrong about pure evil.

Rye was a lot of things, a lot of things she couldn't know yet, but he wasn't a sociopath or a murderer. She'd read about Christine's autopsy, the drugs she'd had in her system, her history of mental illness. She'd watched a ten-minute video of an episode of a crime show he'd pulled up on YouTube, a team of attorneys explaining how he couldn't have done it. The video had half a million views.

Diagnoses: Acute grief from the deaths of his wife and young daughter three years ago. Survivor's guilt. PTSD from being accused and convicted of their deaths and subsequently falsely imprisoned.

~

"This is all so gut-wrenching, and I'm sorry...I'm just so sorry you've had to deal with this," Tallie said. "Did you tell the cop who pulled us over who you really were?"

"Yes. And he recognized my name immediately. Googled me as I sat in his patrol car, and he got the same pitiful sorrow in his eyes everyone gets when they hear the story."

Tallie changed the expression on her face, careful to not have those pitiful-sorrow eyes when she asked him, "Weren't you worried someone would recognize you when we were at the party? The unicorn...my friend who thought you looked familiar? Did anyone say anything?"

Rye shook his head. "No one said anything, but there were a couple of times this weekend when people looked at me too long. In the pub...and an older woman stopped me in the grocery store. It's usually older people. Old people love the news. Li said something about me looking familiar, though. And I thought your mom definitely recognized me when she came over. I thought your neighbor did, too. She looked at me weird."

"Well...just so you know, my neighbor looks at everyone weird," Tallie said.

"Noted," Rye said.

After a moment he launched into why the letters were so impor- tant to him. He told her he got rid of everything else that belonged to Christine and Brenna except the wedding ring and those butterfly wings. And that the letters, although simple and, in Brenna's case, unfinished, were his first attempts at sharing the part of his heart that had gone mute. He hated that he couldn't even bring himself to finish Brenna's letter, and the letter he'd written to Christine embarrassed him because it didn't say enough. How could it? No matter how hard he tried, he couldn't get it right. Like he'd failed her all over again.

"I know they didn't seem important, but I'd never even tried to write Brenna a letter before. And I'd started letters to Christine in the past, but that was the first one I'd been able to finish... if it's even finished... I don't know." He paused and looked up before continuing. "The letters aren't the same thing at all, but just in general... I'm tired of people going behind my back and reading shit about me and knowing everything or *thinking* they know everything. I didn't even get to tell you their names myself. You saw them first," he said.

"I'm sorry I read them," she said, attempting to fully understand his frustration as well as she knew her own.

"Well... I overreacted."

"Tell the truth: Did you really send your parents that suicide letter?"

"Yes," he said. "I'm being honest with you about everything now."

He kept talking. Told her where the money had come from. Told her he took antidepressants for about a month years ago and hated them. Told her he didn't even smoke weed anymore. He was prescribed the beta-blockers after everything because he thought his adrenaline would never let off turbo-boost.

Tallie smoked another cigarette and another with Rye as she listened to him. She had to force herself to think of him as *Rye*, and she'd gone from angry to sad to frustrated, braiding those emotions into one thick mess, only stopping when she fell into the habit she was so used to. What she got paid hundreds of dollars by the hour to do: To be a therapist. To listen. To ask the right questions. To listen and ask the right questions some more.

~

Tallie would've rallied and protested for Rye's release if she'd lived in that town. She pictured herself staying up late, squeaking a black marker across white poster board. *#FreeRyeKipling.* Rye was arrested and tried because of racism. She could only imagine how hard it'd been for him, growing up in a little, mostly white town like Bloom, marrying and having a baby with the town princess like that.

~

"As far as honesty goes...I wouldn't believe any of this if I hadn't read it myself," Tallie said to him, holding up her phone in the owl-light. The sky was lowering. She focused on the two pretty nurses—one zaftig, one skin and bones—sitting on a bench on the other side, smoking and speaking quietly in their cartoon-printed scrubs. A ring of white lights encircled them, like little moons. "I mean, obviously I understand why this would've sent you to the bridge," she said, understanding fully now why he'd been so calm about Lionel catching fire. When he'd seen all he'd seen, what could possibly shock him?

"Thursday was my birthday," he said, looking up. Four words revealing yet another cavernous truth.

"You were going to jump on your birthday."

"Christine and Brenna...it was October. Even the sound of the fallen leaves reminds me of them. I can't escape."

"I can't even imagine how unbearable it seems...how hard October is for you," she said, falling into her rhythm of repetition again, signaling to her clients that she heard them. Rye's eyes were red in the whites, rimmed with violent pink.

"I told myself if I could feel better, after being out of prison for a year...back in the world...I'd stick around. But this week came, my birthday came, and I didn't feel better. Every day I had to look for a new reason to stay alive, and it became more and more difficult to find one." He paused and took a tender breath in. He told her his parents had tried so hard to help, but he'd been completely closed off. They didn't know what else to do, and neither did he. "I thought grief would kill me, and I wanted it to, but spending time with you...being there to help Lionel out...this weekend happened."

"Well, I'm listening, and I hear you," Tallie said.

"I had no clue what I needed, and you helped me—"

"But I still don't understand what you talking to my ex-husband has to do with all this," she said, aggressively fizzing out the *s* sounds so he couldn't be mistaken about how she was feeling.

"It doesn't. I have no excuse. It was a stupid thing, and it got out of hand—"

"What did you say to Joel?" she asked.

Rye talked, told her about the emails and Joel's replies. He told her about telling Joel she was considering adopting a baby and that she had a boyfriend, too. She scratched at her neck, which had become unbearably itchy, and before she could open her mouth to say anything, he apologized again.

"I betrayed you, thinking I knew what you needed after only knowing you for a couple of hours, and I'm a total asshole for it."

"Correct," she said, scratching, wishing he could feel it, too. "And who was this supposed boyfriend?"

Rye looked at her.

"You?"

He didn't say anything.

"Rye—"

"I'm so sorry."

"So you told him everything. All the stuff I told you, when I thought we were getting to know each other, the things I didn't want him to know. The things I could've told him myself but didn't want to," she said, nodding angrily.

"What he has with her...he always thought it'd be you. *Wanted* it to be you," Rye said.

"He said that, even now, after everything?" Tallie sniffed and wiped her nose with an old tissue she found at the bottom of her purse. She smelled the dirty musk of tobacco on her fingers, and it nauseated her. What the hell had she been thinking? How had she lost control all weekend? She'd never smoke again. Never.

Before she could stop him, Rye began reading to her from his screen. Joel's emails, spilling his heart. She listened to the words of a kinder, less defensive Joel. A contrite Joel.

"He thought he was talking to you, finally being able to tell you these things. I was going to send you these emails when I left. I thought they'd make you feel better," Rye said when he was finished. "I told him men need to get better at taking care of the women they claim to love so much, and I said it to myself, too, about Christine. But it was arrogant of me to assume you wanted what I didn't get. I mean, like...closure."

"Look, I had closure in my own way with Joel. And I'm incredibly angry with you right now, but from what I've just read and from what I've seen in you...all I'm saying is it's not your fault if someone you love is mentally ill. Sometimes there's nothing any of us can do. And that's the most terrifying thing about it all," she said.

After some quiet Tallie asked, "What email address did you use?"

"TallieCat007."

A birdlike squawk of a laugh shot from Tallie's mouth, taking her by surprise. She wiped her eyes.

"I made it that first night. I was drunk on wine, and you were in your bedroom. Joel kept responding, grateful you'd reached out," Rye said.

"Grateful *you'd* reached out," Tallie corrected him sharply. "And you did it...knowing I'd hate you once I found out—"

"*Do* you hate me?" he asked. "I understand if you do."

"I don't know, Rye. I introduced you to my *entire family* as Emmett. You met my neighbor! I'm so embarrassed about this. I look like an idiot."

"No. You could never look like an idiot. Don't take the blame for something that's not your fault. Isn't that what you'd tell me?"

"Oh, I'm doing exactly that. I'm going to tell Joel I knew about it. I'll apologize, and it'll be over and he'll go home," Tallie said. No way would she let Joel know this happened behind her back.

"You don't have to. I'll man up and apologize."

"No, you won't. I'll take care of this," she said, imagining Joel up there, moving behind the stone and glass of the hospital.

~

"Yeah, so were . . . were you pretending everything this weekend?"

"No, Tallie. I wasn't pretending everything this weekend."

~

Rye followed Tallie into the stairwell heading to the burn unit. She hadn't asked him to, and she hadn't turned around to look at him until she stepped back and stood next to the fire extinguisher in the glass box on the wall.

"Listen. That was a big deal for me . . . what we did together. Letting you come into my bedroom. I don't do that. I've never done that before with someone I'd just met . . . with someone I wasn't in a relationship with," Tallie confessed. Flashes of him with his mouth all over her in her bedroom lit across her brain. Equal parts guilt and shame and excitement. Seeing his naked body—not so unlike her beloved *David*—smelling it, tasting it.

"Tallie, it was a big deal for me, too. Seriously," Rye said, touching his chest with one of his bandaged hands.

"I didn't even know your real name then. I didn't even know who you were. You could've told me, and I would've been fine with it. I just wish you'd told me," she said. The hypocrisy of what she was saying thick in her throat as Rye reached out for her. "Don't—" she said, turning away and opening the door to the hallway. Dazed, she went to the bathroom to hold a cool, wet paper towel to the back of her neck.

~

"Joel, can I talk to you?" Tallie said when she found him. She stood over him, sitting in the hallway, scrolling through his phone.

"I just talked to your dad . . . that was interesting. I mean, he obviously didn't kill me, but he said I was the last person he expected to see here. I told him I'll never stop caring about your family or you," Joel said.

"Did you see Lionel?"

"Yeah. I talked to him and Zora. Your dad left, but he'll be back with Glory. And your mom and Connie stepped out, too. Your mom told me I was still an asshole, by the way. She told me if I came here to break your heart some more, I can go to hell. So good to know she hasn't changed. And River's gotten so big, I—" Joel said, stopping himself. Joel, knowing so much about her family, knowing the name of her mom's best friend, and remarking on how much River had grown in the past year made her blood itch. She felt faint, but she'd never fainted. The dizziness would simply pass like it always did, without taking her with it. Joel looked at Rye, neither of them saying anything.

"If I could just talk to you over here," Tallie said, refocusing.

Rye took Joel's seat when he got up, and part of her worried that Rye would bolt, even though he'd promised not to leave without telling her first. Did that still count? She looked back at him before she walked around the corner with Joel.

~

"Here's good," Tallie said as Joel sat in another one of the chairs in the hallway. She skipped a chair and sat, leaving a block of space between them that may as well have been a million miles. "Joel, the emails were a prank. Immature. And I'm sorry. Rye was drunk and joked about emailing you, pretending to be me. And once I found out he'd done it, I didn't stop him. It was stupid, and it got out of hand." She stared at her ex-husband, shaking her head. "I can't even believe you're here. And don't get me wrong. It's kind of you. I believe you came here out of the *kindness* of your heart because I know how much you love Lionel—"

"A prank? You hate pranks," Joel said, guffawing. "You're serious?" he said after examining her face for what felt like a full minute.

"I'm serious and I'm sorry. It was so stupid," she said.

"Wait. What did you get out of this?"

"I had some questions . . . and you answered them."

"Why didn't you ask me yourself? Why'd you get this guy to do it? I'm so confused right now," Joel said.

"He was pissed after I'd told him what had happened between us, and I let him speak for me because he was able to do it without holding back. Writing you myself would feel so serious and *involved*—"

"This guy was all over the news years ago. Some really awful shit. He could be a total lunatic with what he's been through. Therapy or not, you purposely surround yourself with crazy people who suck you dry, Tallulah," he said.

"He's not a *lunatic*. You think I surround myself with crazy people, which is a horrible thing to say, by the way, and I think you're always out there looking for the next new thing. New job, new state, new wife . . . everything is fine until you get bored, right? Nothing can ever be good enough for you!"

"That's not true," Joel said softly, shaking his head. Tallie had hurt him, and she was only a little sorry about it.

"Joel, I'm not arguing with you here like this. I need to move on." She put her hands out toward him, pushed that energy back. He could keep it. She wasn't his wife anymore; he was no longer her problem.

"Yeah . . . you need to move on, but you still log in to my Facebook account. Aha. Understood," he said. His tone, their fights, the way he stayed ready to jump in with full force—all of it rushed at her and would've knocked her down had she not been sitting.

"You were perfectly fine taking the time to email me, Joel, when you could've been hanging out with your wife and baby," Tallie said.

"Oh, wow. Are you accusing me of being neglectful?"

"Think about it. Do you really want to ask me that question?"

"Are you accusing me of being inappropriate? There was *nothing* inappropriate in those emails," Joel said.

"I'm not accusing you of anything anymore, Joel. We're well past that."

"Good, because you and your boyfriend—"

"Look, quit it. I don't know how serious it is. I still see Nico sometimes, too. Wait. This is none of your business! Why am I telling you these things?" she said, feeling wildly protective of Nico. She sure as hell didn't want to talk to Joel about Nico. Nico was hers, and she didn't want Joel attempting to darken any part of him in her heart.

"Imagine that. Nicodemus Tate. Well, that's where you wanted to be all along, right? Good for you, coming full circle," Joel said, frowning and nodding.

"Oh, fuck off, Joel. You had your midlife crisis, and now you have your baby, so give it a rest! You have no right—"

"I just didn't think you'd accuse me of being inappropriate when you're sleeping with one of your *patients*, because that's highly inappropriate, not to mention you're ruining your career," Joel spat out. Tallie was looking down.

And when she looked up, Rye was standing there with the word *patients* hovering above him before it froze him where he stood. A whirling riot of honesty stole her breath.

RYE

Patients?

"Yep. Right. I'm one of her *patients*," Rye said, glaring at her before turning to Joel, who looked away. "And as one of your patients, Tallie, would you please come with me to get my stuff from your car? Because I'm leaving. I have to go."

Goodbye; I'm going to the fucking moon!

"Rye," she said as he walked toward the stairwell doors. He stood at the end of the hallway looking out the window, listening. He was all exposed nerves, like his superpowers had just come in.

(The thermostat is set to exactly seventy-four degrees in this hospital. A siren, slowly getting closer. Squeaking sneakers, high heels. A rolling cart. A man down the hallway clears his throat. Pen on paper. A crying baby. A chair makes a shrieking scrape against the floor. Tallie and Joel are talking. Everyone is always. Fucking. Talking.)

"I have to take care of this. Are you staying here?" she said to Joel.

"Do you *want* me to stay here?" Joel asked.

"Joel, I'm done playing games. I've had, like, two hours of sleep. I don't have time to argue with you. Stay or don't, but I'll be back," she said.

"Fine. Okay. I'll be here," Joel said quietly.

268

Rye shoved open the door. Down and down the stairs with Tallie behind him, saying his name.

"Rye, stop," she said as they stepped onto the sidewalk.

"You're a doctor? Not a teacher? You lied, too! I came clean, and you said nothing," he said.

"You didn't exactly come clean…you got caught. And I'm not a doctor. I'm a therapist."

"You're a *thera*…You're kidding," he said. She had to be kidding.

"No. I'm not kidding. I'm a licensed therapist, and like you, I didn't want you to know, because I knew you'd treat me differently."

"So this was, what, pro bono work for you? That's the only reason you were being so kind to me? Did you know who I really was?!" Rye said. He couldn't remember the last time he'd felt so stupid. A *therapist.* Everything she said, everything she did: fake. She'd been sneakily practicing on him. Impossible conspiracy theories formed in his brain. Had someone sent her after him? Had someone been following him? Watching him?

"No! Absolutely not. The connection we had was real…*is* real. I wasn't pretending," she said. Rye sat on the ground, put his back on the stone.

"I told you I wasn't pretending, either. But now it's done. Will you give me a ride to the bridge, please? I could walk or hitch, but it would be delaying the inevitable, and honestly, at this point, I'd like to get it over with," he said. Everything was a tinderbox; everything could go up in flames, not just Lionel. Him, Tallie, the hospital, the entire world. This was it. It was time to go.

"Get *what* over with?" she said frantically. "You really think I'm going to *help* you?"

"I'm done with talk therapy, Tallie. It didn't work for Christine, and it's not working for me."

"Emmett…*Rye*, you want me to take you to the bridge, then let's go. Let's go to the bridge," she said, wrestling with her purse to find

her keys. She jingled them out, held them up. "Let's fucking go."
She began walking toward her car, and he stood.

"Sounds good," Rye said, following behind her.

When they got to her car, she opened the trunk and doors for him.

"Stay here. I'm going to tell Joel goodbye. Just be here in the
car when I get back, and I'll take you wherever you want to go,"
she said.

"Is this *Therapist* Tallie talking now?" he asked. "More fake intimacy?" All her sincere moments had come through a professional
filter. Nothing about their weekend was real. He couldn't believe
how guilty he'd felt for lying to her when she'd been lying the
whole time, too.

The world was shit, and everyone was a liar.

"Is this *Clementine Emmett* talking now?"

"I'll wait here. I'm done talking," Rye said, yanking his stuff from
the trunk and slamming it closed. His hands still hurt. So what?

"Promise you'll wait here," she demanded, looking right in
his eyes.

"Yeah," he said. He sat in the passenger seat, closed the door.
When he looked in the side mirror, he saw Tallie walking toward
the hospital.

*(Tallie tries the stairwell door, but it is locked. She goes around to the
front entrance. A car door slams. A truck engine starts.)*

~

"I didn't see you in here when I walked out," Tallie said when she
returned to the car.

Rye had put the seat back, closed his eyes.

"I told you I'd wait" was all he said. He wasn't going to let her
get anything else out of him. Game over. She started the engine.

TALLIE

Inside the hospital, Tallie had found Joel sitting in the hallway with River on his lap like some sort of bizarro-world *Madonna and Child*. She put her hand on River's head when she got to them. Joel bounced his knee, causing River to giggle with glee. The mirth echoed down the hospital hallway.

"Zora stepped out for some fresh air," Joel said.

Tallie sat in the chair beside him.

"Listen. It's really nice of you to fly all the way out here and show up," she said, too tired to argue anymore.

"Hey, what can I say? I wouldn't have felt so comfortable if I hadn't hoped you were reaching out to me, but...a prank is a prank, right?" he said before making a gushy airplane noise at River, who got a kick out of it.

"Auntie Lulah, can I play games on your phone?" River asked Tallie, and she handed it over to him, letting him know she'd be leaving soon.

River sat in his own chair next to Joel, who was relaxed and looking at Tallie with the brown eyes she'd lost herself in so many times before. Those brown eyes she'd married; those brown eyes that had broken everything.

"But the emails didn't sound like you. Not all the way. Didn't seem like something you would do. Wishful thinking, maybe...that you'd write and want to forgive me after...everything," Joel said.

"Well, maybe you wouldn't know what I sound like now anyway. Maybe you don't know me anymore, Joel. You have a new life, and I'm allowed to have a new life, too."

Joel took a deep breath in acceptance and put his arm around the back of her chair. "I'm glad I came to see Lionel."

"*She* doesn't care that you left?" Tallie asked.

"No. She knows Lionel is like a brother to me."

"Did you tell her about the emails?"

"No."

"Whoa—not even one full year into your marriage and you're already keeping secrets? Tsk, tsk," Tallie said. Joel didn't say anything, just touched his beard. "Rye is not one of my clients. I call them clients, not *patients*. I've told you so many times and you forget. And he's not missing. It's none of your business, but he has issues with his family, and he's taking care of them."

She pictured Rye in her car. She imagined him gone already, breaking his promise, finding his way to the bridge alone or getting lost in the dark. She looked at the clock on the wall.

"I apologize, truly. I'm just confused. Everything is *really* confusing right now."

"Because you shouldn't be here, Joel," she said. He didn't object, just cleared his throat.

"Your cats. How are your cats?"

"They're fine."

"They don't miss me?"

Tallie laughed a little and shook her head. "How's your horse?" she asked.

"It's...it's not my horse. It's hers."

"Right. Got it."

272

"Hey, so...you're thinking of adopting a baby?" Joel asked after a minute of silence.

"I am."

"With Nico...or this guy...or?"

"Alone!"

"Gotcha."

Bless his heart, she thought. Joel, relieved she wasn't having a child with someone else so he wouldn't have to feel the way she'd been feeling.

"Yeah, well...I saw the latest picture of Pearl. She's pretty. Got your hair." Tallie touched his ponytail, looked at the clock again. Her eyes stung from exhaustion and bewilderment. Who was she? Where was she? What had happened? She sniffed and turned away. "I've got to leave and take Rye...back. I don't know what else to say."

"So whose year is it? Gus or Judith?" Joel asked, knowing too well about her parents' alternating-years rule for the Halloween party.

"This is the year of Gus and Glory."

"Good ol' Gus and Glory," he said. "What was your costume?"

"Rye and I were Mulder and Scully."

"Aha. And just so you know, my parents asked about Lionel. I told them I was coming."

"Your mom thinks you're nuts," she said.

Joel nodded. "Well, they love you."

"Are they doing okay?" she asked.

The urge to cry still hung over her. She'd loved Joel's parents and missed them. Joel's mom had cried when they got divorced. She'd come over to the house with a bottle of wine after Joel had moved in with Odette. Talked for hours, telling Tallie about the men she'd known in her past who had tried and failed to be good husbands. She didn't try to persuade Tallie to give Joel another chance, but she let her know how much she and Joel's dad had loved having Tallie as their daughter-in-law all those years. It'd meant a lot to Tallie for

Joel's mom to show up like that. And even still, Joel's mom texted and called Tallie occasionally, checking in.

"Yeah, they're good. Thanks," Joel said.

"Know how mind-boggling and surreal it was for me seeing a picture of your mom holding your daughter?" Tallie asked.

"I'm sorry you saw it."

"It's on your Facebook page."

"Tallie—"

"They're really great grandparents," she said, interrupting him.

Tallie and Joel stared at each other as if their history played on a film between them, the two of them separated by that flickering screen. She thought of the emails Rye had shown her—that tender, apologetic Joel. She looked at him, knowing that *that* Joel was in there somewhere behind those eyes.

"I learned my lesson, but I learned it too late," he said.

"I don't know what to say to that, Joel."

"Will you at least unblock me from your phone?"

"For what?"

"I don't know, Tallie. Just because?"

"I will as soon as I get it from River." She nodded and leaned over to see River's face flashing with cell phone light.

"I like your glasses, by the way. They look good on you," Joel said, taking his time looking at her. "And about what I wrote in those emails—"

Tallie held up her hand. "I really can't talk about this right now. I have to go. The whole thing was stupid. It's done. We have to make a deliberate decision to move on...but I'll unblock you," she said. "River, I need my phone now. Your mommy will be up here soon." She held out her hand to him. Once River gave it to her, she let Joel watch her unblock his number. "And you'll change your Facebook password? I'm deleting mine."

"On it," Joel said, taking River on his lap and giving him the phone from his pocket. Joel told Tallie he was going to hang around a little longer and that Ben and some more of Lionel's friends would be coming tomorrow.

"Text or call me if you want to," Tallie said, "to let me know when you're coming back up here...before you leave town."

"Yeah. Of course," Joel said, touching the top of River's head before lifting his hand and holding it still, frozen in a wave.

~

Tallie's phone lit up with preciousness as Aisha's face filled her screen. She swiped to answer it, walking fast through the parking lot.

"Girl. I can't talk for long right now, but I have so much to tell you. You wouldn't believe it. Like, *so* much," Tallie said.

"Okaaay. Is Li all right? As soon as I turned my phone on when I got back home, it blew up with texts saying his costume caught fire at the party. But he's in the hospital now?" Aisha said. Aisha's voice did a good job of bringing Tallie to reality. She walked to the car, filling her in as quickly as she could about Lionel's accident and Joel showing up. She told her she was giving a new friend a ride and would call her soon, explain everything later. She ended the call, saw her car was empty, and walked closer with a sludgy sick stomach, worried Rye was gone.

But when she peeked in the window, she saw him inside with the seat laid back, one arm thrown over his face, looking like a sweet child she'd do anything for. And all he wanted was for her to take him to the bridge. She'd play along. An embarrassingly bottom-of-the-barrel therapy trick—reverse psychology. *Bridge bridge bridge.* If he wanted the bridge so bad, that's where they'd go.

~

"So after all this, you won't talk?" Tallie said, shattering the silence in her car. Rye remained quiet. "We've talked all weekend, and..."

"We've *lied* all weekend," Rye finally said after a stretch of taciturnity.

"Not everything I said was a lie. Yes, I lied and said I was a teacher. Maybe it was unethical for me to not disclose that I'm a therapist, but I'm not perfect and never claimed to be. I'm a professional secret keeper," she said, wildly gesturing with a free hand before putting it on the stick shift. "I guess you are, too, now."

Rye turned to her as she stopped at a red light. He had the same haunted, heavy look he had on his face when she found him Thursday evening. Gone was the *Emmett* in her kitchen, the *Emmett* making biscuits and charming her mother yesterday morning, the dashing *Emmett* the night before in his suit at Lionel's party, kissing and kissing her. *Bridge* manifested himself as they neared the Ohio River. But. She couldn't control him. He'd been an unknowing participant in talk therapy. They were soon to part ways. If he didn't want help, she couldn't force him. She had to get some rest because she would be waking up early for her morning appointments. She had a life, and it was just as important as everyone else's. Rye needed to take care of himself the same way she did.

"Look. I've apologized. You've apologized. So that's it," Tallie said, minutes away from the bridge.

"So that's it," he said quietly, parroting her to the glass of the passenger window.

Those minutes were biblically torturous, as if they'd been planned out by some cruel god. The tension, thick and solid, as if the car had been filled with concrete.

As they approached the bridge, Tallie thought she might puke. If she could stop the car and lean out, purge herself, she could feel better. How was *he* feeling? Angry but relieved? Sad but angry? Humans could feel a million different ways at the same time. It wasn't like one emotion politely cleared out to make way for another. Most often they smudged together like daubs of paint, mixing and making new colors and feelings altogether.

A few cars—some red taillights and the occasional flash and disappearance of headlights. The night had fallen like a lid on a pot. The bridge was lit up, and there was a skinny walkway and crisscross of metal that was merely aesthetic. Rye had climbed over the railing easily on Thursday. If someone were determined to jump from the bridge, the railing would be of no consequence. Tallie pulled her car aside and shut it off, punched on her hazards the same way she'd done on Thursday. All roads led back to that bridge in an ever-widening gyre.

"Here's your bridge," she said, nauseated. She hoped he'd back off and finally let this go once he saw it. That's what she prayed. She needed water. There was an old water bottle in the driver's-side cup holder. It crinkled in her hands and she took a plasticky drink, choked it down. She needed fresh water, food, a solid ten hours of sleep.

Rye stared straight ahead.

"Okay."

"Okay, then."

"Thank you," he said when he looked at her. He put his hand on the door handle without pulling it.

"This is what you want? Really, Rye? This? What do you want, Rye? What do you want?" Tallie said with a swelling panic, like an orchestra tuning before playing the discordant devil's chord. Nope. No way could she let him get out of the car.

"I mean it when I say thank you. And here: this is for you, too," he said, unzipping his backpack and pulling out the envelope of cash. He held it out for her, and when she wouldn't take it, he put it on the dash.

"I'm not taking your money. I told you this," she said.

"What do you charge for a therapy session by the hour? Two hundred dollars? Seventy-two hours together at two hundred dollars an hour, that's fourteen thousand, four hundred dollars. There's around ten thousand in there. I'll mail you the rest," he said.

The delicate, low orange light of the streetlamp—numinous and scumbled—pressing his window like a promise.

"Rye, you're not my client," Tallie said, remaining as calm as possible. She knew how important it was when speaking with someone who was upset. *She* was upset, but there was no one there for her. She was alone, very alone, shuttering her windows from the raging wind of her own strong emotions for the greater good. Again.

"I'm not taking the money back," he said, looking at her with soft eyes, not the hard, haunted ones she'd seen earlier.

"Can I take you somewhere else? Let's not do this. Where else can I take you? I'm sure you're as exhausted as I am. We're running low on sleep and high on every possible emotion."

"I forgive you. I'm not mad at you. Honestly. Thank you, Miss Tallie," he said, pulling the handle.

"Rye, I'm not mad at you, either. I forgive you, too. And I'm not giving up on you! I'm not," Tallie said, finally crying in a series of fragmented sobs. Primitive, desperate sounds escaped her mouth.

"Thank you so much, Miss Tallie," he said, stepping out of the car with his jacket and backpack.

Tallie swung her legs out of the car, walked through the dread. A truck zoomed past with deep bass rattling its fiberglass before the world went quiet. The rain had put the earth through a full rinse cycle; the river perfumed metallic. She felt as if she could reach out and touch the black velvet darkness. She wanted to snatch it back like a curtain and reveal another world where this wasn't happening.

"Rye. Please don't do this. I won't let you do this," she said, raising her voice as he continued walking toward the railing.

Just quiet.

She prayed the first Bible verse that came to her mind, aloud. *Abide with us: for it is toward evening, and the day is far spent.* Rye stood still, listening. He turned around and closed his eyes to the night. Was he smiling?

RYE

Arcadia. Simple, peaceful. With his eyes closed, Rye saw the lake restaurant and the Honeybee House. The green hills behind it. A happy Christine and their smiling baby, Brenna—*Sunshine.* He floated through the moments of peace he'd had *before.* And he saw Tallie's house, smelled those autumn candles and the rain. That suspended space of calm away from the noise of the world, the noise in his head. He was so tired.

Weightlessness.

Gravity.

Eternity tapped his shoulder, seduced him to turn around.

No more observations.

Nothing to report.

"Rye," he heard Tallie say.

"Rye," she said louder. He'd turned away from her, felt her hand grab at his back.

"Rye, please get in the car."

TALLIE & RYE

They stopped for coffee on the way to Bloom. Tallie was okay with Rye cracking the window, smoking in the car. She held her hand up at him, refusing when he'd offered her a cigarette. They'd been mostly quiet. They'd cried privately, together, both trying their best to conceal it—wrung out. Bloom was three hours away, and they drove south, Tallie smoothing her car down the interstate at seventy-five miles per hour until it was time to turn off the exit ramp. Rye had listened to her make three phone calls. One to her mother. One to her father. One to Zora. In all three, explaining to them she'd be back at the hospital first thing in the morning before her appointments.

When they were stopped at a red light, she'd texted Nico, asking to see him on Monday evening after work; he'd said of course and called her *lieve schat*. Told her to talk back soon, and she promised she would. She'd asked Zora how Lionel was doing and, when she got off the phone, relayed the information to Rye in a casual tone that made him ache for those slow moments before Lionel caught fire. The same way his body and heart ached to turn back time and walk into his Honeybee House, hug his wife and daughter. Protect them somehow. The same way his body had ached those mornings after spending all night working heavy construction. The same way his body had ached when he was ill and sweating with stomach flu in prison. The same way Tallie's body and heart had ached, trying so desperately to get pregnant. The same way Tallie's heart had ached when Joel had moved in with Odette and when he'd told her he'd gotten Odette pregnant.

Tallie's car hummed with ache as they drove to Bloom.

~

Rye's dad opened the front door wide and clutched his chest, threw his arms around his son. How long had Tallie been crying? And Rye's mom, in her flowered nightgown, walked into the kitchen and turned her head, covering her mouth and crying when she saw them. Tallie stood there spent and broken, the lamplight glowing up at Sallman's *Head of Christ* hanging on the wall.

RYE

Rye, back home, promised he'd keep in touch with Tallie. He promised he'd find a therapist, and if he couldn't find one he liked, he'd contact her and let her help. Before she left him at his parents' house, he'd walked her to the car and asked if it was okay to hug her.

"Are you serious?" she asked before reaching out to him. Their lies, their mistakes, their anger dissolved into stardust and shimmered its way above them as they held each other.

"You're too tired to drive."

"I'm running on adrenaline at this point. I'll keep the windows down, turn the music up," she said. "And after everything, I'm being completely honest when I tell you I'm so glad I met you. I mean, life is short, clearly, but I want to live it. I was open with you, and you hurt me, but I don't regret any of this."

"I'm sorry I hurt you. I can't say that enough."

"And I'm sorry for not being up front with you."

"I betrayed your trust after you were so kind to me," he said.

"Yes. And I forgive you. That's how forgiveness works. Do you forgive me?"

"Easiest thing I've ever done."

"See?" she said. And after she nested herself inside the car she said, "Goodbye, Rye."

"Goodbye, Tallie."

He watched her drive until her taillights blurred, until she turned and disappeared.

~

Before he crashed in his old bedroom at his parents', he looked at the picture of Tallie and the one of them together that she'd sent him, to make sure he hadn't imagined it. He went through his backpack, pulling everything out and putting it in a pile next to the bed. The envelope of cash was in there, and he didn't know how or when Tallie had snuck it back in. His parents stood in the doorway, not wanting to let him out of their sight.

(And there is something new: the postcard of Klimt's The Kiss, *slipped into the Bible behind Brenna's purple-crayoned coloring-book heart.)*

PART FIVE

TALLIE

In November and December, Tallie checked in with Rye often. Winter was hard, and she wanted to make sure he was okay. He always responded to say hi and ask how she was doing. They exchanged the same sort of texts, with Rye reminding her that she mattered, too.

happy thanksgiving!

Happy Thanksgiving!

how are you? how are your hands?
not small talk. i really mean it. i
always think of you, pray for you.
tell me how you are pls.

I'm ok. My hands are fine. I
appreciate you thinking of me. I think
about you too. I hope you're good.

i'm v good. talk anytime, ok?

Ok, I will. Thank you, Tallie.

~

merry christmas, rye. i know it's
brenna's birthday. how are you?
big talk!

Merry Christmas. Thank you for
remembering. I'm ok. I love big talk.

~

are you taking care of yourself?

Trying my best. Heard One
Direction yesterday and smiled.
What have you done.

oh woooow! so proud of you. good
boy!

Forever trying to impress you,
good girl.

~

your feelings are just as important
as everyone else's.

So are yours. :)

~

He'd sent her recipes for his favorite ramen soup, the best spicy-hot
chicken, and the cognac sauce for his steak. Occasionally in the middle
of the night, she'd wake to a *hi* text from him, and she'd *hi* him back.

288

big hearts in my eyes when you
reach out first! forgive my
therapist-talk but honestly, it's so
reassuring. feels significant, so i
let it in!

Let it in, let it in. Glad to hear it.
And all right then . . . consider it
meticulously noted. :) Btw, I told
my new therapist he reminds me
of you. A good thing. A really good
thing. Thanks again for helping me
find him.

oh wow i'm so stoked to hear this!
he's a gem and so are you. a
perfect match!

You're the gem.

jsyk, i miss you.

Just so YOU know, I miss you too.

i like you, Rye.

I like you too, Tallie.

~

And sometimes.

are you ok?

Close.

~

Tallie told her family just enough about Rye, letting them look up his case for themselves. She let them know he'd been trying to start fresh: that was why he'd called himself Emmett and lied about where he was from. Lionel said he didn't care what his name was; he was his buddy for life after saving him. And her mom swore she'd thought it was him but didn't want to say anything. As if she could ever keep her mouth shut about something as huge as Tallie hanging out with a guy who'd been accused of murdering his family. But it bothered Tallie very little, her mom claiming that. She was determined to go easier on her.

After love, forgiveness is the strongest glue holding every family together.

~

In the new year, TLC Counseling Services added two more therapists, and Tallie stayed busy with work, coming home to her house at night tired and satisfied. Some evenings she came home to Nicodemus Tate bundled up, sitting on her porch in the cold or in his white Jeep, waiting for her. They'd go inside and make dinner. Make love in her bed before falling asleep and wake to have their coffee together in the morning before going to work.

She and Nico had fallen together completely, Tallie finally admitting to herself and to him that yes, he was her boyfriend. She'd told him everything about Rye, even the embarrassing parts. She told him that she and Rye were kissing when Lionel's costume caught fire.

Tallie was clear with Nico about not wanting to get married again and needing her freedom, always. And she made sure he knew she would remain in contact with Rye because he was her friend. "I understand. I know you. I know who you are," Nico had said.

And as soon as he'd said that, she knew she would marry him some-day. Maybe. Probably. His vim was heady and arresting. Dreamy. Enough. She loved Nico to distraction; she'd easily agreed not to sleep with anyone else. They'd finally gotten the timing right, and now they could set their watches to it.

"*Ik hou van jou*," he'd said after he'd given her a key to his place.

"*Ik hou van jou*," she'd said after she'd given him a key to hers. She'd said it in Dutch and English. French, too.

I love you, Nico. *Je t'aime, Nico. Je t'aime follement de tout mon cœur.*

~

When it got warm again, Tallie and Nico went to Florence to eat and drink and visit *David* at the Galleria dell'Accademia di Firenze. "You have to do things when you have a chance to do them," her dad had told her when she'd mentioned wanting to go. The advice was so simple that it rang poignant. She'd been focusing on remaining heart-open and ready for anything. Zora had gotten pregnant not long after Lionel's last skin-graft surgery, and although Tallie couldn't have been happier for them, it reminded her of what she wanted but didn't have, the things she hadn't done yet.

And Florence! A lovely escape, with its palaces, gardens, and medieval cathedrals. Bistecca alla Fiorentina and Chianti by candle-light, strong espresso out of small white cups, and tiramisu under wide-striped patio umbrellas. Cobblestone streets slicked wet with Italian rain. Moonlit Nico-kisses: astral, sparking the dark. He'd bought her a *blu e corallo* Pucci scarf made of Italian silk, and she'd worn it around her neck, wrapped it around her hair, tied it around her wrist so she could feel it cool in the warm wind. She'd gifted him an austere moon-phase watch the color of night.

"*Orologio*," he'd said, putting it on, after his *grazie* and *lo adoro*.

"*Prego*. Tennis players love *orologios*."

"*I tennisti adorano gli orologi,*" he'd translated properly in a deep, singsongy lilt.

They stayed at the Villa Cora and swam there in the pink rose garden, Tallie loving how Nico's ropy body cut through the pool water, how he'd pull her close—both of them sun-kissed and weightless—grab behind her knees, and wind her slippery body around his like an octopus. And afterward, in their room, he'd peel off her bathing suit and his, hang them to drip in the heat. Sunshiny Nico-kisses: celestial, lemon-bright. Sex and naps smelling of coconutty sunscreen, windows open, white curtains breezing, waking to red wines and dinners.

He'd started wearing a masculine square onyx ring on his middle finger, and Tallie found the sharp contrast of the sight of it plus the tinkling it made against the wineglass brutally romantic. Nico tried his best to teach her some useful Italian phrases, but she was too easily distracted by the lightness of his tongue, the handsome smush of his mouth when he said them.

Ti amo tanto, Nico. Ciao bello. Ti amo pazzamente con tutto il cuore.

～

She'd put her head on Nico's shoulder and cried on the plane ride home until it sank all the way in that Florence was a real place that existed and she could go again. It didn't disappear simply because she was leaving it. And there were so many other places she hadn't been! She wanted to go back to Italy and see Scotland and Paris and Australia, too. She'd fallen in love with a sunny Australian soap opera on Netflix and tacked a postcard of Coogee Beach on her bathroom wall.

She considered her future with Nico and adopting a baby, how those two things had seemingly converged in a blink. She'd completed her home-study portion of the adoption process, and the birth mother she'd chosen was due near summer's end. Nico had been supportive all along and wanted to stay updated on everything, but they hadn't discussed in full detail what their lives would look like moving forward. Together.

You are the true love of my life, he'd said.

nico, i do want to be yr only girl…forever, she'd texted him in the dark of the first night they'd spent apart since returning home.

you already are, lieve schat.

~

Tallie deleted her social media account and finally donated the rest of Joel's stuff to Goodwill, all of it. She hadn't talked to him since he was in town to see Lionel; she and Joel had met for a quick coffee before he left Louisville. It'd been okay and sneakily healing, sparking her dreams of writing a book on comfort and creating safe spaces and mental health.

She'd made little waterproof note cards that said: *You are not alone. You matter. You are so loved.* The suicide hotline number appeared underneath, and she left them tied with lilac ribbon to prevention the bridge where she'd met Rye. She'd also written several letters and made as many calls to the mayor's office petitioning for higher railings on the bridge.

~

She hadn't heard from Rye since the beginning of spring, right before she left for Florence. There were times when she scanned the *Southeastern Kentucky News* online and the obituaries, hoping not to find his name. Every night, she prayed he was okay. Her phone calls and voice mails and *hi* texts went unanswered.

She rewatched the crime-show documentary clips about his case. Rye in a backpack in his high school hallway, Rye in a suit in the courtroom, Rye standing in front of the lake restaurant, Rye crying at his sentencing. Rye with Brenna on his shoulders, his hands hold-ing her tiny feet, next to Christine, smiling sweetly in front of their yellow house. The torn photos of their family—Rye, alone on one side with Christine and Brenna on the other—floating downward in slow motion in the Ken Burns effect. Clips with titles like *Mystery in Bloom*, *A Long Walk in October*, and *Double Death*.

She knew from their last texts that Rye had moved to Nashville and liked his job at the restaurant where he cooked. Also, he'd met a woman. Tallie's stomach had tickled with surprise and jealousy, but she told him she was happy for him and meant it. Then Rye went radio silent. She wrote him about Florence and the food and the art attack she had when she finally saw *David*—how her heartbeat quickened and she felt like she was floating, how they stood there for hours with Nico reminding her to take breaks, to close her eyes when she needed to, to stay hydrated; how he put the oyster crackers from her bag into the cup of her hand one by one, reminding her to eat them—but Rye hadn't responded. And she'd sent him a picture Zora had emailed her. A photo someone had taken of her and Rye at Lionel's Halloween party: Mulder and Scully, embracing on the patio. They were smiling and unaware of the camera, lost in each other's eyes.

She'd tracked down what she thought was his parents' phone number, but it'd been disconnected. She searched Google in vain, not finding anything new. She reread article after article about his trial because it made her feel closer to him. She missed her friend and continued texting him, even when he didn't respond.

> hey rye remember it's ok to let ppl
> take care of you. this is exactly
> what you would say to me.
>
> you matter.

i hope things are ok. i miss you
and think abt you a lot. so do the
cats. say hello to nashvegas.

lionel called you "my mysterious
superhero" friend the other day.
he's right! he asks abt you. he'd
love for you to call him!

did you ever finish prisoner of
azkaban? give me yr address so I
can send you a copy?

heard sam cooke today and
thought of you. it was raining too.
you'd be so proud of my gutters!

happy birthday rye! sending you
love! <3

∽

happy halloween eve, rye! sunday
afternoon in louisville at the speed
art museum tomorrow? a few days
late, but we could celebrate your
birthday! one o'clock? by the
brancusi, you can't miss it. we
could make buttermilk roasted
chicken.

and only if you felt up for it, we
could drop by lionel's party? he's
still having it, of course. he's unstoppable. but i won't make you

put on a costume, i PROMISE!
everyone would just like to see
you.

also! i have a surprise for you.
please come?

easy heart.

don't dream it's over.

tender loving care.

pls talk to me.

i also want to say this bc you are
my friend: i love you. i do. i love
you, rye and i care abt you.

rye, pls?

She left him a voice mail, too, and obsessively checked her phone
for the rest of the day, praying for a response.

RYE

Dear Mom and Dad,

It's time and this is goodbye. I'm sorrier than you know about having to write this. I don't want to write this. I don't want to do this. I'm so tired and nothing is working. I miss Christine too much. I miss Brenna too much. And nothing I can do will fix that. Except this. If I do this, maybe I can start over somewhere in the afterlife. Try again. I don't want to do this. I love you both so much. I can't express how much. You've never stopped being there for me and I know you never will. This shatters me and my heart is already irreparably broken. I want you to know how much I love you and how much I will miss you when I'm gone and the rest of the money is in my closet. Top right corner under my yearbooks.

From: JoelFoster1979@gmail.com
To: Talliecat007@gmail.com
Subject: Re: i still care about you too

Tallie, Ben told me about Lionel's accident. I tried calling. How bad is it?? Please let me know how he's doing? I'm thinking of flying down there.

From: talliecat007@gmail.com
To: joelfoster1979@gmail.com
Subject: Re: i still care about you too

Hey Joel. This is Rye Kipling. I'm deleting this email account, but I wanted to say I'm sorry for any trouble I caused. And to reassure you that your secrets are safe with me. What you wrote about Lionel and the woman in NYC, what you wrote about him knowing about you and Odette. Tallie never saw that stuff and I'll never tell her. There'd be no point. Again, I'm sorry. I don't know how else to end this except by saying that.

From: JoelFoster1979@gmail.com
To: Talliecat007@gmail.com
Subject: Re: i still care about you too

I appreciate it.

Rye had been admitted to a psychiatric hospital in Nashville for a short stay after his return to Bloom. The psychiatrist his parents had found thought it best for him to have focused treatment, and Rye went willingly. After being released, he made his new home there in Nashville, cooking at a trendy new restaurant that served food on cutting boards and had more than twenty locally brewed beer options. Hipsters, tourists, industry insiders, and country music lovers kept the place popping, more than happy to spend fifteen dollars on a tiny bowl of slow-cooked collard greens and bacon.

His parents visited him often. Hunter and Savannah came to town, too. Rye held their daughter and spoke softly over her, listening and retelling them everything about Tallie and the Halloween party. How the weekend changed his heart.

Hunter and Savannah's baby girl was Daisy Christine.

~

The picture Tallie had taken of them and the one she'd taken of herself were still on his phone. So was the one she sent him that someone had taken at Lionel's party. He considered keeping them there forever. He loved forgetting about them, then remembering. At times he'd search Google for Tallie, not happening upon much. He'd search for Lionel, too. There'd been a small article written up in the newspaper when Lionel was released from the hospital, although he'd also been in touch with Tallie then, and she'd told him. There was another write-up about Lionel attending a ribbon-cutting ceremony after the new year and another one in the summer about his wild, sprawling home in *Architectural Digest*. Lionel, a pregnant Zora, and River sat on their long suede couch, smiling at the camera. Rye went out immediately and bought the print copy of the magazine, read every word about the house he'd been in, which seemed like a dream on Halloween night. The article had mentioned the accident, with Lionel saying a friend of his sister's had basically saved his life. After Halloween, he and Lionel had texted and talked occasionally, Lionel telling him during that first conversation that he knew the truth about who he was and didn't give a shit about any of it—Rye was his friend for life.

~

Lionel had called Rye after the holidays and asked him if he'd ever considered opening a restaurant of his own. They spoke at length about how—when and if he was ready—Lionel would love to help him out and be one of his investors. Lionel floated the idea of Rye opening another lake restaurant or a fleet of food trucks. Rye was stunned with gratitude and told him he'd definitely be the first person he called once he could get to a proper headspace about something that huge. And the last time they talked, Lionel had reminded Rye that he had an open invitation to come to Louisville and hang at his place, but Rye hadn't responded. He kept the copy of *Architectural Digest* by his bed in his new small, cozy apartment, and he'd gotten a candle that smelled like one of Tallie's. He'd never lit it, but he liked to take the top off and sniff.

~

He went quiet on Tallie, too, feeling like it was better for her to move on. She had a great life, and he worried his darkness would swallow her up. He had nothing to offer her, and she had so much. And besides, what were they to each other? Friends? Casual acquaintances? Two people who'd hooked up and spent a wild, weird weekend together? More than that? Nothing? It was spring, and he hadn't seen her since that Sunday after Halloween. And every time he picked up his phone to respond to her, a voice in his head told him it was the wrong time.

He thought of her every day. He tried not to dwell on whether she was seeing Nico or anyone else. He didn't know if what he felt was jealousy, but it was close enough. For so long he thought nothing mattered. How could it? But he knew Tallie mattered. Her kindness and patience and forgiveness had changed his life by making him want to keep it.

With his parents' support, and after finding new medication that worked, he'd gotten through the holidays and found himself lifted at the promise of warm weather. He met a woman in the spring whom he enjoyed spending time with after work. She was pretty and smart and funny, and they'd see lighthearted movies together and go for long trail walks, but her pharmaceuticals sales job took her away to Indianapolis. She'd hinted that maybe he could come with her, but he didn't want to leave Nashville yet. He'd made a close friend at the restaurant where he worked and liked spending time with him and his wife, their families. Rye's apartment was a ten-minute walk from the restaurant, and he enjoyed the familiar, comforting chaos of his cooking schedule, plus the rituals of grabbing Saturday afternoon coffee at the joint on the corner before work and the walk back to his place late on Sunday nights. Staying busy during the week with only Mondays and Tuesdays off helped keep his mind as occupied as it needed to be. When he wanted to be around people, he could do that. And when he wanted to be alone, he could make that happen, too.

Rye joined a small church in his neighborhood, and some of the people in the congregation knew his story. He tried his best to take 1 Thessalonians 4:11–12 to heart. *Make it your ambition to lead a quiet life, to mind your own business and to work with your hands, just as we told you, so that your daily life may win the respect of outsiders and so that you will not be dependent on anybody.*

He began painting during his hospital stay. Art therapy. He didn't think about it too hard, just put his brush to the canvas, loving the feel of it. He'd simply paint an entire canvas one color, then cover it with another. His apartment was filled with canvases leaning against the walls. Some of them hanging. The smell of paint soothed him, reminding him of dreams and a future he'd previously kept unwritten.

Rye melted, cooling hard and flat when he saw a kid Brenna's age, and he knew that would never go away. *Brenna would be seven;*

Brenna would be seven and a half. And the same thing happened whenever he encountered a woman who reminded him of Christine. *Christine's eyes, Christine's hair, Christine's face. Christine would be thirty.* The stabby math of grief would never add up. It would always be as if Christine and Brenna had gone on a long trip without him, never to return.

But one day. One day, he'd get his ticket, too.

~

He'd gotten Tallie's art museum voice mail and texts and thought of writing her back I love you too and I'll be there if you're sure it's okay. Wrote and deleted it four times before putting his phone down, leaving it unsent. After hearing about it, Hunter had urged Rye to go to Louisville. "It sounds like she really cares about you...you have to accept that. There's no way around it. Do you care about her? If you care about her you should go, simple as that. She asked you to. Dude. Go!"

A SUNDAY AFTERNOON IN LOUISVILLE AT THE SPEED ART MUSEUM

Rainy. Halloween. Tallie hung around the Brâncuși until 1:15, walking over to visit the Chagall, the Pollock, and the Picasso beforehand. She had her daughter, Andromeda Lee, slung around her; Andromeda, who was now three months old. Tallie had adopted her from a teenage mother in Louisville she would stay in contact with and took the baby home a day after she was born. Her family and girlfriends had thrown Tallie and Andromeda a bringing-home-baby party, showered them with clothes, chiming plush animals, and bamboo blankets, soft and small. Nico was there, too, filling her home with so much love, swelling her heart.

Nico was there more often than he wasn't, the three of them making a nest in her bed, a new family in her home. And Andromeda looked every bit a celestial being—tufts of black curls, glowy gold-brown skin—a baby girl made of starlight. Nico was entirely smitten, calling her *popje* in a moony, bite-size voice he used only for her.

~

Tallie swayed to keep her daughter sleeping and satisfied by the Brâncuși in the gallery bustling with families and couples, docents in the doorways. She looked one last time, thinking of how much of a blessing it'd be to see Rye's lilac puff floating through.

~

There was a gold canvas gift in Rye's truck. He'd painted it for Tallie—the color of her energy. He saw her immediately, through the crowd. She'd cut her hair. Gold was how he felt when he looked at her, how he felt when he thought about telling her he was taking Lionel up on his offer of investing in a restaurant. She was magnificent under the gallery lights. Sfumato, a tender work of art. When she turned, he could see Tallie had a baby slung around her with lavender fabric. She swayed by the Brâncuși as if blown by the slightest breeze. He whispered her name.

~

Rye.

Rye was there with sunflowers, and he was real. His eyes weren't haunted; he looked healthy and good. She wanted to run to him and tell him. Instead, she watched his mouth move from across the room. Was he saying her name?

~

When he got to her, he said hi and smiled. "You don't know how good it feels to see you."

"You don't know how good it feels to see *you*. You stopped talking to me."

"I'm sorry I haven't been responding, but... I've been thinking about you. A lot."

"Happy birthday, Rye. And wow, you look really—"

"You do, too. I—"

"This is Andromeda, my surprise."

~

Rye put one hand on the lavender half-moon curve of Andromeda's back, his finger in her tiny fist.

The baby, sleeping, squeezed it tight.

(See. There is soft light. There are small mercies.)

AUTHOR'S NOTE

Dear Reader,

I'm a firm believer in holding fast to good, lovely, beautiful things as much as I can in this world, even when times are hard. I want to comfort my characters when they are sad, depressed, or grieving. I love filling my books with coziness, warm drinks, and sweet conversations, even when I am making my characters' worlds crumble around them. In life, I try my best to look for the light and to look for small mercies, even when things are dark and scary. It's important for me to leave this book on that: a hopeful note. If you are looking for a sign of hope, a sign of light, a sign to hold fast, please let this be it. New mornings mean new mercies! And if things do get too dark for you, please speak up and reach out for help. You are not alone. You matter. You are so loved.

x,
Leesa

National Suicide Prevention Lifeline: 1-800-273-8255

ACKNOWLEDGMENTS

Big love and thanks to my agent, Kerry D'Agostino, for being sunshine and for every little bit of hard work, patience, care, and thoughtfulness you pour into this world. Big love and thanks to my editor, Elizabeth Kulhanek, for being so incredibly lovely, fantastic, and such a joy to work with. I couldn't ask for more, really. To papers under pillows and kindles of kittens!

Thank you to everyone at Curtis Brown, Ltd.

Thank you to my beyond amazing publicist, Linda Duggins, for being the best. XO! Thank you, Alli Rosenthal and Alana Spendley, for being so wonderful to work with. And many thanks to Barbara Clark, Tareth Mitch, the art department, and the legal department at Hachette Book Group and Grand Central Publishing.

Special thanks to my dear friend and *lieve schat*, Stephanie Graf, for answering my questions about the Dutch language.

Special thanks to my BFF, Elisabeth Clem, for the *X-Files* inspiration always and forever (among other things we could talk about all night).

Special thanks and love to Wendy C. Ortiz.

I listened to Jake Gyllenhaal sing "Finishing the Hat" from *Sunday in the Park with George* about a million times while writing this novel, so I want to thank Jake Gyllenhaal and Stephen Sondheim for that. "Look, I made a hat!"

Oh, Sam Cooke, my heart. Thank you, Sam Cooke.

And thank you to Vincent van Gogh for his art and letters. I treasure them and him in a very special place in my secret heart where no one can touch them.

Thank you, dear reader. I hope you are cozy.

Thank you to my family. I love you.

R and A, I love you madly and will always write it here to be in my books forever.

And Loran, I couldn't do this without you. Who would make my tea? Who would make dinner? Thank you for doing those things and thank you for all you do for me, for us. Most important, thank you for loving me like Jesus, for being you, and for being mine. Love you forever.

ABOUT THE AUTHOR

Leesa Cross-Smith is a homemaker and the author of *Every Kiss a War*, *Whiskey & Ribbons*, and *So We Can Glow*. She lives in Kentucky with her husband and children.

Facebook: LCrossSmith
Twitter: @LeesaCrossSmith
Instagram: @LeesaCrossSmith